girl

Who Gave

Him The

Moon

Book Two
in the
Zodiac Series

An Atlantis Entertainment Novel

J. S. Lee

Axellia Publishing

First Edition, February 2019
Published by Axellia Publishing

Print ISBN: 978-1-912644-22-3
eBook ASIN: B07MVC6DFB

Cover design by Natasha Snow Designs;
www.natashasnowdesigns.com

Edited by C. Lesley
Proofread by S. Harvell

This book is a work of fiction. Any references to historical events, real people, or real locations are used fictitiously. Other characters, names, places and incidents are the product of the author's imagination. Any resemblances to actual events, locations, or persons—living or dead—is entirely coincidental.

CONTENTS

DEDICATION

For Adena, Melinda, and Heather
Thank you from the bottom of my heart!

And for Byungchan (Victon)

THE ATLANTIS ENTERTAINMENT UNIVERSE

Young Adult Contemporary Romance
(As Ji Soo Lee)

Zodiac

The Idol Who Became Her World
The Girl Who Gave Him The Moon
The Dancer Who Saved Her Soul
The Leader Who Fell From The Sky

Coming Soon

The Boy Who Showed Her The Stars

K-101

For those of you unfamiliar with K-pop / K-dramas / Korean culture, here's a short handy guide:

Names

Names in Korean are written family name then given name. It's not uncommon to use the full name when addressing a person—even one you're close to.

이민혁 is the Korean way of writing Lee Minhyuk, but his stage name would be written as 킹 (a king in Korean is wang—왕)

백송일 is the Korean way of writing Baek Sungil

김재훈 is the Korean way of writing Kim Jaehoon

민태경 is the Korean way of writing Min Taekyung (TK)

If you are interested in how to write and pronounce the characters names, please go to https://www.jisooleeauthor.com/characternames.html

As Lucinda is American, her name would be spelled out phonetically to become 루신다, or as King calls her, 루나 (which is also a Korean name).

Surnames (Family names)

As the western worlds combined, we ended up with a lot of variation in surnames. In Korea, although there is variation, you will find a lot Kims, Lees, and Parks.

BTS, for example have Kim Namjoon (RM), Kim Seokjin (Jin), and Kim Taehyung (V). They all share the same family name, but are not related.

To try to keep things as easy to follow as possible, I have tried to make sure that all characters don't have the same surname *unless* they're in the same family. The one exception to this is Minhyuk and Seungjin. (To cut a very long story short, in the first version of this book, Minhyuk's name had to be Lee. Then I scrapped the whole story and re-wrote it. As I'd already published Zodiac 1, it was too late to change it. One day I may share that version with you).

Oppa (오빠), hyung (형), noona (누나), and oennie (언니)

This one gets a little confusing at first. The first thing you need to know, in Korea, age is a very important thing. It's not uncommon for you to be asked your age before your name because you need to be spoken to with the correct level of respect (known as honorifics). To show this, there's actually several ways to speak to address a person and it usually depends on your age (an exception to this might be in a place of work where someone younger than you is more senior to you). But I'll keep this simple and limit myself to terms used in the book.

Traditionally, oppa, hyung, noona, and unnie are terms used to describe your older sibling—depending on what sex you are and what sex they are. If you are male, your older brother is hyung and your older sister is noona. If you are female, your older brother is your oppa, and your older sister is unnie (technically, 언니 when Romanized is oenni, and 형 is hyeong, but unnie and hyung have become the more standard way of writing this). However, this can often be transferred to people you are close to. A girl will call her older boyfriend oppa. An idol will call his older groupmates hyung.

Sunbae (선배) and Hoobae (후배)

Along the same vein, sunbae (senior) and hoobae (junior) may be used as an alternative when using experience as a basis, rather than age.

Teacher (선생, 선생님, or 쌤)

A teacher in Korean is a seonsaeng. Because teachers are a respected profession, you will often find 'nim' (님) tagged on the end—선생님 / seonsaengnim. In America (or other western countries), teachers are often called Mr. (or Mrs. Etc) Family name. In Korean, they will be called Family name Teacher. If was a teacher, I would be Ms. Lee, or in Seoul, Lee Seonsaengnim. Even teachers will address other teachers this way.

This might differ with a student addressing the teacher if they have a good relationship with a teacher, to become ssaem (it's like an abbreviation of seonsaengnim), and then I would be Ji Soo ssaem.

The reason I'm including this is because one of the teachers will be referred to as Woosung ssaem.

Other

Comeback: this is an odd one for most people. Your next single isn't just your next single. It's a comeback—and it doesn't matter if you've waited two months or two years.

Kakao: Kakao is a messaging app similar to Whatsapp or Wechat.

SNS: What we would call Social Media, Koreans use the term Social Networking Service. Included in this would be **V Live**, an app which allows Korean idols to communicate with their fans (a bit like Instagram Live)

화이팅: Fighting, or 'hwaiting' is a word commonly used as encouragement, like 'good luck' or 'let's do this'.

Maknae: a term used for the youngest member of a group.

'Ya!': The Korean equivalent to 'Hey!'

Abeoji: Father

Eomeoni: Mother

제 X 장: Chapter (pronounced jae X jang)

Character Bios are also available at the back of this book

More terms and information is available on Ji Soo's website:
www.jislooleeauthor.com/k101

제1 장

Lucinda

After more than six months of planning, and having my parents nearly change their minds twice, I was finally in Seoul. It was strange doing the journey by myself. Being a dancer, I was used to travelling by myself to get to competitions, especially because both of my parents worked, but this was the furthest I'd been by myself.

The flight from Newark, New Jersey, had been long, but relatively smooth. I'd slept most of it, trying to get my body to adjust to the South Korean time zone, seeing as it would be early evening when the fourteen-hour flight landed. As soon as we'd landed, I'd taken my phone off flight mode and found a dozen messages from my parents and my sisters. I quickly messaged the group chat, even though it was late back home, and let them know I had arrived safely.

The bags seemed to take forever to unload: two full cases and my carry-on bag. It was a lot of luggage for a vacation, but I wasn't here for a vacation.

I heaved the bags onto a cart and pushed them outside to the taxi rank. I'd promised my dad I would get a taxi from the airport to my hotel, regardless of the cost. It didn't take long for me to be in a car and leaving Incheon for the long drive to Seoul.

I sat back, trying to take everything in—until the taxi driver asked me why I was here. He'd used broken English, but when he didn't seem to understand my response, I switched to Korean. That earned me a wide grin. "You know Korean?" he asked.

"Yes. I've been learning for several years now," I replied.

"K-pop?"

I chewed at my lip. Then I nodded. That was the simple answer. The actual answer was much more complicated than that: I had fallen in love with a boy.

Lee Minhyuk.

Since I had turned thirteen, I had been attending the New York Dance Academy vacation programs. That was where I had met Minhyuk. I'd known right from that first moment that I was in love with him. He'd come all the way from Seoul, by himself. By comparison, I had travelled less than an hour from upstate New York. After the first program, I had begged my parents to let me return for their Easter program the following year. Minhyuk had come back.

We'd been the same height—the shortest in the class—so the teacher had naturally paired us up together. After that, we'd spent our free time together. When he'd returned home, we'd started writing each other.

His letters had been in Hangeul—Korean. Mine,

in English. At first, most of my time had been spent trying to decipher the little symbols, then slowly, in my spare time, I'd started learning Korean.

My reading, writing, and listening were quite good. Or, at least, I thought my listening was good. Just from being in the airport, I knew it wasn't good enough. Everyone talked so fast! I'd also discovered that my speaking wasn't brilliant. After learning mostly from a book, with the occasional conversation with Minhyuk, my pronunciation wasn't brilliant. But the taxi driver seemed happy enough.

I finally arrived at the hotel and checked in. My room was high up and gave me a great view of the city. It was early evening and I was hungry. But first, I needed a shower.

I pulled my cases onto my bed, seeking out my wash things, then took a long hot shower. Once I felt I had washed all the grime of travel away, I got out and I dried my hair. My hair was long and blonde, and unlike both my older sisters, it needed attacking with flat irons before I could leave the room. By the time it was suitably straight, it was dark out and my stomach was growling.

I left the hotel, my feet already being led by my nose.

My hotel was in Gangnam, on the south side of the river, and close to the school I would be attending. But I was going to worry about that later.

I pulled out my phone, wishing for the umpteenth time that Minhyuk had his own phone.

There was a reason we were writing letters.

Minhyuk was an idol.

Even saying that out loud seemed crazy.

When I had met him, he hadn't been. In fact, it wasn't until last summer that I found out that was what he wanted to be. I thought he had just wanted to be a dancer, like me.

Turns out, that wasn't quite the case.

He had gone back to Seoul, auditioned for one of the biggest entertainment companies, Atlantis Entertainment, and passed. He'd debuted only a few months ago.

Unfortunately, part of being an idol meant that he wasn't allowed a cell phone. There were a lot of other strict rules too—including not having a girlfriend …

Even keeping it to myself still had it sounding crazy.

I walked down the street, settling on a coffee shop. I was in the mood for an iced americano and a sandwich. Settling into a couch in the window to wait for my order, I sent a message to Sungil.

Sungil was one of Minhyuk's best friends. He wasn't an idol, but whenever I wanted to get in touch with Minhyuk quicker than waiting for his hand-written response, I would message Sungil.

Thankfully, both Sungil and Minhyuk knew I was coming to Seoul. Unfortunately, Minhyuk had a scheduled promotion and hadn't been able to meet me at the airport. That was fine. I didn't really want him seeing me after fourteen-plus hours of travel. I wanted the opportunity to clean up and look cute for him first.

We were going to meet up tomorrow at lunchtime, but I had promised I would send a message to Sungil to let him know I had arrived safely.

Sungil's response arrived at the same time as my sandwich. **OK.**

Sungil wasn't the chattiest of people in his messages. I had a feeling he would be like that in real life too.

Despite having had a long sleep on the flight, after having something to eat, I was suddenly exhausted. Exploring could wait. Instead I returned to my hotel room and collapsed on the bed, fully clothed.

2

When I awoke the following morning, it was with a nervous excitement thrumming through me. I showered and dressed, selecting the outfit I'd chosen two weeks before even packing my suitcase. For one of the few times in my life, luck was on my side. I didn't have to battle with my hair, and it fell shiny, sleek and straight, with minimal effort. My make-up was on point (years of dance competitions meant my make-up skills were pretty good), and there wasn't a single zit on my face.

A couple of days before I had flown out, Minhyuk had messaged (via Sungil, of course), to ask me to meet him by the Hannam Bridge over the River Han. It was a short walk from my hotel, and outside, the weather was sunny, but warm. Even the humidity seemed to be on my side today.

I arrived at the 7-Eleven we'd agreed on, with plenty of time to spare. I went inside, buying a bottle of water (I wasn't going to tempt fate. If I managed to spill this down me, at least it would dry without leaving a mark), then I went back outside to wait on a nearby bench.

It was a late Monday morning, so the traffic

wasn't bad, but there were plenty of passersby for me to people watch. I earned a few stares, which was a little strange, but I ignored most of them. The city was busy, like New York, but otherwise, I hadn't been anywhere like it before: I liked it.

It wasn't until I had been staring across the river at the far side that I realized I had been sitting there for a while. I pulled out my phone and checked the time. Minhyuk was late.

As my stomach sank, I wrapped my arms around myself. He would have been caught up, that's all. There was no way he or Sungil would have allowed me to travel halfway around the world by myself to stand me up. Korean guys were even more protective than American ones.

But that didn't stop the evil voice in the back of my mind from speaking up, telling me I was crazy. Who went to the other side of the world, to a country where their first language wasn't the same—just for a *guy*?

"Minhyuk is not that kind of person," I muttered sternly, silencing the voice of doubt. It had only been twenty-five minutes.

After forty minutes, I stood, growing restless, and then started pacing back and forth, feeling fidgety. I normally started my day off with a run, and with travelling, I hadn't had a run since Friday. I just had to burn off the restless energy.

Forty minutes turned into an hour, and then an hour and a half. I made a second trip into the 7-Eleven to use the bathroom and to buy another bottle of water. By late afternoon, I was hot and hungry, and contemplating returning to my room. I'd sent a message to Sungil, but his response had been that he hadn't seen

Minhyuk and had no way to get in touch with him.

Just as I started walking away from the bench, a car squealed to a halt in front of me. I stared at it, blinking; as did a few onlookers. A person jumped out, hidden beneath a baseball cap, sunglasses, and a face mask—but my attention was distracted by something glinting in the sunlight: a bracelet. I would recognize that bracelet anywhere. I had a matching one.

"Minhyuk!" I cried excitedly as I started to run over to him.

The car drove off, just as I stopped in front of Minhyuk. The last time I had seen Minhyuk had been January, just before he had debuted. Even though we had continued to write and message each other, and even though he constantly told me he loved me, all of a sudden, I felt shy.

Shy and anxious.

What if someone recognized him.

Would he get in trouble?

Had time and distance made his feelings stronger, like they had mine?

Had he been late because he was changing his mind about me?

"Hullo, Luna," he said, softly. He didn't even look to see if anyone was watching us as he wrapped his arms around me, hugging me tightly. "Let's go for a walk," he muttered in my ear.

He stepped back, his hand wrapping around mine, and led me down a path, away from the road. "I missed you," I told him.

Minhyuk let out an impatient grunt and abruptly tugged me off the path, into the bushes. I started to squeal in surprise, but the sound died in the back of my throat as Minhyuk turned to me, pulling his mask off. While one hand remained wrapped around my hand, the other reached up, settling gently on my cheek. Then he leaned forward and kissed me.

That annoying little voice shut up in an instant as the doubt evaporated.

I sank against him, kissing him back as fervently as he was kissing me. This was far from the soft and tender kisses I remembered.

He was kissing me like … like a boyfriend who hadn't seen his girlfriend for seven months.

Finally, he pulled away, but both hands remained. "I missed you," he said, breathless this time. "I love you."

It was like those seven months hadn't happened. It was like someone had clicked their fingers and it had changed from winter to summer overnight; that New York and Seoul had simply switched places. Time and space had evaporated. All that existed was him. "I love you, Lee Minhyuk," I told him, finally giving him the hug I couldn't give him earlier.

제2 장

Minhyuk

My schedule changed at the last minute. The radio show I was supposed to be on first thing in the morning had changed to an early afternoon appearance. With no way of contacting my Luna, and a giant clock hanging on the wall, tormenting me, all I could do was pray that she would still be there when I finished.

I loved being an idol. It was everything I wanted, and more. It was a very regimented lifestyle, with very strict rules and restrictions, but I loved it.

Until I needed to use a phone.

I didn't mind most of the time. I knew what I was getting into long before I signed my contract. But, while I was kept busy with training, practicing, recording and performing, there were many days where I was too tired to lift a pen, but it didn't mean I wasn't thinking of Luna. There were times when I crawled into bed and I knew she would be awake in America, yet I couldn't send her a quick text message telling her I missed her.

Phones had been confiscated the moment I

moved into the Atlantis dorms. It was the same situation for all the trainees. I, like Bright Boys, had various social media accounts, but none were being managed by me, which meant I still had no access to any SNS.

I also couldn't ask my manager to use his phone. Although my manager, Seok Kyuhyuk, was a lot more understanding than Bright Boys' manager, the same rules applied to me as they did to them: no dating.

My Luna had to remain my secret.

It was a rule that applied to most idols, especially when they first started out, so it wasn't a shock to me. In fact, it wouldn't have been an issue until Luna had confessed to me. I hadn't thought she had felt the same as me; I thought my love was one-sided.

As soon as I discovered it wasn't, I told her I was going to become an idol and the idol life meant no dating. That lasted … all of ten minutes. I decided to try; Luna was worth it.

I suppose, back then, I also hadn't been aware of the consequences. I knew of dozens of idols who were dating. You just had to make sure you kept it secret. At that point I was still a trainee anyway. I hadn't debuted and released my first single so no one knew who I was. Plus, Luna lived in America—it wasn't like we could be spotted in public.

She told me she was going to visit me. A part of me wished it could be for longer than two weeks, but the other part of me was relieved. I didn't want to have to creep around in the shadows to be able to spend time with her.

When I'd finally finished at the radio station, I walked outside and found one of my best friends,

Sungil, leaning against his car, waiting for me. I turned to my manager. "Am I done now, hyung?"

Seok Kyuhyuk looked over at Sungil with a slight frown. Kyuhyuk was one of the few managers who liked Sungil but was aware of what the other Atlantis employees thought of him. "You have a curfew, King."

I nodded, thanked him, then hurried over to Sungil. "I am so glad to see you."

"Noona messaged me," he told me.

'Noona' was a term guys used when referring to girls who were a little older than us. Seeing as there was no way of knowing exactly who we were talking about, Luna had become Noona between the two of us: a codeword so no one at Atlantis would find out, especially as she was younger than both of us. As everything was going through Sungil, nothing would be traced back to me.

Hopefully.

"How fast can you get me there?" I asked as we got in the car.

Sungil shot me a look. "Depends on how much of a scandal you want to be caught up in for being in a speeding car, hyung?" He grinned. "I can get you there in half the time it *should* take."

I sighed, hanging my head. "Don't break the law." He leaned forward, asking his driver to step on it.

It wasn't until we got near that I thought about calling her. Considering how calling her was all I could think about in the station, I was surprised.

I was also nervous. What if she hadn't waited?

The car squealed to a halt. "I owe you one," I told Sungil.

"Hold up," Sungil said, grabbing my shirt before

I could open the door. When I paused, he reached over, dropping a cap on my head. He held up a mask. "You're an idol in public. Meeting in a public park was not the smartest of ideas. Go somewhere quiet and send her in public places. And whatever you do, don't go back to her hotel."

"Sungil!" I exclaimed. "I'm not going to—"

"Go!" he instructed me. "Let true love happen."

I paused again, tilting my head at him. "Since when do you believe in true love?" He'd never told me why, although I had suspected it was something to do with his parents, but Sungil was a skeptic who was constantly claiming true love didn't exist.

"It doesn't matter what I believe," he shrugged. "Besides, I promised I'd be your guy. Now, go. She's been waiting long enough, and you only have a couple of weeks before she goes back home."

I gave him a grin then jumped out of the car.

Luna saw me straight away and came charging over. To me, it was like she was moving in slow motion. Her hair had grown, now halfway down her back, and was so blonde it was almost white. Her cheeks had a slight flush to them, making her blue eyes seem deeper than they were. It was like a black and white memory was filling with color. She was the most beautiful girl I'd ever seen.

I started to open my arms, ready to catch her in the embrace she was charging for, but then, she stopped, just in front of me. The hell with that. "Hullo, Luna," I said, grinning behind my mask. 'Hullo': the first word I had ever said to her, and being shy and nervous, had managed to mispronounce.

I grabbed her and pulled her to me, inhaling

deeply to refamiliarize myself with the scent that was distinctly Lucinda Williams: strawberries and something sweet I could never put my finger on. "Let's go for a walk," I muttered, as a sense of what I could only describe as familiarity and safety flooded me.

We were still on the side of the road, and thanks to Sungil's not-so-discreet car, I hadn't made a subtle entrance. It didn't look like anyone had recognized me; I owed Sungil for the cap and mask.

I took Luna's hand in mine, marveling at how small it now seemed. When we'd first started dancing together, it had been the same size as mine, just like she had been the same height as me. I had grown another few inches, so Luna was now a whole head shorter than me. My hands had grown too.

I led her away from the road, along an empty path towards the river. Then, at the last moment, I changed my mind. The riverbank sidewalk and cycle path were always busy. If we went there, there was a greater possibility of someone seeing me and recognizing me.

"I missed you."

I glanced down and found Luna staring up at me. I could see it in her eyes. She had missed me as much as I'd missed her.

I glanced around. This area was deserted, but there were also trees and bushes lining the path. It was not the romantic setting next to the river that I wanted, but it was private. I led us behind a large bush before someone came along.

Luna let out a small yelp, and I turned, ready to apologize. The words died in my throat when I saw how close she was to me. I was sure I was supposed to be a gentleman about this, but I couldn't help myself. I yanked my mask off, pulled Luna close to me, and kissed her.

The feeling of her in my arms was everything. I had her for two weeks and I wanted to spend as much time as I could like this. "I missed you," I said, before I could catch my breath. "I love you."

"I love you, Lee Minhyuk," she said. Those words… if she hadn't wrapped her arms around me first, I would have pulled her to me instead.

Two weeks was all we had.

I wasn't going to waste a moment of it. "I'm sorry I was late," I told her. "My schedule changed last minute."

"I wasn't worried for a moment," she said. She frowned and looked around, before giggling. "Minhyuk, we're in the bushes."

"I'm sorry," I hastily apologized again, mentally kicking myself. This wasn't romantic. This was … a bush. I tried to lead her out, but she didn't move.

"This is perfect," she told me, trying to lower us both to the ground. "I just want to spend time with you, and this is kind of hidden away."

"Wait," I said. I let go of her hand so I could pull my shirt off. It was one that had been provided to me by a designer and would have been worth a pretty penny, but I laid it on the dry dirt ground for her to sit on.

"I like your T-shirt," Luna laughed as she sat, nodding at the words on the T-shirt my overshirt had covered. 'Sorry I'm late: I didn't want to come'.

Horror rippled through me. "No, that's not why I was late!" I protested. "The stylist put me in this. I was late because the radio had to move the pre-recoding of my show and then the host was late so—"

"Minhyuk, it's fine!" Luna assured me as she pulled me down beside her. "I've done my research since January. I know how busy you can be. I also know that we're going to be restricted with what kind of things we can do, and places we can go. I'm just happy that I've managed to get a couple of hours of your time."

I felt guilty again. "I'm sorry. I feel like I'm your imaginary boyfriend."

Luna cocked her head, then poked at my side. I couldn't stop the ridiculously high-pitched squeal that escaped me as I rolled away: I was incredibly ticklish. "Wow …" she said, gaping at me. "I was just prodding you to make sure you were real, but that was …"

An evil glint appeared in her eyes. "Lucinda, I can see what you're thinking, and don't you dare."

She blinked her eyes at me innocently. It was like a scene from a cartoon, and yet, I swallowed: that was working. I was going to be in trouble if she used that on me.

Before I could pretend the look wasn't working, she lunged at me, her hands sliding up my sides and under my T-shirt.

Why did I have to be ticklish?

I lurched to the side, avoiding her arms, then circled back, grabbing her hands. Once secure, I pulled her back against me. "That's not nice," I told her, sternly. With a quick movement, I moved both her wrists into one of my hands and then settled the other on her hip. "How do you like it?"

She shrugged against me. "I'm not ticklish."

How could a person not be ticklish? "That's not

possible," I said, twisting my head so I could look at her as I ran my hand up and down her side. She just stared up at me, blinking slowly … those eyes were going to be my undoing.

With some skillful maneuvering, mainly so I could break the stare, I abandoned her side and reached down, tugging off one of her Nikes. I traced a finger up and down the sole of her foot.

There wasn't a reaction. She just stared at me like I was crazy.

"I feel nothing," she pointed out, despite my best efforts. The worst part was that I was sure she wasn't even pretending. "OK, I feel your finger, but it doesn't tickle. Honestly, I'm not ticklish."

I let go of her so I could move in front of her. I could feel my disbelief turn to outrage. "How can a person not be ticklish? What kind of human are you?"

"According to you, I'm some sort of alien," she told me, matter-of-factly.

The ticklishness was momentarily forgotten as I stared at her in confusion. "Alien?"

She nodded. "You keep calling me a Moon Princess. If I'm some princess of the moon, I'm sure that means I'm some kind of alien."

"Oh, that's not why I call you my Moon Princess!" I exclaimed, then quickly clamped my mouth shut, embarrassed.

"Then why?" she asked. "Why that? Why Luna?"

I shook my head. That was one secret I wasn't sharing with her.

"Rookie mistake," Luna suddenly declared, launching herself at my ribcage.

Another high-pitched squeal escaped me before I

could stop myself. Somehow, I managed to extract my limbs from hers, swiped at her shoe, and leaped to my feet, bounding away from her. When she gave chase, I darted out of the bush, running to safety in the middle of the grass. While she'd stayed short, my legs had grown, and it was easy to get some distance between us.

I held the running shoe up. "Play nice," I told her.

Luna cocked her head, an evil grin appearing. "That doesn't scare me!" she declared before toeing off her other shoe and kicking it towards me. She laughed at me, then charged, heading straight for me. I didn't move. At the last moment, I doubled over, catching her slim waist against my shoulder, and then I stood upright, slinging her over me. "Minhyuk!" she yelped.

"Why are you running around in bare feet?" I demanded. "You could tread on something and hurt yourself. You're a dancer. You should take better care of yourself." I walked over, collecting the other shoe and started carrying her back to the bushes.

"You're the one who took my shoe off first," she pointed out, her voice slightly muffled from behind. "And you made a fatal mistake."

I discovered what that fatal mistake was, midway through walking back into our little hideaway. Before I could set her down, she reached out, tickling just above my hips.

I let out another shriek, jerking my body, trying to move myself out of Luna's grasp as I tightened my grip on her so as not to drop her. Luna was sneaky. Her hands went straight back up under my T-shirt. The sound that came out of me was almost a scream. The next thing I knew, we were falling sideways. At the last minute, I twisted my body and we fell into a bush rather than the hard grass we had been playing on.

"Are you OK?" I asked from beside her, desperately scrabbling to try to get out of the bush, but half under her, not really succeeding.

"You really are ticklish, aren't you?"

I stared up at the sky through the trees that had been sheltering us. With a grunt, I tried to sit up and failed again. "Yes, and I'm not sure how I feel about you knowing this weakness!" I cried in exasperation.

Luna leaned over and patted my stomach, sympathetically. Or, at least, I assumed she was trying to be sympathetic, considering my reaction was to writhe and giggle.

"You have the cutest giggle," Luna told me as she rolled over and out of the bush. She walked over to me and held out her hand. Pouting, I folded my arms and pulled a face. "Of course, if you think you can get out by yourself?"

That's what she thought ...

I reached up and grabbed the hand she was offering, but when she started to pull me up, I tugged her towards me. Luna fell onto my chest, only just stopping herself from headbutting me.

I don't know how this was different from anything we had been doing until now, but my heart was racing with her lying on me. It wasn't comfortable— there were branches and twigs sticking in my back—but I was in no hurry to get up. I closed my eyes, trying to get myself to snap out of it.

Her hand playing with my hair had my eyes opening in an instant. "You're handsome," she murmured.

I made the mistake of meeting her gaze.

Or maybe it wasn't a mistake.

"What are you thinking?" she asked me.

I smiled. "That these two weeks are going to go by too quickly and if there's any way I could cancel any of my appearances, I would." Her cheeks flamed, and she looked away. "What are you thinking?"

She opened her mouth, and then stopped, shaking her head as she tried to pull away from me. I reached up and wrapped my arms around her. "Minhyuk, this can't be comfortable for you," she protested, squirming in my arms.

"What are you thinking?" I asked again.

She leaned forward and kissed me. I kissed her back. We didn't have much time together before she would have to go home. I didn't want to spend the little time we did have being sad about her leaving.

Much as I loved kissing Luna, and I really, really did, I was about to collapse. I was being propped up with the strength of my core, and three branches which were digging into me—one in a truly inconvenient location.

Gently, I pushed Luna up, feeling bad at the disappointed look she was giving me. "I really need to get out of this bush," I informed her. Before my stomach muscles collapsed on me, I eased her back, and then accepted her help to get out of the bush. My feet were barely on the ground before I was kissing her again. I was going to take every available opportunity to do just that.

제3 장

Lucinda

A week flew by before I knew it. I got to see Minhyuk more than I expected, but not as much as I wanted. Tonight, he had a surprise for me. I had one for him.

I'd managed to keep it a secret from him since January. It wasn't just that I had gotten my parents to agree to a two-week vacation in Seoul. I'd convinced them to let me attend the Seoul Leadership Academy for the rest of my high school education.

Because it had taken a while to complete the paperwork, and I had wanted to finish out my Junior year in New York, I'd waited until the summer until I moved. Of course, because the academic year followed the lunar calendar, now I was here, I would have to complete the second part of my Junior year again.

It also meant that after completing my senior year, I would be returning to America part-way through what would be my freshman year of college. Only, I was OK with that because I was going to audition for Julliard.

My hope was to learn some new styles of dancing while I was here to make me stand out from all the other dancers who would be applying to Julliard.

I'd been keeping it a secret from Minhyuk partly because it hadn't felt real until I was on the plane, partly because I wanted to tell him in person.

Tomorrow was the day I was going to move into the dorms. I was nervous and excited. It was almost like going to college early. I had my list of roommates; *three* of them.

Tonight, we would be alone, and I would tell him then. The last time he had spoken to me, he said he was going to take me somewhere, and although he refused to tell me where, he had told me to wear something nice.

I spent a lot of time getting ready. I wasn't one for dresses, but I'd bought one before I'd left. Like the outfit I had chosen for meeting Minhyuk, I had spent as much time picking this one out too. It was a pretty summer dress that was smart enough that I could have worn it for a dinner out with my parents. A pearl pink with a knee length skirt and a halter neck top.

I went down to the hotel lobby and found Sungil waiting for me. I walked over, chewing at my lip.

"You look pretty," Sungil said.

"Are you here to tell me Minhyuk has had to cancel?" I asked him, glumly. He'd had to cancel on me once already this week because of his schedule. I couldn't fault him for it, but it didn't mean I wasn't disappointed.

Sungil arched an eyebrow. "Do you really expect him to come to a *hotel* and pick you up?" I ... hadn't thought about that. I shook my head. "I'm here to bring you," Sungil continued.

"Do you know where I'm going?" I asked in surprise.

"I have to, to be able to take you there," Sungil pointed out.

I hadn't spent any time with Sungil, but I was certain I wasn't creating a good first impression of myself. I wasn't the most academic of people, seeing as I spent a lot of time out of school, dancing, but I wasn't an idiot.

"I'm sorry," I told him. "I'm just a little surprised to see you, that's all."

Sungil nodded. "King wanted to pick you up, but I told him that wasn't a smart move. Besides, he has to get ready."

"You know he hasn't told me anything," I told Sungil as I followed him outside to where his car was waiting. The driver opened the door and I got in, sliding over.

Sungil got in beside me. "King wanted to surprise you."

"Why do you do that?" I asked. "Call him King," I added when Sungil tilted his head.

"That's his name," Sungil responded.

I shook my head. "His name is Minhyuk."

Sungil sat back in the seat, crossing his legs. "As far as Atlantis is concerned, that became his name when he signed the contract. He asked that I call him that too, otherwise I'd call him Minhyuk."

I frowned as I stared out the window. That had never occurred to me. I called him Minhyuk because that was who I knew—not King. King was the boy the fans loved. Minhyuk was the boy who loved me.

He'd never mentioned it, but I wasn't sure I'd

ever be able to call him King.

The car eventually pulled up outside another hotel. I couldn't help but look at Sungil in surprise. "You're bringing me to a hotel?" I said, staring over at him.

Sungil looked up from unbuckling his belt and caught me chewing my lip. I knew my gray eyes were wide and unblinking as they stared at him. "I'm bringing you to King," he said, getting out of the car.

I hurried after him, coming to a stop when something flashed in my face. All of a sudden, there were people with microphones and cameras pointing their equipment in my direction. A dozen people started firing questions at me at the same time. I had no idea what Sungil was up to, but right now, I really wanted to get back in the car.

As if he knew what I was thinking, before I could change my mind, Sungil was by my side. "Just smile," he told me, leading me into the lobby.

"What is going on?" I hissed at him. "Why are we at a hotel? Why are there photographers here? I thought Minhyuk would get into trouble if anyone knew about me."

"Which is why you are here with me," Sungil responded, calmly, leading me to one of the elevators where a bellboy pressed the button for us.

It wasn't until we were both heading to the penthouse, that I turned to him. "Where is here?" As soon as the doors pinged open, Sungil darted out, leaving me in the elevator.

I stepped out, looking for Minhyuk. Instead I was greeted by a room full of strangers. As the only white person, I was already gathering curious stares.

So much for bringing me here with him.

I sucked in a breath and held my head up. I wasn't unused to attention. I was a dancer and I competed. A lot. People were always watching me. It didn't take long for people to decide I was unimportant and return to whatever they were doing.

The room was also full of reporters and cameramen. Most of the crowd were middle-aged men and women in suits and smart dresses. There were hardly any people my age. "Where the hell have you brought me?" I asked a potted plant in English.

From the other side, the head of a guy my age popped out. "Me?"

"No, sorry," I apologized in Korean. The guy stepped out and tilted his head. His hair was all gelled up, and he was wearing eyeliner. Far from wearing a suit like everyone else, he looked ready to hit a club. He was also really handsome, I realized as I felt my face heat up.

The boy cocked his head. "Are you asking the plant?"

I half turned my head to look at the small bush beside me and felt my face continue to burn. I gave the boy a shrug. "Yes. I gave up a date with a tree for this guy," I replied, hoping all the Korean I'd learned before coming out here was sufficient enough to make a joke.

The boy laughed. It was warm and genuine. As was the look he gave me. "You're not like most of the people here."

I glanced around. "Thank you. That means the night cream is working. I'm really forty-eight."

The boy laughed again. "And now I don't know which honorifics to use."

"How offended would you feel if I said don't use

any?" I asked him, feeling myself relax.

He gave me another thoughtful look. "Are you younger than me?"

I shrugged. "I turned seventeen in June," I told him, reverting to English. "Wait, how good is your English?"

"My name is Yung Dongyeol." The grin returned.

"I'm ..." I frowned, pulling a face. "Yung Dongyeol?"

"You're called Yung Dongyeol too?"

"Lucinda," I hurriedly shook my head, finally recognizing the boy in front of me. "Yung Dongyeol, as in one of Bright Boys' vocalists?"

Surprise appeared on Dongyeol's face. "You know who I am?" When I nodded my head, he smiled. "Are you a Dazzle?"

Dazzle was the name of the Bright Boys' fandom. I laughed. "I guess I am," I told him. Before I could offer up any more information, Dongyeol was suddenly surrounded by four other guys, all around his age, and all in similar states of dress: more members of Bright Boys.

The immediate area became very noisy as they were all excitedly chatting to Dongyeol. My Korean was good, but they were talking far too fast for me to follow properly. Judging from the looks the five of them were sending my way, the snippets of conversation I was able to understand, and how twitchy Dongyeol was becoming, I knew they were teasing him about me.

Then one of them said something, which, when Dongyeol responded, made them fall quiet. Finally, one with reddish hair, Apollo, one of the rappers, stepped forward and peered at me. Keeping my feet firmly planted where they were, I leaned my head back, away from him. "Dongyeol says you're dating a tree."

My mouth fell open. "No!" I objected. Then I grinned. "I turned the tree down to come out with the bush," I informed them, using both hands to indicate to the plant beside me.

"She's cute," Apollo declared to Dongyeol, as another swung his arm over Dongyeol's shoulder. "It's a shame she has bad taste."

I realized then that they didn't know who I was. "Take that back," I demanded in mock horror as I cupped my hands over a pair of imaginary ears the bush had magically sprouted. "You'll offend my date."

Another member, Seungjin stared at me with wide eyes. "I wish I could take a picture of this."

"Hey! Where's your phone?" Dongyeol asked me.

It was in my pocket. It was also full of pictures of me and Minhyuk—including on my homescreen. "I didn't bring it," I lied in a panic. If they didn't know who I was, that meant Minhyuk hadn't told them about me. "I was that excited that I forgot to bring it," I added.

"About us?"

"No," I shook my head. "About George."

"Who is George?" i asked. While Seungjin was my age, the others were older. Ryan, Dongyeol, and Apollo would have been the year above me at school, and Yongsik at college … if any of them were still attending school, that was.

I pointed at the plant. "My date: George Bush."

There was a moment of silence and then the group started laughing. "I like this girl," Ryan declared.

"Lucinda?" Still smiling, I turned in the direction of the voice and found Minhyuk watching me, his expression somewhere between surprise and amusement. I was certain mine was too: I think that was the first time I had heard him call me Lucinda and not Luna. "You made it."

"Hi, Min … King" I corrected myself. That sounded even more foreign than Minhyuk calling me Lucinda.

"How do you know King?" Apollo asked me.

I glanced at Apollo, then at Minhyuk, staring at him helplessly. I didn't want to say anything that would get him in trouble.

"The New York Dance Academy," Minhyuk offered to the confused faces. He turned back to me. "I'm glad you could come. It has been a while since I saw you last."

It had been last night.

The others *definitely* didn't know who I was.

I nodded. "Sungil brought me."

Minhyuk sighed. I was sure it was a sign of relief. "Where is Sungil?" he asked, looking around the room.

"Sungil?" Apollo asked me.

I turned, grinning. "The tree."

When Dongyeol burst out laughing, all the other boys looked confused. "I have no idea what that means," Minhyuk told me.

I shared a look with Dongyeol, then shook my head at Minhyuk. "It's a long story," I told him, before turning back to Apollo. "Sungil is my friend. I know him through Min … King."

"Minhyuk?" Apollo asked, looking at Minhyuk.

I quickly cleared my throat before I got Minhyuk in trouble. "What is going on here?" I asked Minhyuk, glancing at the boys, then at the people surrounding them, who suddenly seemed interested in the group. As I scanned the room, I realized a lot of them were looking at me.

"You really don't know?" Yongsik asked, surprised.

"Did Sungil not tell you?" Minhyuk asked.

I managed to shake my head in response as Apollo spoke up. "Is Sungil your boyfriend?"

"Yes," Sungil declared, glowering at Apollo as he suddenly appeared and joined my side.

I stared up at him, my eyes wide. I could see why he was saying that, but really he could have just said we were friends. This was going to get messy, especially when they all found out I was staying in Seoul. I turned to Minhyuk. "King—"

"*That* Sungil?" Seungjin said loudly, cutting me off.

"I was looking for you," Sungil said, addressing Minhyuk and ignoring Seungjin. "Sorry we're late. She took forever to get ready." I looked around the room, ignoring the incredulous look Minhyuk was giving me. "There are a lot of people here tonight." Sungil glanced at the other boys and nodded a greeting. "I didn't know Bright Boys were here. Where's Jaehoon?"

"We're here to support our friend," Dongyeol, his hair now bright red, declared, grinning at King. "Jaehoon is here with Hyunseo, somewhere."

At that moment, the lights in the room dimmed and everyone went silent as someone bounded onto the stage which had been set up at the far end of the room. The man took to the microphone beside an elegant grand piano and started speaking. "Welcome ladies and gentlemen, on behalf of Atlantis Entertainment." I turned my attention to the stage, glad that he was speaking clearly so I could follow. "We are happy and humbled that you would spend your evening with us, here at the Regency Hotel."

I glanced around, trying to work out what was happening. Thankfully, everyone else had their attention on the small stage.

"… By welcoming King to the stage to share with you his next comeback, Moon Princess," the MC continued.

제4 장

Lucinda

My mouth dropped open as the room burst into applause. Minhyuk left us, walking over to the stage and joining the MC. There was a pause and then music started playing. Minhyuk bowed to the audience and then sat down at a large, white, grand piano.

Oh my goodness, I was finally going to be able to see Minhyuk perform live. I had been set on doing that for a long time and had hoped that studying out here would give me that opportunity.

I shook my head, turning my attention to the stage and Minhyuk. With him being sat at a piano, I had been expecting him to play something classical. Instead, the melody of an upbeat pop song filled the room from the giant speakers either side of the stage. Part way through, the backing track kicked in, and Minhyuk left the piano to start dancing.

I'd trained with him for several years, so I knew he could dance. He'd choreographed a few of our routines in the past. I'd bought his debut album and watched as many of his stages on YouTube as I could. But still, watching him sing and dance at the same time was amazing.

Minhyuk was amazing.

Minhyuk—King—was a pop star, and as far as I was concerned, one of the best.

And then, I started paying attention to the lyrics. I could feel my eyes grow wide. I'd never heard this song before. The odd lyric was sung in English, and although I would have to hunt down an English translation of it to confirm, I was sure that he was singing about a faraway love. Specifically, his love of a Moon Princess and the great distance between them.

The song was about me.

The song ended, and the room exploded into applause. I joined in, clapping as hard as I could. King had surprised me, but in a good way, and I was incredibly proud of him. The lights came back on and the next thing I knew, Sungil had grabbed my wrist and spun me to him. "You're crying."

I pulled my hand free and brought it to my cheeks. They were wet. Quickly, I wiped them away, shrugging. "I liked the song," I said as I realized Seungjin was watching me.

"The song made you cry?" Seungjin asked, clearly not believing me.

"Who is crying?" Minhyuk asked, as he rejoined us, accompanied by the two remaining members of Bright Boys; Hyunseo, the leader, and Jaehoon, Minhyuk's other best friend.

"Me," I admitted. I leaped over to him and threw my arms around him to hug him. Then, I stepped back, quickly realizing what I was doing and swiped at his arm.

"When you said you sang, this is not what I thought you were talking about!" I exclaimed in a panic.

"Do you sing?" Dongyeol asked, curiously.

"Not exactly," I replied.

"Is anyone else curious?" Apollo asked, speaking more to his groupmates.

I waved my arms as I shook my head. "Oh, I'm a nobody. I'm not a singer."

Apollo and Dongyeol shared a look. "Noraebang!" Dongyeol declared.

I glanced at Minhyuk, biting at my lip. I really needed to talk to him, and I wasn't sure what he had planned, so I didn't want to agree to anything.

"I have to be here for another hour maybe," Minhyuk declared. "But after that, let's go find a noraebang and have some fun."

I sighed. "What is a noraebang?" I searched my brain for the translation. I had come across it in my studying, but for the life of me, I couldn't remember what it meant.

"Find out later," Apollo teased.

Z

True to his word, Minhyuk was only gone an hour, but it was a very strange hour. Minhyuk didn't speak that often of Bright Boys. I'd learned more about them in the letters from the early days of them all being trainees—before they were Bright Boys. The descriptions from Minhyuk had been brief. Most of his conversations were about Sungil and Jaehoon.

The members of Bright Boys were all ridiculously attractive, but so was Sungil. Sungil had trained with them all too, but something had happened and now he was just an ordinary person like me. Minhyuk had mentioned it briefly—it was something to do with Sungil's father not wanting the heir of his company being an idol.

I wasn't sure if there was more to it or not, but Sungil spent most of the hour with Jaehoon, looking almost uncomfortable at being there. That automatically made me feel bad. If I'd have known, I would have insisted on taking a taxi rather than making Sungil be somewhere he didn't want to be.

When Minhyuk rejoined us, ready to leave, I followed him and the others outside, using the back entrance to the hotel where we flagged down a number of taxis. Everyone pulled out caps and masks. Sungil made me stay by his side. "If anyone sees, they will think you're with me, rather than Bright Boys or King," he explained as he handed me a cap and mask. It didn't go with my dress, but I pulled them on.

Being an idol was crazy—and I wasn't one.

It wasn't until I was in the back of the taxi with Minhyuk, Sungil and Jaehoon, that I could sense Minhyuk relax beside me. I turned to him, keeping my voice low. "That song," I started.

"Shut the front door!" Jaehoon exclaimed, making me jump. "You're her."

I stared at him, eyes wide. "Me?"

Jaehoon's attention was on Minhyuk. "It is, isn't it? She's your Moon Princess."

Minhyuk grinned. "This is my Luna," he nodded, reaching for my hand.

I could feel my cheeks heating up. "Why do you call me that?"

"Because the word sounds prettier than it does in Korean," Minhyuk replied.

I shook my head, turning slightly in my seat. "I mean, I understand Luna, because it could be short for Lucinda, but why Moon Princess?"

"You don't know either?" Jaehoon asked, surprised.

"No," I said, looking back at Minhyuk. He just shrugged at me. I could see he wasn't going to tell me, so I sat back. "Do the others know about me then?"

"No!"

The response came in surround sound with Minhyuk, Jaehoon, and Sungil replying loudly. I held my hands up. "OK, note to self: don't mention anything to the others."

"We're not allowed to date. It's in the Atlantis contracts," Jaehoon said. I nodded, knowing this already. "The company actively checks up on us, and they already have our phones, as you know, so while we don't think any of the others would say anything, this way it doesn't put them in a position where they would have to lie."

Minhyuk laced his fingers through mine. "I know it means sneaking around for you, and I'm sorry."

"Is this going to get you in trouble?" I asked him. "Not this," I said, holding up our hands. "I mean going to a noraebang …" My eyes widened as I remembered what it was. *Karaoke.*

"Possibly," Minhyuk said, thoughtfully. He squeezed my hand at my panicked expression. "But I wanted to be able to take you out somewhere, and this was all I could think of. Plus, it means I get to show you off to my friends." He leaned over and kissed my cheek.

From the other side of the car, Jaehoon mimed sticking his fingers down his throat, while Sungil rolled his eyes. "Get a room."

Once more I could feel my face heat up. I was sure I was the same color as Apollo's hair. "They're just jealous," Minhyuk whispered in my ear.

We arrived at the noraebang and Minhyuk let go of me. I shoved my disappointment aside: I knew that was going to happen. I followed Sungil into the non-descript building and up two flights of stairs.

The ten of us poured into the room where I was pushed to the front. "This isn't quite what I had in mind," I muttered as the boys all piled onto the seats that lined the walls. With a shrug, I turned to address the room. "Prepare to have your minds blown."

With that, I bounded over to the machine and searched for a song, grinning when I discovered they had the one I wanted. I picked up the microphone and took my position on the small stage, only to discover the boys were whispering amongst each other.

All of them looked worried. My grin widened as the opening bars started. The song I had chosen was a rap song. And even if it was an American rap song, it was still difficult. But I could sing—well, rap—it.

I watched as Jaehoon glanced at Minhyuk. Then Minhyuk leaned forward to catch Ryan's attention. Wordlessly, he nodded his head in my direction. I opened my mouth, ready to sing, when Ryan joined me, taking the other microphone. "What are you doing?" I asked him, missing my cue.

"Helping," he offered. I gave him a look of confusion and he smiled. "I'm one of the rappers in Bright Boys."

I frowned, ignored the song, and grabbed Ryan's hand, pulling him off the stage to where the machine was. "Can you sing?" I asked him, releasing my hold on him.

"You know we're an idol group, right?" he asked, pointing over at the rest of his friends who were watching with interest, trying to hear what was being said over the backing track that was still playing.

"That doesn't necessarily mean you're also a vocalist," I mumbled, my cheeks flaming. "What I mean is, how high can you sing? Can you manage female vocals if I switch this to a duet?" When he stared at me in confusion, I scrolled through the karaoke machine, pointing at a duet. "Can you manage this part?" I asked, pointing.

Ryan stepped forward, squinted at the machine, and then turned to me with a look which said he thought he was mistaken in the part I was pointing at. "Are you sure you don't want me to do that part?" he said, pointing at the rapper's name.

"Nope," I shook my head. "That's mine."

"You want to rap the male part, and have me sing the female part?"

I raised a shoulder. "Only if you think you can keep up with me?" I selected the track and bounded back onto the stage. Ryan followed after me, clearly still unsure how serious I was being. The track started playing and when the female singer's part started, he missed the cue. Yes, he had definitely been certain that I was going to sing.

I elbowed him, then shook my head. I cleared my throat and started singing, catching up with the song. I can't sing, and I was massacring it. The part was high, and I didn't need to look at the winces on everyone's faces to know I was missing every note. I leaned over and raised Ryan's microphone, waving my arm at him. Finally, Ryan started singing.

I stopped, surprised. He *could* hit the high notes. I recovered quickly, ready for my part. I couldn't sing, but I wasn't too bad at rapping. I wasn't good enough to make a career out of it (not that anything other than dancing had been my intention for as long as I could remember), but I was good enough that every single mouth, Ryan's included, was hanging open in disbelief.

That was partly why I did it. Even back home, the expectations were that I looked like I fell into the Taylor Swift category of pop music, especially with my blonde hair. The dress I was wearing was cute and girly and did nothing to alter that image either. They'd have been even more surprised if they'd have let me continue with my initial selection—the rapping of Eminem in this song was reasonable, but the other one was much quicker, and I could keep up.

I continued rapping, stepping off the stage, ignoring the lyrics on the screen as I knew the song by heart. I reached out, stole Apollo's cap, and stuck it on my head, returning to the stage, just in time for Ryan to take over with his part. While he sang, I danced about to the side. It felt awkward because I was rapping at the same time, but I was a dancer.

The room was singing along with us and I was suddenly grateful that I was able to do this. I still needed to talk to Minhyuk, but there would be time tomorrow. For now, I was enjoying myself. Sure, the circumstances that had led to this were a little strange, but it felt like I was home, surrounded by friends.

Bright Boys would leave at the end of the night, and I'd probably never see them again, but they were all so friendly; even Apollo who had seemed shy, was really just quiet. Minhyuk looked relaxed around them, too. The only person who didn't seem to be relaxing was Sungil.

Several songs later, I grabbed two drinks from the tray which had been delivered while I had been singing and joined Minhyuk, offering him one. "You can rap," he said, taking the bottle of Fanta.

I nodded. "Not what you were expecting, I take it?"

"You surprise me a lot," he admitted, so quietly, I barely heard it over Ryan and Apollo who were now rapping.

The music suddenly stopped, and Jaehoon pulled a face, announcing something I didn't quite catch. I yawned and stretched. "I'm guessing that's the cue to leave?" I asked as Minhyuk nodded, glumly. We left the karaoke bar to find a small minibus and a very irritated looking man waiting for us.

I barely had a chance to look at him before Sungil stepped in front of me, spinning me around so I had my back to the man. "Who's that?" I whispered at Sungil as he pulled me against him.

"I'm sorry," he apologized, sounding as uncomfortable as he looked. "That's Oh Seokbeom. He's Bright Boys' manager." I tried to peer over my shoulder, but he held me tighter. "He is the one who saw you in New York."

I was the reason why Minhyuk had never debuted in Bright Boys. Last year, he had been at New York Fashion Week and I had sneaked into his hotel to meet him. We'd been caught and Minhyuk's punishment was not debuting. Instead he'd had to wait months and then he'd been debuted as a solo artist.

I could feel my heart pounding in my chest and it wasn't because of Sungil's embrace. I ducked my head, resting it against Sungil, praying that Oh Seokbeom wouldn't come over and recognize me. I did not want Minhyuk being punished again.

"Just stay there," Sungil murmured.

Behind me I could hear the guys being reprimanded as they were ushered onto the minibus. "Are they going to be in trouble?" I asked, quietly.

"Oh Seokbeom is a strict and grumpy manager, and they wouldn't have come out if they were going to get in trouble. We're not far from the dorms. Hyunseo would have gotten it approved first," he assured me.

I knew the moment the minibus was out of sight because Sungil released me, stepping back so suddenly, I nearly stumbled.

"I'll take you back to your hotel," Sungil told me.

제5 장

Minhyuk

Although it was a Sunday, I was unable to find time to see Luna during the day. I had no scheduled appearances, but I had to be in the studio, working on my comeback. My performance of 'Moon Princess' had been a test run. The choreographer had been there, but he had decided my moves needed tightening. While I wanted to see Luna, especially because time was running out before she had to go back to America, my comeback was just as important.

It wasn't until the evening and I was in my room that plans changed. I had a room to myself in the dorms. It wasn't big, but it wasn't much smaller than the two rooms Bright Boys shared—at least this one only had me in it.

While we were trainees and rookies, we had rooms. When we became more established and earned a bit of money, Atlantis would move us to a higher floor in the dorms where we would get a small apartment between us. I'd seen Onyx's. Theirs was big and they had a room each, plus they had a TV area and a kitchen.

We had to go down the road to Atlantis Entertainment's offices to use their cafeteria.

I was getting ready to head down, and conveniently meet up with Sungil on the way so that I could check to see if Luna had sent me any messages, when I heard the commotion.

Bright Boys were on the same floor as me as they still only had rooms rather than apartments too. I stepped out into the hallway and found Hyunseo, Bright Boys' oldest member and leader, backed up against a wall with Jaehoon and Ryan pinning him back against the wall.

"Let go of me!" Hyunseo yelled. "I'm going to kill him!"

"Which is precisely why we're not going to let go, hyung!" Ryan shouted back.

"She's gone!" Hyunseo continued to yell, still struggling to break free of Jaehoon and Ryan's hold. "My parents sent her away and it's all his fault, not hers. He's going to get away with it."

"Hyung!" Jaehoon snapped. "If you do anything now, it will be you who gets in trouble, not him.

"Jaehoon is right. If you want justice, you need to get Mina to go to the police. If you do anything, it's going to reflect on us too," Ryan added.

Hyunseo's struggling lessened. "She's my sister," he said, the anger leaving his voice to be replaced by desperation.

"And it's up to her," Ryan said, again. "I know it's not what you want to hear, but she needs to be the one to go to the police."

A door opened and Dongyeol stepped out. "What's going on?" he asked me, joining me in the doorway. Hyunseo, Jaehoon and Ryan were oblivious to our presence.

"Hyunseo has a sister, right?" I asked.

Dongyeol nodded. "Mina. Why? Did something happen?"

"Is she dating someone?"

Dongyeol nodded again. "Min … Min Gukyung? His younger brother goes to SLA. I think he's your age."

"Taekyung?" I asked, searching my brain. It had been some time since I had last attended school.

"I guess?"

"I think something happened between Mina and Gukyung," I explained. In front of us, Hyunseo was slowly starting to calm down.

"So, it's settled then," Ryan suddenly announced. He turned to me and Dongyeol. "You will both come, right?"

"Sure," Dongyeol agreed.

I had no idea what I was agreeing to. "Yes."

"Great. Get ready and we'll go."

"Go … go where?" I asked.

"Club Zero."

"Hyung, I have plans," I said, slowly, thinking of Luna.

Ryan pulled a face. "You have something scheduled?" Ryan was the Chinese-Korean member of the group. He'd been born in Hangzhou, a city not far from Shanghai, but had moved to Busan when he was six. He was fluent in Mandarin, Korean, and English, and had a strange accent which captured all three.

"No," I said slowly, catching Jaehoon's eye.

Before Jaehoon could jump in and help me, Dongyeol clapped a hand on my shoulder. "Then there isn't a problem."

"Are we old enough for Club Zero?" I asked, grateful that, for once, no I wasn't.

"We don't need to worry about that," Ryan replied, vaguely.

"I'm supposed to meet Sungil," I said in a last-ditch effort to get out of this.

"Brilliant," Dongyeol smiled. "Bring him along."

I had to bite back the groan. "OK," I relented, hoping that Luna would understand. At least Sungil would be able to send her a message for me.

Z

That was harder than planned. When they discovered I was going to meet Sungil at Atlantis, the group decided to go with me. I wasn't sure why. There were more likely to be fans lurking around. It also meant that I couldn't explain fully to Sungil. Sungil sent me a questioning look, but all I could do was shrug at him as Dongyeol clamped a hand on his shoulder, declaring we were going clubbing.

Although I kept my fingers crossed that the club wouldn't let us in, especially considering Seungjin was with us and he didn't look old enough to be there, the bouncers didn't even ask to look at our IDs, ushering us through to the back.

A new unease settled over me while I was in there. Our contracts had never specified that we were to stay out of nightclubs, but one of the members of H3RO, Nate, had been caught fighting in clubs. My manager had told me the only reason why he wasn't in the trouble he should have been was because H3RO were on a hiatus.

Although I could have had a drink, I chose not to. Dongyeol and I were the only ones not drinking. It wasn't because I didn't drink, but because I didn't want to be caught drinking. I was surprised to see Seungjin drinking—I wasn't sure that even his father, the Chairman of Atlantis Entertainment would help him out if he got into trouble over that one. "Are you sure you should be doing that?" I asked him.

Seungjin shrugged. "It's just a beer, King."

I sat back, keeping to the back of the booth we had claimed. I realized that I didn't care for nightclubs. They weren't my thing. If anything, I'd rather have been in one of the Atlantis dance studios, dancing. That wasn't true—I'd rather have been with Luna.

I was grateful when Hyunseo finally decided it was time for us to get back to the dorm. Whatever had gone down with his sister, the beer and the dancing seemed to have cooled him off. The later it was getting, the more aware he seemed of us younger members. "It's close to curfew," he announced loudly, over the music.

I was on my feet in an instant, happy to get out of there. It was too late to get in touch with Luna now, and I didn't want to get in trouble for breaking curfew and risk not being able to see her. She was only going to be here for another five days.

Outside, we waited for our Ubers. The first one arrived and people bundled into it. Somehow, I was left on the sidewalk with Hyunseo, Sungil, and Jaehoon. Sungil wasn't going in the same direction as the dorms—his house was in the Hanman district on the other side of the river.

I should have known everything was going too

smoothly.

One moment we were talking about the next Bright Boys comeback—it was supposed to be in October and they were getting the first listen of their song this week—and the next, Hyunseo had gone barging past me, shoving me so hard in the process that the only reason I didn't go flying into the road was because Jaehoon grabbed me.

"Are you kidding me? How dare you show your face?" Hyunseo roared, amongst a mouthful of expletives.

I turned in time to see him disappear around a corner. Jaehoon, Sungil and I looked at each other. Then, in silent unison, ran after him.

We were too late.

A guy was on the floor, Hyunseo standing above him, ready to hit him. Jaehoon charged over, tackling him out of the way before he could strike. "Get off me!" Hyunseo bellowed.

Sungil and I ran over to help Jaehoon. "We need to get out of here before anyone sees," Sungil told him, dragging Hyunseo away towards the street.

While Jaehoon helped him, I ran over to the guy on the floor. I didn't know him, but my money was on him being Min Gukyung. He was alive but unconscious, sporting a split lip and a nasty red mark below his eye.

"King, leave him!" Jaehoon yelled at me.

"I can't!" I shouted back. "He needs to go to a hospital!"

"We'll all get in trouble, and then you'll have to answer questions with the police."

I stared down at Gukyung, torn. It felt wrong leaving him, but if I had to answer questions from the police, I wouldn't be able to lie. Hyunseo would be in trouble—we all would be.

The decision was made for me. Hyunseo stormed over, grabbed my upper arm, and pulled me away. We fell out onto the street, just as our Uber pulled up. All of us, including Sungil, jumped into it.

The ride back to the dorm was spent in silence. It wasn't until we got out that Hyunseo spoke. "Inside." I think his instruction was aimed at Sungil who was about to order another Uber. Dutifully, we followed him inside, slipping back into silence. Instead of going up to the dorms, we went to the basement.

"Hi guys!" Xiao greeted us cheerfully as we passed the gym.

The basement of the dorm building held two gyms—one for males, one for females, and past them, the old dance studios. In a remodel, the dance and recording studios had been moved to the Atlantis building, but one remained, hidden away at the back.

Xiao, the Chinese member of Onyx wasn't the only person we passed. Because the gym was in our building, it was open twenty-four hours. Rookies, trainees, idols—we all kept strange sleeping habits, so it wasn't unusual to see so many people.

We all bowed respectfully to our sunbae—our senior—as we passed, but didn't stop to chat, like we would have done. Xiao, unperturbed carried on his way to the gym.

Hyunseo led us to the last room, opening the door. This was H3RO's dance studio, another of our sunbae groups. I hadn't seen them around for a while, thinking about it …

We walked in, waiting patiently for Hyunseo to

close the door behind us. When he turned to us, he did so with his head bowed. "I am sorry," he said. "I should not have put you in that position."

"Who was he?" Sungil asked. "What was all that about?"

Hyunseo sucked in a deep breath before looking at us. "My sister's ex-boyfriend. He hit her," he said, simply.

Beside me, Sungil's hands curled into fists. "Then I'm sorry we stopped you," he growled.

"No," Hyunseo said, firmly. He ran a hand through his blonde hair. "You did the right thing. I should never have brought you into this in the first place."

"I don't think anyone saw anything," Jaehoon said, quietly.

We all looked at him. "I hope not," Hyunseo said, looking ashamed, hanging his head again. "But if they did, if Min Gukyung reports this—if *anything* comes of this, I need you all to promise me that you say you know nothing."

"He attacked your sister," Sungil scowled.

"And I attacked him," Hyunseo corrected him. "I'd do it again, too, but only if you three weren't there. If anything happens from this, I want you to promise me you will say you didn't see anything."

"He attacked your sister!" Sungil objected again.

"Which is precisely why you can't say anything!" Hyunseo snapped back. "She's gone. She's not even in Seoul anymore, which means she's not going to the police. If her name comes into this, if anyone finds out, her name is going to be all over the news, and because of me, because of who I am, it is going to get blown out of proportion. I failed to protect her once. I can't do it again."

"It shouldn't come to that," Jaehoon said, diplomatically. "No one saw us."

"Except Gukyung," I muttered, softly. When Hyunseo looked at me, I held my hands up. "I won't say anything. I promise."

Jaehoon and Sungil echoed my words.

"I'm sorry," Hyunseo said, again. "And if anything does come of this, I promise you that I will deny you were involved. I was the one who reacted recklessly. You won't be punished for it."

I left the studio believing him.

제6 장

Lucinda

I'd arranged with the hotel that I could checkout after lunch. They organized a car to take me and my luggage over to the school and dropped me off. I stood outside the gates of the Seoul Leadership Academy, staring up at it in confusion.

The pictures online didn't quite match up with what I was seeing. Online, it was described as an exclusive international school, and with the tuition fees almost the same as the private school I had attended in upper New York state, I was expecting it to be as well looked after.

It wasn't.

The sign was peeling.

The gardens which lined the path, and then the thirty-something steps up to the dorms were full of weeds. Inside, the furniture in the lobby had seen better days: it needed a lick of paint at the very least.

I wasn't too worried. There had only been a handful of international schools in Seoul that would take me because of my grades. It wasn't that I was stupid, but I had missed a lot of school over the years as I travelled to competitions, and that had pulled down my GPA.

SLA was also close to the Atlantis Entertainment building. I wasn't out to stalk Minhyuk, but I had done my research. It would be easier for him to explain why he was around his management company, than if he was regularly seen in other areas of the city. Another advantage was, if he was keeping odd hours and I had to sneak out, I wouldn't be travelling all over the city to see him.

I leafed through the pack I had been given when I had checked in, fishing out the sheet of paper with the six-digit code on it to unlock my room. Once open, I pushed my cases in and stopped, examining the room.

It was big. Just by the door was a private bathroom. Peering in, it had one shower and toilet, but two sinks and a large mirror. In the main room, on either side, was a set of bunkbeds. In the middle, separating them, were four desks. Opposite the bathroom was a small kitchen area. Kitchen was generous. There was a water fountain for boiling and chilled water, a sideboard, and a small refrigerator.

I was also the first to arrive. My pack said that all three other beds would be occupied. I looked around, and picked one of the beds, opting for the top bunk.

I'd been told when checking-in and getting my room assignment that there would be nothing open on the campus until the following morning when the school officially opened. Seeing as I had a few hours to kill before I would hear from Minhyuk, I decided to explore the campus and get a feel for the school.

It wasn't that much bigger than the one I had

attended back in America, only it went up, rather than out. My school had buildings no bigger than two stories. Here, the school had six floors. The first floor had the cafeteria and auditoriums. The second floor had the library and what looked like the teacher's offices. Floors three through five had the homerooms.

Unlike back in America where we moved around for each class, here we had one room and we stayed in that while the teachers moved. The only exception was for science: the labs were on the sixth floor. That amused me at first, until I realized that if there was some form of accident and the school needed to be evacuated, you wouldn't need to get everyone out past a floor that was on fire.

My homeroom was on the fourth floor. The classroom was empty, but open. Aside from being on a higher floor, it was very much the same as every other classroom I'd been in.

From up here I could see the grounds better. Behind the school was a running track—one big enough for a soccer pitch in the middle of it. Scarlett, my sister, would have liked that. If you kept going, the buildings on the other side belonged to the Seoul Leadership University.

There wasn't much else to see, so I walked back to the dorm to unpack. When I returned, my other roommates still hadn't moved in. I pulled out my laptop, put on some music, and busied myself with emptying the cases and hanging my clothes up.

It was strange seeing so few belongings when, back home, I had a walk-in closet, with the attic above the double garage housing even more clothes. They were mainly old dance costumes though. My life had been condensed into two cases.

Once I'd moved the empty cases to a closet at the end of the corridor where they were supposed to be stored, I sat down at my desk. Minhyuk (or rather, Sungil) still hadn't messaged me and it was getting close to dinner. The facilities on campus wouldn't be opening until tomorrow with the rest of the school, so if I was going to eat, I would have to go off campus to find something.

I wasn't sure what Minhyuk wanted to do, so I figured I would give it another hour. In the meantime, I decided that I would research dance classes. The one downside to the school was that it was academic and not performance based. This wasn't Julliard.

Seeing as I had come out here with the second intention of learning a new style of dance, I wanted to find somewhere quickly. I lost myself in an internet blackhole, jotting down a few places here in Gangnam, and a few more around the city. Although I was sure I would be able to navigate the public transportation systems easily enough, I figured staying close by—if I could—would have its advantages.

I was going to run the studios past Minhyuk before committing anyway. He was a dancer, so I figured he would know where to avoid. Thinking of Minhyuk, I reached for my phone: still nothing. With my stomach now grumbling at me, I decided it was a good idea to go eat. I grabbed my purse and headed out of the school.

The hotel I had been staying at had been close enough to the school that I'd had the opportunity to walk around and explore a little of the area while Minhyuk was busy. On one occasion, I'd come across a fried chicken shop called Roosters. I'd only just eaten at the time, otherwise I would have tried it then, but now I was in the mood for chicken. I was always in the mood for chicken; it was my favorite.

I walked into Roosters and eyed up the menu. "Would you like any help?" a voice greeted me in English.

I glanced over at the guy behind the counter. He was about my age and taller than me, although I was about as tall as most of the Korean girls, so that didn't mean much. He was good looking, although his features were much softer than Sungil's, and more youthful than Minhyuk's. I walked to the counter and gave him a grateful smile. "Thank you, but I speak a little Korean," I told him, in Korean. "Could I have some dakgangjeong?" I requested, selecting the sweet crispy chicken. "And a Coke."

"Grab a seat," the guy said, before disappearing into the back.

I took a seat at one of the tables close to the counter. There were a couple of people in there, but they were sat in groups of threes and fours. The guy reappeared a few moments later with a can of Coke and a straw, setting them on the table in front of me. "Thank you."

"Are you travelling by yourself?" he asked, curiously.

I shook my head. "I'm here for school."

"Oh, where have you and your family moved to?"

I shook my head again. "It's just me. My family are back in America."

The boy narrowed his eyes, thoughtfully. "Have you come to be an idol?"

I laughed. "No. Don't worry: I know enough to know that's not a possibility."

"But you're here by yourself?" he pressed, looking surprised.

"TK!" a voice called. We both looked behind the counter and found an older guy watching us. His apron was smeared with flour and he was giving 'TK' a disapproving look. "Don't disturb the customers."

"It's OK," I called back to him. "He's not disturbing me."

The chef leaned on the counter, looking as surprised as TK had. "Your Korean is very good."

"That's kind of you to say, but I know it's far from perfect."

"Are you on vacation? Where are your parents?" he asked, looking behind me as though they were going to magically appear.

"My parents are back in America. I'm here for school," I said, repeating the answers I had given TK. "Seoul Leadership Academy."

Both the chef and TK looked at me in surprise. "That's the school TK attends."

The chef's expression remained pleasant, but TK's suddenly went cold and I couldn't work out why. "I need to restock the fridge," he grunted, disappearing into the back.

I glanced at the chef, who shrugged. "That's not my story to tell."

As if that didn't sound ominous. Up until that moment, I hadn't felt too nervous about my first day at school. Now I had a dozen different thoughts and scenarios running around in my head.

"Let me get your order for you," the chef

continued before he followed TK into the back. I scratched at the back of my neck before popping the can open and jabbing the straw in. When my order arrived, it was served by the chef and TK was nowhere in sight. "Don't take it personally," he said, setting the food in front of me.

It was a little hard not to, but I distracted myself with sweet, sticky chicken. It was delicious. The only problem was, would I come back? TK hadn't exactly made me feel welcome.

I looked at my phone. It was getting late and I still had no message from Minhyuk. I typed out a message to send, via Sungil, and stared at it before hitting send. In the end I deleted it without sending it: it wasn't that I didn't want to seem needy, but rather, if Sungil knew anything, I was sure he would have sent me something by now.

"Yoo Chaewon."

I looked up at the chef, blinking at him in confusion. "Excuse me?"

"I am Yoo Chaewon. You're welcome here any time," he said, handing me a takeaway menu. "We deliver too."

"OK," I said, slowly, taking the piece of paper from him.

"Don't be too quick to judge TK," he said, nodding his head towards the back where I was sure TK was hiding. "He's shy."

"Sure," I muttered, sticking the menu in my purse. "The chicken was delicious. Thank you."

I returned to the dorms shortly after. The later it got, the more I realized that Minhyuk wasn't going to message tonight and I still had school in the morning. I pushed the dorm room door open and stepped in. When I saw there was another girl in the room, I stopped. "Oh, hello!" I greeted her, giving her a warm smile. Finally, one of the other three roommates was here.

The girl was shorter than me by a couple of inches. She was also quite overweight, with a round face hidden behind thick bangs and a short bob which didn't really suit her. The girl looked at me with her eyes wide, then muttered something in Korean.

"I'm sorry, but I didn't hear you," I apologized. I walked over to her and offered her a hand, still smiling. "I'm Lucinda. Lucinda Williams."

"Hong Baekhee," the girl returned, although she didn't take my hand.

"Becky?" I repeated, recognizing the name from the welcome pack. "Welcome, roomie," I added, before wrapping my arms around my roommate.

Baekhee wriggled backwards, out of the embrace. "Baek*hee*," she said.

"I'm sorry," I apologized. "My pronunciation is a little off. *Baekhee*," I repeated. I glanced down at the suitcase and piles of boxes that Baekhee had brought. "I don't really have a preference on a bed, so if you want the one I took, it's all yours," I offered, pointing at the one I'd had set up.

Baekhee slowly looked over at the far bunkbed, then back to the one I had claimed. "The others haven't moved in yet?"

I shook my head, scratching at the back of my neck as I tried to recall the other names. "Cho Miyeon and … Han …" I frowned. "Eunbyeol?"

"Han Eunbyeol," Baekhee confirmed, so quietly

I struggled to hear her. "They changed the assignments."

"Baekhee, are you okay? You look like you're going to pass out."

"I'm fine," Baekhee snapped, waving her arms at me to get me to back off. I did, taking two steps away from her as she turned and hurried from the room, slamming the door behind her.

I stared at the closed door, scratching at the back of my neck. "Why do I get the feeling this is going to be a problem?" I sighed. I walked to my desk, where I'd left my welcome pack, and pulled out the roommate list. I stared at the names. "This is going to be a drama-filled year, isn't it?" I asked the empty room.

It was too early to go to bed, but I was bored, and I was confident, at this point, I was definitely not meeting up with Minhyuk. I grabbed my laptop from my desk, bringing it up to the top bunk with me, and loaded up Netflix.

제7 장

Lucinda

I fell asleep watching a movie, only waking up the following morning when the lock to the room bleeped. The door burst open and Baekhee stumbled in, almost hidden behind two large boxes. I jumped down from my bunk and darted over, taking the top one from her. "What have you got in here?" I asked, carrying it over to a spare desk and setting it down on top.

"That is none of your business," a voice declared. I turned, finding another girl in the doorway, two silver suitcases beside her.

I held my hands up at her. "I assumed it was Baekhee's."

"Don't."

I stared at her, lowering my arms. "Well, can I assume you're one of my roommates?"

The girl, her hair tied back in pigtails, looked me up and down, before rolling her eyes. "Great. Another year with unsavory roommates."

"Speak for yourself," I said, growing irritated by

her. She was a pretty girl, but I recognized the makeup skills on her. I had a feeling I was rooming with the mean girl in the school, and if so, that would explain Baekhee's reaction when I said our roommate's names earlier. The question was, was she Miyeon or Eunbyeol. "Are you going to introduce yourself, or shall I give you a name?"

"Don't you know who I am?" she jutted out her hip as she twirled her hand around one of her pigtails. Was she a celebrity?

I rolled my eyes. "No, I just decided to ask for our amusement."

"This is Han Eunbyeol," Baekhee murmured.

"You can shut up and go get the rest of my things," Eunbyeol barked at her. Baekhee nodded meekly, then disappeared from the room.

"Are you serious?" I asked her, staring at her in disbelief.

Eunbyeol wheeled the suitcase into the room and looked at the untaken bunkbed. "This one doesn't face the window. Swap."

I folded my arms, tilting my head. "Is that a request, or a demand?"

Eunbyeol blinked, then sighed. "A request?"

"Then my answer is, if it means that much to you, sure," I said nonchalantly, although I was watching Eunbyeol carefully.

Eunbyeol stared at my bunk bed, before looking at the other, chewing at her lip. Finally, she shook her head. "No, I will take this one," she said, quietly. She pulled her case over to the bed, just as Baekhee appeared in the doorway, struggling with another box.

Frowning, I hurried over and took it off her once

again. "How many of these are there?"

"One more," Eunbyeol announced. She was lying on the bottom bunkbed with her feet dangling over the edge, staring up at the slats of the bed above her.

I rolled my eyes, looking back to Baekhee. "I'll help you."

"And two more cases," Eunbyeol called after us as we left the room.

"I take it you and Eunbyeol have history?" I asked Baekhee as we walked to the elevator.

"Mmmm," Baekhee mumbled, refusing to look at me.

I held my hands up as we stepped into the elevator. "If you don't want to talk about it, that's cool. I don't need to know the specifics. I'm already making my own opinions on the kind of person she is."

Baekhee said nothing and we went down in silence. It was a short trip through the foyer. Baekhee didn't wait, and I hurried outside after her. The sight before me had me sighing.

The dorms were not built on flat ground, but rather on the top of a slight hill. At the bottom was a private driveway for parents to drop off their children … or in the case of most of the students, for the drivers to drop off their employer's children. As such, there were about thirty steps to climb up and down.

Baekhee was already halfway down them, making a beeline for the two silver cases matching the two Eunbyeol had brought in, a large cardboard box on the ground next to them. Shaking my head in amazement, I jogged down the steps and caught up with Baekhee. "Next time get me to help you," I told her.

Baekhee shot me a sideways glance but said

nothing as she walked over to the box. The weather was hot and humid, and she was already looking flustered and sweaty. I chewed at my lip: Baekhee was probably not used to exercise and carrying the cases up would be hard work for her. "I'll take the suitcases," I declared, trying to be helpful. "I haven't been in a gym for a week, so I could do with a workout."

Although Baekhee continued to remain silent, she shot me a grateful look as she picked up the box.

"Are you okay with that, or would you like me to take it up for you?" I offered.

"I can manage," Baekhee finally responded.

I turned my attention to the cases. They were the solid ones with four wheels, not that the wheels would help me here, and were both big enough to come up to my hip. I tipped them on their side, taking them by the handles and tested them. They were heavy, but not heavy enough that I needed to take two trips up the stairs.

Or so I thought.

A third of the way up, I was regretting the decision. I wasn't weak. When I wasn't dancing, I spent a lot of time in the gym: Most people didn't realize how much you needed muscles and strength to dance. However, I had overestimated my ability to carry both of them at the same time, regardless of how balanced I was. I was just about to set one down, ready to carry on with just the one, and then come back for the other, when a hand swooped in, taking it from me.

"What are you …?" the question died in my throat. "Oh, it's you," I said, recognizing the boy from the chicken shop: TK.

"The American," he said, gruffly.

I opened and closed my now free hand, trying to get feeling back in it as I carried on up the stairs. "It's Lucinda, by the way. And for the record, they're not mine."

"They're not?" he asked, following me up the stairs. At the top, he set the case down and pulled up the handle so it could be pulled inside.

I followed his example and then reached for the case he had brought up. "I can take them from here," I said, looking around for Baekhee—she'd already gone inside.

"I've got it," he insisted, shaking his head as he refused to hand the case over, walking towards the elevator

I paused and stared at his back before hurrying after him. "No, they're my roommate's: Han Eunbyeol."

My bad feeling about Eunbyeol increased when TK froze, looking at me like I was the devil. "You're friends with Han Eunbyeol."

"I don't know if I'd say that," I said, ready to ask him what the deal was, but before I could get the words to form, TK had abandoned me. Once more I found myself staring at his back as he hurried away. "Is my roommate the devil?" I asked his retreating back. "Thank you!" I yelled, when he didn't respond.

Baekhee was already in the dorm room, organizing her own belongings when I wheeled Eunbyeol's cases in. "About time," Eunbyeol called. She was still lying on her back, although now her phone was held above her face.

"You mean, thank you, right?" I said, staring at her, pointedly. I wasn't one for confrontation, but there was no way in hell I was going to live in this room with her thinking she was the queen ruling over us.

Eunbyeol propped herself up and looked over at me. "Sure."

Whether for better or worse, I didn't get much chance to get to know either of my roommates. Largely because neither of them were willing to make conversation, but partly because I didn't have much time before I had to get to class. I quickly washed my face and brushed my hair, pulling it back into a messy topknot. By the time I was finished with my makeup the room was empty. Of course, neither of them would wait for me.

I changed into my school uniform, slung my bag over my shoulder and walked to the other building, upstairs to the classroom. Late August in Seoul was hot and humid. I was looking forward to the air conditioning in the classroom.

Only I was disappointed to discover there was none. There were only open windows and a fan in the corner, which did nothing. The room was already almost full. Baekhee was at the front, her eyes fixed on the whiteboard behind the teacher's desk, sitting by herself. I could tell she could see me, but she pointedly ignored me.

Eunbyeol was at the back of the room near a second door, standing with two other girls who were talking animatedly. The three of them stopped when they saw me, sending me an evil glare. I wasn't sitting with them …

Instead, I walked to one of the free seats by the window, halfway back. I sat down and turned to drape my unwanted blazer over the back of the chair and then realized TK sat behind me. "Thank you for your help earlier," I told him.

"Sure," TK muttered, turning his head to stare out of the window.

The next thing I knew, a large mass of a body was storming past me. I turned my head just in time to witness the desk go flying and someone punch TK. "What the hell?!" I yelled, when I worked out the mass was Sungil. "Stop it!"

My shouts were drowned out by another figure wrapping their arm around Sungil's and pulling him back so roughly, Sungil was sent flying into the desks behind. "Enough!" the voice yelled. "Baek Sungil, get out of my classroom, now!"

I stared wide-eyed at Sungil as he picked himself up off the floor, still furious. Sungil had sharp features and high cheekbones, and when he was angry, he looked terrifying. I had no idea what TK had done to deserve the punch, but Sungil's look alone was enough for me to never want to get on the bad side of him. "It's all his fault!" he snarled.

"I don't care whose fault it is," the man, our homeroom teacher, I guessed, yelled back at him. "Unless you get out, you will be the first person in the history of SLA to be expelled before the first bell rings."

Sungil glowered at the homeroom teacher before sending a death glare at TK. "You need to tell him to stop."

"GET OUT, SUNGIL!" the teacher bellowed.

Sungil turned, about to walk out, but he stopped suddenly, staring at me. "Lucinda? What are you doing here?"

"How does he know the new girl?" I heard

someone whisper.

I gave him a small wave, but my verbal response was cut short before it started. "SUNGIL, GET OUT OF MY CLASSROOM!" the teacher yelled again, coming up behind Sungil.

Sungil glowered at him, threw me another confused look, and then proceeded to leave the classroom, kicking several empty desks and chairs out of the way as he did.

"And this is why we shouldn't let scholarship kids into the school," I heard a girl's voice ring across the classroom. Her words were clear and loud; certainly not trying to be discreet. "They do something disgusting and the paying kids who have the right to be here are made to look like they're the bad guys."

The teacher turned to her, looking both disgusted and impatient. "Cha Yerin, if you have an issue with the type of students SLA accepts, then you need to take it up with your mother. Given the fact she is the one who allows scholarships, I would suggest you don't waste her time. Now, stop wasting my time and the class' and sit down." The teacher turned to TK. "Go clean your face."

I stared in amazement. Sungil, the guy who seemed gruff, awkward around girls, but was really a softy, had come in and punched another kid—albeit for reasons currently unknown—and the teacher had just thrown him out of the classroom? If anything like that had happened in my old school, Sungil would have been marched to the principal's office and, at the very least, suspended. TK's nose was dripping blood down his once immaculate white shirt and he was being told to

'clean your face'?
      I was speechless.

제8 장

Minhyuk

It was a little after midnight when I got into bed, and I lay awake, staring up at the ceiling. I had an awful feeling in the pit of my stomach that everything was going to go to hell for Hyunseo. My fears were confirmed when I was pulled out of my restless doze before three in the morning.

With blurry eyes and a muggy head, I got out of bed and opened the door. Oh Seokbeom, Bright Boys' manager was on the other side, glaring at me angrily. "Get to Atlantis. Now."

He stormed off, leaving me staring after him. "I think we're in trouble." I looked up and saw Jaehoon a few doors down, staring at me. Behind him, I could see the younger members of Bright Boys in various states of dress, clearly confused as to what was happening.

Slowly, I nodded.

I disappeared into my room and dressed. It was rarely a good sign when we were summoned to the offices at an early hour in the morning. The fact we were being summoned *this* early was a certainty something was wrong.

I stared at the clothes hung up on the rail in the corner of my room. I didn't have many smart clothes. When I dressed up for events, they were usually provided by the company, and I had to return them after. That being said, if I was being brought in front of management, I needed something a little smarter than the joggers I was currently wearing.

Once dressed in the smartest clothes I had with me, I walked down to the parking lot under the dorms with Bright Boys. Only a few of us knew why we were being taken in, and although there were some confused expressions regarding my presence, no one spoke.

We piled into one of the minivans, the journey continuing in an uneasy silence. Since debuting, both myself and Bright Boys rarely went to Atlantis without going in a vehicle provided by the company. It wasn't a long walk, but this meant we could leave our dorm and enter the main offices via the underground parking lots and never have to step foot on the sidewalk. From a privacy point of view, we didn't have to worry about being seen in sweatpants or without doing out hair.

We were lucky. Some of the other groups at Atlantis, like H3RO, didn't get that luxury. Then again, they hadn't been active for nearly two years, so they didn't have quite the same problem.

At Atlantis, we were taken up to one of the boardrooms on the top floor and told to wait. I slid into a seat at the table beside Jaehoon. "Is this what I think it's about?" I asked in a low whisper.

Jaehoon shrugged. "Oh Seokbeom didn't say earlier. He just told us to get here. He was angry though. He likes his sleep." I had a feeling it wasn't just the lack of sleep that was the problem. Jaehoon glanced around the table at the rest of the group. The other members were talking uneasily amongst themselves, trying to guess why we were all there.

Apart from Hyunseo. He was staring at the mahogany surface in front of him like he was expecting a death sentence.

"We made a promise, King," Jaehoon continued, once he was sure no one was listening. "No matter what, we keep it."

I wasn't going to break my promise. Not at the chance of it hurting Hyunseo's sister. I still wasn't sure of the details, but I *was* sure that she had already been through enough.

With the lack of sleep and the general uneasiness, it took me a while before I remembered Luna. I hadn't asked Sungil to message her last night for me, and I wasn't sure if he would have done so without me asking him to. She had less than a week left in the country and I didn't think I would be able to see her again.

We were kept waiting for nearly three hours: I was convinced they were using the same tactics the police did, and somehow, it was making me feel more and more guilty. Finally, the doors opened and Lee Sejin, the Vice Chairman of Atlantis Entertainment, walked in, accompanied by Oh Seokbeom and my manager, Seok Kyuhyuk. Whereas Lee Sejin and Oh Seokbeom looked furious, Kyuhyuk looked disappointed—I wasn't sure which was worse. We all stood, bowing respectfully, and didn't sit back down.

"Park Hyunseo: my office," Lee Sejin snapped.

Wordlessly, Hyunseo left the room.

"I want to know who was at a nightclub last

night," Sejin continued.

We all looked at each other, then slowly, everyone but Apollo and Yongsik raised their hands. Seokbeom looked at them with narrowed eyes: he didn't trust anyone. "Neither of you two were there?"

"No, hyungnim," Yongsik replied, looking confused and hurt—most likely at the fact we had gone out without inviting him. Although he didn't realize it, he was lucky.

When the rest of us confirmed that neither of them were with us, Seokbeom dismissed them.

"And which of you weren't with Hyunseo when he left the club?" Sejin continued. There was a small vein pulsing below his ears. He looked like he was going to explode.

"We all left together," Seungjin told him. He looked confused too, which meant Sejin hadn't spoken to his brother.

"No, Hyunseo was outside with three other people. Who were they?"

I glanced at Jaehoon, then the pair of us raised our hands. If looks could have killed, our managers would have been arrested for murder.

"Who was the other person?" Sejin demanded.

"No one, hyung," Seungjin responded.

Sejin slammed his hand down on the desk so hard, it boomed, echoing around the room. All of us jumped. "There were three of you!" he bellowed.

"It wasn't any of them," Jaehoon quickly told him. "It was our friend, Sungil."

"Sungil?" Sejin repeated. "Baek Sungil? The waste of space who auditioned with you two?"

Although I didn't like my friend being referred to

like that, I knew better than to say anything. Instead, I nodded. "Yes."

"Does that mean we can go too?" Seungjin asked.

Sejin turned on him. "When you are in this building, I am not your brother. I am your boss," he said, venom oozing from his voice. "And no, you cannot 'go'. You are eighteen and you were in a club, underage. You and the rest of you parasites will wait in here until I have dealt with your leader and these two thugs," he spat. He turned to me and Jaehoon. "Join Hyunseo in my office."

With another bow, Jaehoon and I left the boardroom. "We're in trouble," I said.

We arrived at Sejin's office and were ushered in by his secretary, Park Inhye. Hyunseo was waiting inside and he looked mortified the moment he saw us. "Why are you here?" he asked.

"Someone must have seen us with you," Jaehoon told him. "Sejin wanted to know which three of us were with you."

Before we could say anything else, Sejin walked into his office. Alone. He marched over to the desk in the corner of the room, but instead of sitting down at it, he stood behind, staring out of the window. He had a corner office, one of the biggest in the building. I think the only person with a bigger office was the Chairman himself.

The corner of the room was made up of two floor-to-ceiling walls of window. Lee Sejin stared out at the Seoul skyline of the north bank of the city that was slowly starting to brighten in the rising sun, his hands clasped behind his back. Finally, after what seemed like half an eternity, he spoke. "Just as I was going to sleep,

I received a phone call from a reporter friend. He's based in Gangnam Police Station." Sejin turned to face us. I lowered my head. "Do you know why a reporter at a police station would be calling me at three in the morning?"

I bit my lip, refusing to say anything.

"No, sir," Hyunseo responded for me.

Sejin's eyes narrowed. "Interesting, considering you were the one with the leading role in this story."

We remained silent.

"It seems, Park Hyunseo, that you savagely attacked a member of the public. That innocent member of the public was taken to the hospital, suffering from a fractured cheekbone and a concussion. The police are currently taking his statement before they come to question you."

Out of the corner of my eye, I saw Hyunseo ball his hands into fists, but he remained quiet.

"Do you two have anything to say in the matter?" Sejin asked. When we said nothing, he sat down at his desk. "Very well. As of now, Bright Boys will not be promoting. Lee Minhyuk, your comeback has been cancelled."

"You can't do that!" The objection came from Hyunseo, not me. "I was the one who—"

"You are probably going to be charged with assault, so you can shut up," Sejin sneered at him. "As for you two" he said, looking at Jaehoon and I, "Not only did you not come to anyone with this, but you, along with the other members of Bright Boys were in a nightclub, drinking, *underage*. You can all go back to school and take this time to reflect on your actions, which will be decided upon by the public, so I suggest you keep your noses spotlessly clean." He looked at the two of us. "Why are you still here? Get to school."

I walked out of his office feeling sick to my stomach.

"King—"

"Just don't," I snapped at Jaehoon. I walked off, leaving him outside of Sejin's office, waiting for Sejin to finish up with Hyunseo.

Instead of going to school, I went to one of the recording studios. That was where I was supposed to be today: recording one of the tracks for my mini album. Sejin had already cancelled everyone because the room was empty.

I sat down in front of the mixing board and stared at the microphone in the recording booth. I was so angry, but there was nothing I could do. Sejin was right.

If it wasn't Mina, I would have said something, but I'd met her before, and she was one of the sweetest people I knew. That was one of the things that had been keeping me up all night: she wouldn't survive her name becoming headline news. On the few occasions I had met her, it had been in private locations, away from the public. She wasn't one for fame.

I punched at the side, frustrated. Why had I gone out in the first place? I could have been spending the time with Luna.

Luna …

I leaned forward, letting my head drop. Luna …

제 9 장

Lucinda

Monday passed in a blur. With a summer vacation and not the best attendance previously, by the time classes ended, all I wanted to do was crawl into bed. Instead we already had homework to do, and I had a full book to read (thankfully, I was allowed to read an English version) by the following Monday.

I went to the cafeteria eyeing up the selection. It was some form of tofu soup with kimchi. It was a good thing I liked spicy soup. I picked up my tray looking for a place to sit.

I had joined in the middle of the academic year and I was a foreigner. Everyone had already established their friendship groups and none of them seemed particularly welcoming. My eyes fell on a familiar face, sat in the back corner by himself. I hurried over.

"What are you doing?" TK demanded, paling as I pulled a chair out and sat down opposite.

I shrugged, picking up my spoon. "Eating my dinner: believe it or not, it's something both Americans and Koreans do. Although I will admit, the kimchi is a new one on me." To emphasize the point, I took a mouthful of the soup.

TK's complexion paled further. "You can't sit there," he told me.

I sat back in the chair and twisted the cap off my soda bottle. "Why not?" I asked him, taking a sip and setting the bottle back down in front of me.

TK swallowed nervously. He licked his lips, opened his mouth to speak, then froze, his gaze flying to something behind me. I started to turn but three girls stopped at the end of the table. Instead, I focused my attention on them: Yerin, Eunbyeol, and the third friend.

The three of them were beautiful. They looked like they could have been an idol group. Yerin, in particular, was stunning, I decided. She could easily be a model. She was also the girl who had been glaring at the side of my head from the other side of the classroom, throughout the day.

Her hair was black, hanging in loose waves down to her waist; it looked about the same length as mine when I didn't have it pulled back in a ponytail. She was slim, with thighs that I was instantly envious of. It wasn't that I was overweight, but with all the dancing, and all the time I spent in the gym, my legs had a more muscular shape to them.

The girl to her right, the one whose name I didn't know, was a red-head. Although the auburn wasn't her natural hair color, with the thick bangs and sharp features, she looked like she could have been a model too. Then there was Eunbyeol. Although not quite as model-esque as the other two, Eunbyeol was still exceptionally pretty. She looked the youngest of the three, but it was possible that was because of the pigtails she was sporting.

It took a moment for me to realize that Yerin was talking to me. "I'm sorry," I said, cutting her off. "I wasn't listening."

The girl smiled, but the emotion didn't quite meet her eyes. "I was saying, would you like to join us?" she asked in perfect English. She glanced at TK giving him a sneer, before looking back at me. "You can do better than Min Taekyung."

"Like you?" I asked, only just able to stop myself from scoffing at her.

The look she sent in my direction was filled with venom. "Do you know who I am?" she asked, finishing with a word that I didn't quite catch.

I slowly shook my head. "Should I?"

"Cha Yerin," the girl announced, like I was supposed to recognize that … "My mother is the chairwoman and principal of the SLA." That was her brag? The school was falling apart … but it did mean that I would have to tread carefully. I wasn't stupid. She turned to the redhead. "This is Geom Kareun. Her mother is the famous designer, Geom Jan Di—GJD."

I glanced at the girl next to her and caught her smug smile. Annoyingly, I had heard of GJD. I even had a few tops in my closet.

"This is Han Eunbyeol. Her grandfather is the CEO of one of Korea's leading import conglomerates." Yerin continued, nodding to the petite girl.

"Eunbyeol is my roommate," I pointed out, fairly certain all three of them knew that. "And I'm Lucinda Williams," I said, giving them a half-hearted wave.

"What do your parents do?" Eunbyeol asked me.

"Why?" I turned around in my chair to face her. "It's me in front of you, not my parents. Unless you're fishing to be my stepmother, I don't see what that has to do with anything."

Yerin leaned forward, resting her palms on the table. "That has everything to do with it," she told me in a low voice. "This might be the most exclusive school in the country, but just like outside of these four walls, there is a ranking, the hierarchy, and who your parents are play a large part of it. Isn't that right, Min Taekyung?"

My eyes flicked over to TK. His gaze was fixed firmly on the bowl in front of him, but he still managed to bow his head when Yerin addressed him. "Cha Yerin is in the highest tier," he muttered, like it was the most important fact in the world, and saying it aloud was a great honor.

"That's quite right," Yerin agreed, with a patronizing tone. "Whereas, by comparison, Min Taekyung is only here because his father, the school janitor, got him in on an employee scholarship. Which makes him the scholarship kid. The lowest of all scholarship kids, at that."

"He's the maintenance manager," TK mumbled, so quietly, it was only because I was still looking at him that I realized he was speaking.

I glanced back at Yerin. "I'm clearly missing the part where what your parents do is important to who you are," I frowned. There was a voice in the back of my head bellowing at me to stop provoking the girl in front of me, but my heart was telling me that no one else in the school would stand up for TK. No one deserved this level of crap, especially if it was over what their parents did.

"Spoken like someone who is also here on a scholarship," Kareun sniped. "You certainly dress like someone on one."

I was not deluded enough to think that I came from a family that had anywhere near the amount of wealth that these three girls did, but my parent's income was not lacking. My dad was a successful and popular quarterback for an NFL team, whose career had included four Super Bowl wins. At forty-five, he was still playing football and still carried the record for highest number of Super Bowls a player had played in.

My mom, after managing the first fifteen years of my father's career, had opened a successful sports management agency. Their net worth was enough that me or my sisters wouldn't need to work, but as both of them had come from humble beginnings, were determined to let us find our own feet rather than rely on them. In short, we had money, but they tried not to spoil us. Tried … I knew I had grown up with a lot more opportunities open to me than most people. I think it was another reason as to why they'd consented to let me finish high school in Korea.

Instead of telling them this, however, I shrugged. "I've lost my appetite." Abandoning the bowl of soup, I stood, brushed past Yerin, and continued to the door, ignoring the stares I was earning—from the whole cafeteria.

In the doorway, watching the interaction, was Sungil. His eyes didn't leave my face as I grew close. I glanced up at him. "I'm surprised you haven't been expelled." Sungil shrugged at me. "Don't tell me: your father bought a new wing in the library," I said, making a stab in the dark.

"Hardly," Sungil told me, vaguely. At least he had the grace to look marginally uncomfortable about that. "But you need to stay away from Min Taekyung."

"Why? Are you going to punch me too?"

"Maybe you should ask King," he shot back at me.

"I can't—he doesn't have a phone!" I snapped.

"You do!"

I blinked. What? I lowered my voice. "What happened to Minhyuk? And what has TK got to do with it?"

Sungil gave me a scathing look. "Why don't you go ask your new best friend? Or better yet, use your phone and do an internet search." He didn't give me an option to respond before moving past me, over to the cafeteria hatch. I glanced over my shoulder, spotting our homeroom teacher on cafeteria supervision.

I didn't like Sungil's comments, and the fact I couldn't get in touch with Minhyuk worried me. I also didn't want to disturb TK—yet. Taking a deep breath, I hurried outside, making my way to the bleachers overlooking the track.

I ignored the few messages from my family and friends and pulled up Facebook. I followed a few 'news' sites (OK, they were the equivalent of tabloid trash, but they were good for keeping you updated on what was happening in the K-pop world, even if it was usually click-bait) and wanted to see if they had posted anything.

The little tofu soup I had eaten churned in my stomach at the top article. Hyunseo, leader of Bright

Boys, had been arrested earlier in the morning for assaulting a member of the public.

There were certain family names in Korea which were more popular than others. Kim, Lee, and Park were three of the most popular. BTS had three members with the family name of Kim, and Minhyuk and Seungjin in Bright Boys both shared the family name of Lee. None were related.

The victim was a student at Seoul Leadership University, with the family name of Min. If Sungil hadn't have said anything, I wouldn't have made the connection. Hell, I didn't even know TK was really called Taekyung, never mind Min Taekyung.

And yet, I knew this Gukyung was TK's brother.

My stomach churned uneasily again.

I wasn't sure why Sungil was so angry towards TK. According to the article, Hyunseo had attacked Gukyung, not the other way around. Of course, the articles from this source needed to be taken with a pinch of salt.

What it didn't mention was Minhyuk's name, or his stage name. I moved onto the next site. This one said unconfirmed sources were reporting King and some members of Bright Boys had been involved.

Now I knew something wasn't right. The last thing I associated with Minhyuk was violence. He was thoughtful and gentle.

The worst part was that I had only one way of getting in touch with him: Sungil.

I sent him a message asking him to let me know what was happening. I could see when Sungil read the message, but the response didn't come.

My plans for starting my homework evaporated.

I lost track of time as I paced back and forth on the bleacher level, until, with the night growing in, I decided to leave the campus before curfew hit.

It wasn't until I got to the Atlantis Entertainment building, staring up at the turquoise glass-fronted building, that I realized I'd made one mistake with the plan: the dorms and the offices weren't in the same place. The worst part was that I couldn't go in and ask where I could find Minhyuk, because if I did, then they would either tell me to get lost, or they would work out what I was to him.

I sat down on a bench opposite, glowering at my shoes. The fact Minhyuk was an idol sucked. I still hadn't told him that I was staying. I sat there for a while until I finally called it a night before the police came and told me to stop being a creeper.

I walked back to the dorms, scuffing my heels along the concrete. It was getting late, and I knew I should get back to the dorm, but I was restless, and I knew I wouldn't be able to concentrate on homework, nor would I be able to get to sleep.

When I'd explored the school the day before, I'd found some empty classrooms on the same floor as the auditoriums. They had been cleared of all the desks, although the whiteboards had remained. More importantly, I noticed that they had wooden flooring, and not tile floors like the rest of the school. Which meant there were a couple of decent sized rooms with flooring suitable for dancing on.

That was what I needed to do now: dance. I hadn't done that since being here. I hadn't even been to the gym.

The outfit I was wearing wasn't my first choice

for dancing in, but as it was going to end up in the laundry basket anyway it didn't matter if I got hot and sweaty, which, with the night air still hot and humid, was entirely likely.

I made a detour to the school, walking along the deserted corridors, only, when I got close to the classrooms, I discovered I wasn't the only one who had the idea of using them. I could hear music. I recognized the song as one of f(x)'s. Curious, I made my way to the source of the music.

Like the rooms on the upper floors, this one had two doors and the wall in between, along the corridor, had windows. I peered in. Inside, a girl was dancing, and she had moves that had me entranced. She was tall. Taller than me, at least, maybe by a few inches. Her hair was tied back in loose pigtails, although, unlike Eunbyeol, hers were tied behind her neck.

With her cutoff jeans, high tops, and cropped hoodie—the hood pulled up over a baseball cap—it took me a moment to recognize her from my class. It didn't help that she wasn't wearing the giant owl glasses she had been wearing earlier.

There had been so many new people to remember that her name escaped me. All I could remember was that she had sat right at the back of the classroom and spent most of her time with an earphone in one ear—yet was still able to answer the teacher's questions when called upon.

While I was familiar with the f(x) song, I wasn't familiar with the dance. There was a difference between most boy and girl K-pop groups' dances. The boy groups tended to have powerful moves, often with some form of popping or B-Boying—breakdancing.

The girl groups were usually more girly. The moves this girl was making was more what I associated with the boy groups. And then she did a headspin into a windmill.

My mouth dropped open.

Oh. My. Goodness.

The girl was good. No ... she was amazing!

When she finished, I couldn't stop myself from bursting into applause. Breathing heavily and sweating slightly, she ripped her hood down and stared at me, wide eyed.

I stepped into the classroom, still clapping. "I'm sorry, I was passing because I had the same idea," I explained. "I wanted to use one of the rooms to dance in. Then I saw you dance. Girl, you're incredible."

"You're in my class," she said, regarding me warily.

I nodded, walking over. I offered my hand. "I'm Lucinda."

"You're my roommate!" she exclaimed.

I closed my eyes, trying to remember the final name on the room assignment. "Miyeon?" I asked. "Cho Miyeon, right?"

Miyeon nodded, reaching for my hand. Instead of shaking it, she curled it into a fist, then fist-bumped it. "You're a dancer?"

"Since I was four," I responded. "I started off with ballet then moved into different styles. It's partly why I'm out here: I want to learn more and K-pop is a whole other level of ability."

"You want to be an idol?" Miyeon asked, dubiously.

I laughed. "Oh no, I want to be a dancer."

Miyeon stepped back, gesturing to the music player she had set up. "Want to show me what you've got?"

I grinned, pulling out my phone. I quickly synced up my phone with the Bluetooth and then picked out my song: a song by Avicii. I hit play, found my beat, then lost myself in the music to a routine I'd performed recently in a competition. It wasn't K-pop, but it was more contemporary than classical.

When I finished, Miyeon applauded, before giving me a low, appreciative whistle. "You and I are going to be friends," she declared.

제10 장

Lucinda

Miyeon and I stayed dancing in the classroom until late in the night, at which point, we had to sneak back into our dorm. I fell asleep as soon as my head hit the pillow. Thankfully, there were two of us running late to class the following morning. "It's my second day here," I yelled at her as we charged down the corridor to our homeroom. "I can't believe I'm late on my second day."

"We're not late yet," she yelled, taking the lead.

Our homeroom teacher, Nam Woosung, was in the doorway, about to close the door when the pair of us went sliding under his arm, just making it in in time. "Sorry," I muttered, darting over to my desk. I sat down, realizing the seat beside me that had been vacant the day before was now occupied. By Seungjin. Lee Seungjin, the ridiculously good-looking member of Bright Boys. "What are you doing here?" I asked, bluntly, before I could stop myself.

The answer came from Nam Woosung. "As you may have noticed, we have several returning and new faces in the class. Yes, they are idols, yes, they are human too, and yes, they also need to pass this year, so can you all please keep your fangirling to a minimum so we can all achieve that goal."

I turned in my seat, my eyes scanning the room. Slowly I picked out Jaehoon … and Minhyuk.

Our eyes met. Somehow, he didn't seem as surprised as I expected him to. Then I remembered his best friend, Sungil, would have told him I was here. And yet he hadn't thought to message me?

When I'd looked at moving out here with the possibility of seeing my boyfriend a little more frequently than *maybe* once a year, I hadn't expected him to be attending the same school as me. I certainly hadn't dreamed he would be in the same class as me.

A dream.

That was what this was, right? I was still asleep? I blinked, dropping my attention to Minhyuk's body. Sure enough, he had the SLA school uniform on. I glanced at Jaehoon. He was wearing the uniform too.

For a brief moment, happiness surged through me. And then the implications of *why* they were wearing the school uniform hit me. Whatever had been in the papers had been true. Hyunseo had hit someone—TK's brother—and the others had been involved.

"Oh, no," I muttered under my breath. My gaze switched back to Minhyuk. I was about to mouth 'are you OK?' at him, but I caught the expression on his face: horror.

"Are you joining us today, Miss Williams?" the question was accompanied by a large bang and I whirled in my seat to face the front, finding Nam Woosung standing over me, his hand from where he had slapped my desk, still resting on the wood. "Or are you a Dazzle?"

I was about to point out that Dazzles were Bright Boys' fandom, not King's (he called his fandom 'Crowns') but decided against it. "Sorry, sir," I apologized instead, picking up my pen.

The morning passed by at an excruciatingly slow speed as I spent more time watching the clock above the whiteboard than I did paying attention to whatever lesson was taking place. I didn't even have the opportunity to have a whispered conversation with Seungjin about what was happening.

The mood of the class was strange too. I knew instantly who the Dazzles were because they were constantly trying to catch Seungjin's attention. Or, in Kareun's case, shooting daggers at me.

Just before lunch, a folded-up note landed in the middle of my notebook while Nam Woosung's back was turned, writing on the board. I looked up, trying to work out where it had come from.

Minhyuk?

I hurriedly pulled the piece of paper open, spotting all the hearts before any of the words on the page.

"Lucinda Williams!" Clutching onto the note, I whipped my hand off the table, hiding the paper in my lap. "Nice try," Nam Woosung continued. "But the policy in this class is if you are caught with a note, I will read it out to the class." He walked over to my desk and held out his hand.

I clung onto it. The last thing I wanted was for Minhyuk to get into trouble for sending a note to me, especially not when I hadn't even had chance to see what was there.

And then a hand shot out from beside me, snatching the note from my hands. Beside me, Kareun held the note up. "It's a love letter!" she cried. The class burst into giggles, aimed at me. I tried to sink into my seat, wanting to hide my red face under my desk.

Nam Woosung took the note from Kareun. "'Today is the best day ever. To see you in my class, looking so handsome in the uniform, makes me so happy! Seungjin, oppa, you make my world complete.' I never knew you had such strong feelings for Seungjin."

My head shot up, staring wide-eyed at the teacher. He thought I had written that? "I didn't …" I turned in my seat, looking at Seungjin who was giving me the strangest look. I couldn't say I blamed him. "I don't–"

"You two can discuss your relationship status after the class," Nam Woosung interrupted me as another chorus of laughter erupted.

I would be dead before then. Cause of death: embarrassment.

"When is your birthday?" Seungjin hissed at me as Nam Woosung returned to the front of the class.

"June."

"I'm not interested in dating."

I nodded, not sure if I was wincing or grimacing. I was willing to bet Seungjin was older than me, and that was the only reason he was OK with me calling him oppa. Except I hadn't … "I understand." I turned my attention back to the lesson, or at least, attempted to follow what was happening while I waited for the floor to swallow me up.

The bell for lunch couldn't come quick enough, and even though I was on my feet barely seconds later, when I turned, Minhyuk was already running for the rear classroom door. He didn't think I liked Seungjin, did he?

I started to follow after him but was stopped by Yerin, Eunbyeol, and Kareun stepping in front of me. "Friend," Kareun declared with a fake smile, placing an arm over my shoulder and flashing a grin at Seungjin as he collected his things. As soon as he was gone, she dropped her arm and glowered at me.

"Whatever you're thinking, you stop it now. You have no chance with any of Bright Boys. Idols don't date girls like you." Yerin's statement had a hint of a threat to it.

I blinked. "Yerin, I have no interest in Seungjin."

"He's not good enough for you?" Kareun asked, outraged.

"Not at all!" I objected. "He is incredibly handsome, but he is not my type," I told her without lying. "I didn't write that letter."

"Then why did you have it?" she demanded.

"I thought it was ..." I trailed off. If I said I thought it was for me, would she ask who I thought would have sent it? I didn't want to risk it—I didn't want to risk Minhyuk.

"Seungjin, Jaehoon, and King—they're all off limits to you." Kareun shoved me backwards and I fell heavily into my seat.

"Stay away from them," Yerin added, before leading the three of them from the classroom.

I closed my eyes and let out a long breath. No wonder Minhyuk wanted to keep us a secret.

Minhyuk!

I got to my feet and raced out of the classroom to

the cafeteria. Minhyuk wasn't there. I carried on outside, hurrying to the covered picnic tables, finally finding him on the last one with Jaehoon, Seungjin, Apollo and Dongyeol. Apollo and Dongyeol were in the year above, but clearly, they had been sent back to school too.

I wasn't surprised to see the outside area was packed, mainly with girls. As I scanned the tables, I could see that so many of them were trying to catch the boys' eyes. Fans. Despite the fact they had been caught up in a scandal that had sent them back to school, the girls (and some guys), were still interested. That was a good thing … right?

For me, not so much. It meant that talking to Minhyuk wasn't going to be easy, but I needed to speak to him. I owed him an explanation.

I slowed, walking over. The conversation at the table stopped. Only Dongyeol greeted me with a smile, although Apollo didn't look irritated or annoyed like the others did. Including Minhyuk.

"You never said you went to school in Seoul!" Dongyeol exclaimed. "I thought you were here on a vacation."

"You're not the only one," I heard Minhyuk mutter under his breath.

I was surprised at how cutting his words were, but I forced the smile to stay on my face as I nodded at Dongyeol. "I honestly didn't expect to see you again," I told him. "But I had been hoping it would be a surprise for my friend."

"Sungil?" Dongyeol asked.

I stared at him blankly before I remembered that Sungil had been acting as mine and Minhyuk's buffer. I quickly nodded. "Sure." Before I could dig myself into a lie I was going to regret, I turned to Minhyuk. "Could I speak to you please, Minhyuk?"

"King," he said, shortly.

"I … huh?"

"My name is King," he said, his tone not losing any of the ice.

That hurt. I was surprised at how much. I knew that Minhyuk wasn't allowed to date, but it wasn't like I was suggesting anything was happening between us by using his name, was I? It had never been an issue before now, and if it was, why hadn't he said something sooner? We'd spent an evening in a noraebang with most of Bright Boys where I had been calling him Minhyuk and he'd never said anything then.

The worst part wasn't that he wanted me to call him King. It was weird and felt unnatural to me, but I was happy to call him that if calling him Minhyuk was an issue. The worst part was the look he was giving me.

Minhyuk—my first boyfriend, my first kiss, my first love—was looking at me like I was nothing more than a crazy fan, invading his personal space. For the first time I felt like I was looking at King, the idol, not Minhyuk my boyfriend, and I had *never* felt like that before.

I bit my lip, swallowing a large lump from my throat. "King," I said, softly, not quite able to make my words the same volume they had been moments ago. "I'm sorry. King, could I speak to you, please? In private," I added.

"Why does she want to speak to *King*?" I heard Seungjin ask Apollo, sending me a look of distrust.

Minhyuk stared at me, then slowly, silently, rose to his feet and walked away from the table, not waiting to make sure I was following him. Eyes were on us as I hurried after him. He led us to a quieter area, then suddenly, he spun on his heel to face me. "What are you doing here?" he hissed at me.

"I was going to tell you," I told him. The lump was back in my throat. "I wanted to tell you at the weekend. It was going to be a surprise."

"A surprise? Are you stalking me?"

My mouth fell open. "Stalking?" I spluttered. "No, I just … I was … I knew we would struggle to see each other, but … I just wanted to be closer to make it easier." I shook my head as my vision started to get a bit blurry. "Minhyuk—"

"King!" he snapped.

"King," I repeated, confused as to why he was being so mean. "I thought you would be happy."

"I'm not," he snapped. "And I didn't appreciate finding out from Sungil!"

I always thought that I wouldn't be the girl to cry over a boy, but I could feel the tears streaming down my cheeks. I reached up to wipe them away. For half a second I saw a glimmer of something, something of the Minhyuk I knew, and then it was gone. "I'm sorry," I whispered. "I didn't know you would be attending SLA too. I wanted to tell you the other night, but I didn't hear from you."

There was the longest pause while Minhyuk stared at me. "Well I am, and while I'm here, you and I can't be together," he said, eventually.

Before I could even make sense of the words, he was gone. I stared at his retreating back, feeling like he had shoved his hand through my ribcage and plucked my beating heart out of it, taking it with him.

제11 장

King

Mid-September

"You really need to snap out of it, King," Sungil declared. He was lying on the couch, the PlayStation controller in his hand, but his attention was on me and not the television.

"She's right in front of me, and I can't be with her," I said, miserably. "Not that I think she even wants to be *near* me anymore."

Sungil set the controller down on the floor, rolling onto his stomach to look at me. "You have been avoiding her since you found out she was at SLA," he pointed out. "How can you tell if she's avoiding you if you're avoiding her?"

I shot him a scathing look before getting up and walking over to the kitchenette. I grabbed a couple of bottles of chilled coffee from the refrigerator before returning to the small sofa. I knocked one against Sungil's shoulder, frowning when he hissed in pain. "What's wrong with your shoulder?"

"Nothing," he said, vaguely. He twisted round into a sitting position and moved over so I could sit next to him. "Thanks." He took the bottle from me and tried to twist it open, wincing as he did so.

I unscrewed the lid on the bottle in my hands before swapping it with Sungil's. "What did you do to your shoulder?" I asked again.

"I went home," he shrugged.

I sank back into the sofa with a long sigh. Sungil's family was rich. Not well off, but *rich*. His father was the Chairman of the Baek Group—an enormous conglomerate—making Sungil the richest chaebol in the school. By a considerable amount.

Sungil had auditioned with me and Jaehoon for a spot at Atlantis. He'd made it too: Sungil had a powerful vocal range. He was a better singer than I was. Only, he'd done it without his father knowing. He'd managed to be an Atlantis trainee for about three months before his father found out and dragged him out. Being an idol was not a suitable career for his son.

I knew Sungil had been miserable about it. He still was, although he was getting better at hiding it. He hid it better than his father's behavior anyway.

Sungil had secrets. Secrets that I had only discovered by accident, and he didn't know I knew about. When he was little, his mother was in a car accident. According to Sungil, she had died. Three years ago, I discovered that wasn't the case. She was alive, but disabled, living in a care home in a facility outside the city.

If that was what Sungil's father did to his wife, I wasn't surprised Sungil did what his father said. I had no proof, but Sungil always seemed to return to school with bruises that only ever appeared after Sungil had been home.

"Have you heard anything from Atlantis?" Sungil asked.

I shifted my weight and allowed Sungil to lean back against me. "Silence," I replied. "It's the same with Bright Boys … which I'd instead of the backlash from the fans. I'm not sure either of us will have any left by the time this is over." I glanced down at Sungil. "At least you've avoided that side of things."

"I'd rather have millions of angry fans than one of my father," Sungil muttered, darkly.

Millions was probably an exaggeration in my case, but I understood what he was saying. I gently lowered my hand on his shoulder. "How bad is it, Sungil?"

"I've read the comments," Sungil said. He leaned forward to set the bottle of coffee on the floor, conveniently removing my arm from his shoulder. It was as bad as I suspected then. "You're not looking too bad. Hyunseo's statement helped."

That wasn't what I meant by that question, but I took the cue that Sungil wasn't going to talk about it. "I have a bad feeling about it all that I can't shift," I admitted.

Atlantis was doing very little to help Hyunseo, and in some respects, I almost couldn't blame them for that. To everyone else it looked like Hyunseo was doing nothing to help himself, and his silence was only confirming the guilt. The day we had returned to school, he had spent it in the police station. According to Dispatch news, sources were saying he had said nothing other than Jaehoon, Sungil, and I were not a part of it.

After a month of the same vague answers,

Atlantis had assigned him his own lawyer: a trainee who had been interning at the company. She was pretty, but that didn't mean she was any good at law. As Hyunseo was at the heart of the investigation, SLU had refused to let him in, so instead of returning to college, he was at home, living with his parents. None of us had seen him since.

"I've taken to checking the Bright Boys fan café and fan sites," Sungil continued. "The café is silent. None of the members have posted anything, which isn't surprising considering you were all forbidden from doing so, but I keep looking out for something about Hyunseo."

I nodded. "Me too," I admitted. When Atlantis liked you, they would move heaven and earth for you. When they didn't, you were dead to them. Actually, that wasn't fair. A lot of the people that worked at Atlantis Entertainment were decent people. I'd seen that first-hand. The problem came from the top with the Vice Chairman, Lee Sejin. "Seungjin has been going home every weekend to see if he can get his father to change Sejin's mind. That's where he is now." That was why I had such a bad feeling about this situation.

When we'd returned to the Seoul Leadership Academy, it had been the day after school had started. It had worked out well for some of us. Jaehoon, Seungjin and I were the same age, so we'd all ended up in the same dorm room; the one Sungil and I were in now. Sungil was in another room, three doors down, with some other guys from our year, but spent most of his free time with us.

Apollo and Dongyeol were in the year above, also sharing a room. Ryan, who should have been here, had gone back to Busan where his mother lived. At least we were all close.

But close wasn't the Atlantis dorms.

I let my head fall back onto the back of the sofa. "She moved to another country for me," I muttered.

"You didn't ask her to," Sungil was quick to point out.

"It doesn't make me feel any less of a jerk," I shrugged.

"That's crazy sasaeng behavior," Sungil said.

I flicked his ear. "Luna is not a sasaeng. She is sweet and supportive, and I was the jerk who broke her heart."

"So, unbreak it," Sungil shrugged. "I told you, King, I've got your back on this. I can go back to pretending we're dating and you can be present as my chaperone. That would probably score you brownie points with your fandom."

I chewed at my lip, allowing myself a moment to consider it, and then shook my head. "I can't do it. I can't lie to my fans, and Luna is too sweet to get caught up in a scandal. It's not fair on her, and I'm not sure she would handle the pressure."

Sungil moved back, his neck twisting awkwardly to look at me. "She moved halfway around the world for you. She might be sweet, but she's tough enough to handle that."

I stared at him. He was right, and I knew it, but it was easier to think of her as this sweet, naïve girl. I'd signed up for this life and she hadn't. I'd read some of the comments made about myself and Bright Boys, and no one deserved them—not me, not Bright Boys … It was like the internet forgot we were real people with feelings.

"My manager said Sejin was contemplating our futures," I told him. "I was being included with Bright Boys in that, so if I mess up again, it's not just my future at stake. And I've already had two strikes."

The door opened and Jaehoon walked in. He glanced at the two of us on the couch and sighed. "Room for another?"

Sungil and I looked at each other. We barely had a chance to move before Jaehoon dropped on the sofa between us. "Atlantis pushed back Jiwon's solo album."

My mouth dropped open. "Jiwon? But Onyx are Atlantis' favorite."

Although Atlantis Entertainment did have a girl group, Cupcake, the rest of the groups on the roster were boy groups. The first-generation group was B.W.B.B., who had most of the members in the army serving their mandatory enlistment, but was still the company's biggest and most popular group. After that was Onyx. It was only because B.W.B.B. wasn't promoting that Onyx was earning more for the company, and as such, they were treated like royalty by Atlantis. It also helped that in the three years since their debut they hadn't been caught up in a single scandal.

Which was why I was so surprised they had pushed back the release of his debut album.

"But I was a feature artist on one of the tracks," Jaehoon reminded me.

And suddenly I wasn't surprised.

"They'd do that?" Sungil asked.

Jaehoon nodded. "They're making Ruzt take my part."

Atlantis also had a few solo artists. Ruzt was one

of them. From Jiwon's perspective, this was an amazing thing for him. Ruzt was a ridiculously talented rapper and producer, and rumor had it he was being lined up as a judge on the next season of 'Show Me The Money'—after winning it himself a few seasons ago.

"I'm sorry, hyung," I muttered. The whole thing was a mess.

"This would be so much easier if Hyunseo just told the truth," Sungil grumbled.

"We promised we wouldn't say anything," Jaehoon pointed out.

"That doesn't mean Hyunseo can't say anything," Sungil retorted.

Jaehoon turned, his back to me as he glowered at Sungil. "He's doing it to protect his sister."

"I know what he's doing! But the thing is, Min Gukyung attacked Hyunseo's sister. If Hyunseo tells the prosecution that, they will be much more lenient with him, and you guys will stop suffering. It would be one thing if it was just Hyunseo, but it's all of you."

"It wouldn't work like that," Jaehoon said, shaking his head. "You know what would happen: the world would blame Mina."

Sadly, I thought he was right.

"We need to do something," Sungil told him. He maneuvered himself around and stretched out his legs over both mine and Jaehoon's laps. Not only was he the oldest of the three of us, he was also the tallest with ridiculously long legs. I always looked so short next to him. "And I've been thinking about that."

Jaehoon settled back into the sofa and folded his arms. "We're not making an anonymous tip-off to the papers, hyung. We promised Hyunseo."

Sungil shook his head. "I don't agree with it, but I'm not going to break my promise."

"What are you thinking?" I asked, curious.

"If we can't get Hyunseo or Mina to come forward, we need to go to the source," he explained.

I frowned. "Min Gukyung?"

Jaehoon rolled his eyes. "That's a stupid idea. If we do that, we'll get in trouble for intimidating a witness or something, and then we'll be in even more trouble."

"I don't mean Min Gukyung."

I stared at Sungil, then realized what he was implying. "You cannot go after TK!" I cried. "You've already been in trouble for punching him."

Sungil shrugged. "Worth it."

"No, it's not," I disagreed. "Violence is what got us here in the first place. It's not going to get us out of this mess."

"Then what is the answer?" Sungil demanded. "We just sit around and let the situation fester like an infected wound? Sitting around and ignoring it won't fix it. We need to go after the cause of the problem."

"I don't know what the answer is," I sighed.

"Maybe Seungjin can help us," Jaehoon muttered.

Sungil scoffed. "Seungjin?" he rolled his eyes. "He's only in Bright Boys because his father is the Chairman of Atlantis, and his brother is the Vice Chairman."

"Yeah, and that's why he's back at school with us."

"I think if Seungjin being in the group was going to help, something would have happened by now. I get the impression his brother doesn't think much of him either."

"I'm not talking about his brother," Jaehoon said, mysteriously.

Sungil and I both looked at him. "What do you mean?"

Jaehoon shook his head. "I promised Seungjin."

"Since when are you BFFs with Seungjin?" Sungil asked, his eyes narrowing.

"Since I've spent the last year sharing a room with him," Jaehoon retorted. "He's not that bad once you get to know him, and I can assure you, he's getting no special treatment, nor has he ever. In fact, he's always back at home *because* he's trying to help us. But he told me a secret, which I can't repeat because I promised."

I pulled a face. "What does that even mean?"

"He found something out, and he's still trying to work out what it means, but I think he's got something that can help." Jaehoon frowned and looked at Sungil. "And Seungjin is not my *BFF*, for the record. You two are still my one true pairing."

Sungil rolled his eyes, swinging his legs off us and getting up. He shot Jaehoon a scathing look. "Corn cheese has less cheese in it than you do."

Corn cheese was just that—corn, cheese and a bit of mayonnaise: a side dish. It was delicious and full of cheese. Much like Jaehoon. I laughed.

"And your lack of it is why you're single."

"Maybe the girl of my dreams is lactose intolerant."

I laughed so hard I had tears streaming down my face. Slowly the other two joined in.

Life was not great at the moment. I wasn't sure what was happening with my career, and I'd had to give up my girlfriend, but at least I still had my two best friends.

제12 장

Lucinda

I lay on my bed, staring at the ceiling. It was the weekend so I didn't need to get to class, and I also didn't need to leave my bed. That was what I had done every weekend since Minhyuk—*King*—had broken up with me.

I had become one of the girls my friends and I used to mock.

It was stupid, and I knew this, but everywhere I went, I was reminded of him. He was in my class, his face (and half of Bright Boys') was constantly all over the news … it was hard to get over someone when everything reminded me of him …

It was harder when you had no one you could talk to about it: no one had been allowed to know we were dating, and no one could know that we had broken up. Much as I was hurting, I wouldn't do that to him. Not with everything else he had happening in his life right now.

I wasn't just hurt. I was angry too. I hadn't realized it until a few days later, but the night Hyunseo attacked someone was the same night I was supposed to meet King and tell him I was staying. Instead of meeting me, he'd gone out to a nightclub. Yeah, I was hurt *and* angry.

And there was nothing I could do about it.

I stayed in bed until my stomach forced me out. I climbed down from the top of my bunk and skulked over to the kitchenette, pulling a convenience store kimbap out. I had bought it earlier in the week, so I gave it a sniff before eating it. It wasn't the freshest, but I was certain it wasn't going to kill me.

"You're really going to eat that?"

I turned, finding Miyeon at her desk, studying. I had no idea where Eunbyeol or Baekhee were; I vaguely remembered hearing them leave earlier in the morning. I shrugged at her before taking a bite of the triangular shaped stuffed rice snack.

Miyeon set her pen down, fixing me a concerned look. "I've not asked, because I didn't want to pry, but this has been going on too long. What is wrong with you? All you do is go to class, then come home and go to bed. I thought you liked dancing—you're good at it—but you never come and dance with me."

I walked over to the edge of her bed and perched on the corner of it. "I broke up with my boyfriend," I admitted.

"And that means you're going to spend all your time in bed, feeling sorry for yourself? You're in a new country; you should be spending your weekends going out and seeing it. And even if you don't want to do that, you shouldn't be wasting your time in bed." She flipped her textbook closed and stood, moving over to me. She snatched the half-eaten kimbap from my hands and tossed it in the trashcan. "We're going out." She wrinkled up her nose. "You're having a shower, and then we're going out."

Ignoring my protests, she pulled me to my feet and pushed me towards the bathroom. "Fine," I grunted. "But I don't smell."

"You smell of self-pity and resentment." She shut the door behind her, leaving me in the bathroom.

I looked at my reflection. Maybe she was a little melodramatic, but she was right. Although he had been a large part of the decision to move here, King hadn't been the only part of it. I had wanted to learn new ways of dancing. I had also wanted to explore Seoul, and maybe a few other places in South Korea.

I might not be able to tell anyone what had happened, but I wasn't helping myself lying in bed all the time. I took a shower, imagining the self-pity, as Miyeon had correctly identified it, disappearing down the drain. Wrapped in a towel, I dried my hair, then pulled it back into a pony tail, then escaped into the dorm room to find clean clothes.

"How much better do you feel?" Miyeon asked me.

I pulled my sneakers on and turned to her. "I accept, that in this instance, I was feeling sorry for myself."

"Good," Miyeon nodded. "Now, come with me." She linked her arm through mine, then hurried down to the lift. "How much of Seoul have you seen?" she asked.

"Mostly bits of Gangnam," I admitted.

"Is that it?" she asked in disbelief. "We need to change that."

She led me to a subway station, making me buy a

pass. "You live here. You're going to need one of these." Then she led me down to the correct platform. Miyeon refused to tell me anything more than we were going across the river (or under it). A little over half an hour later, we were topside in a very busy area of Seoul. "Welcome to Hongdae," she announced.

This was a very different area to Gangnam, with a different feel. The amount of people, especially young people, reminded me more of being back in New York, but there was more of a vibe like in Hell's Kitchen. That wasn't quite right—you couldn't really compare the two like that. I suppose the similarity was that I felt more at home here in Hongdae, than I did at the school in Gangnam.

Miyeon led me down the busy streets on a mission, not giving me time to take much in, until we arrived at a small … restaurant seemed a generous term for the place of eating. It was a hole in a wall with some tables outside. "Budae jjigae," Miyeon requested as she pointed to a table. While I sat down, she grabbed two Sprites from a fridge and finally joined me.

"Budae jjigae?" I repeated. I'd not come across that before.

"What is the English?" Miyeon muttered, frowning. "Stew. Army stew. It has ramyun, spam, and rice cakes."

Budae jjigae was delicious. There was a little more in it than Miyeon had said—what looked like sausages, vegetables, and cheese. The freshly cooked food was infinitely better than a borderline-out-of-date kimbap.

Feeling full and even more like the human I used to know, I sat back in my chair, enjoying the slight burn from the spicy meal. "Next time, can we not have something so spicy on such a warm day?" I requested.

Miyeon pouted at me. "Is the Korean food too spicy for the American?"

I laughed. "No, but the weather and the food together is."

"This was supposed to be a sociable meal, but you ate everything so quickly, we couldn't talk. Is everything really OK with you? Is it just the breakup, or are you feeling homesick too?"

"I'm used to being away from home," I shrugged. "I guess, I'm just not used to not having my normal routine to fall into."

"What is your normal routine?"

I grinned. "More dancing, less homework."

"I can't promise less homework, but I can help with the more dancing," Miyeon grinned, jumping to her feet. "Follow me."

Curious, I did. She led me down some new streets, thankfully at a pace suited to our full bellies, and further away from the busy area of Hongdae. I wasn't sure where we were, but the area was feeling a little calmer, if not a little poorer. There were a larger number of buildings either falling into disrepair or boarded up altogether.

Trusting Miyeon, I followed her to one of the boarded-up buildings, around the back to a metal door where she hammered on it. "Miyeon, is this not trespassing?" I asked her, looking around to see if there was anyone watching us.

"No one cares about these buildings," she shrugged. "Not until they decide to do something with them."

In front of us, the door opened up and a tall boy,

who looked a little older than us, appeared. Before I could take in his appearance, he was leaning over to kiss Miyeon. I blinked several times, surprised: Miyeon had never told me she had a boyfriend.

Then again, neither had I.

Miyeon pulled away. "Gunpyo, this is my friend, Lucinda. The American I was talking about." She turned to me as Gunpyo reached for Miyeon's hand. "Lucinda, this is my boyfriend, Ryu Gunpyo."

By now, I recognized most of the students at SLA, even if I didn't know their names. Gunpyo was definitely not a student at SLA. The longer I had been at SLA, the more I realized that the majority of students came from money. There were only a handful of scholarship kids, and thanks to Cha Yerin's vocal disgust of them, I knew who they were. Or, at least, I had a good idea. Yerin thought I was there on a scholarship—I still hadn't felt the need to correct her assumption on that—so the list might not have been entirely accurate.

Not that it mattered, but Gunpyo didn't have the air or attitude of an SLA student. He leaned against the door frame, eyeing me curiously. His expression wasn't unfriendly, but a little guarded. His clothes were brightly patterned, and although they worked, a little tired and worn.

"You're a dancer?" he asked.

I nodded.

"Cool," he shrugged. "Come on in." He indicated I should follow, then, still holding onto Miyeon's hand, disappeared into the building.

Feeling like I was Alice descending down the rabbit hole, I followed. The door had opened to a stairway which led down to the basement. The room was brightly lit. I had no idea where they were getting their power, but there were spotlights on stands around the room.

The room was large, maybe double the size of our classroom. Dotted around the edge were mismatching, broken cupboards—some with doors, most without— and various mats. On the mats, two guys were laid out on their backs, holding comics above their heads as they read.

On the far side of the room, covering the wall, was the biggest collection of mirrors I had seen. In front of them was a girl and guy. The girl was busy teaching the guy a short routine, but both stopped when I walked in. "Who's that?" the guy asked, the question making the two with comic books sit up and look at me with curiosity.

"Guys, this is Lucinda Williams. She's in my class at SLA with me," Miyeon told them. She turned to me. "That's Joo Jimin and Seom Yeosong," Miyeon said, pointing to the girl, then the guy, who had been dancing. She turned to the carpet. "And that's Shim Minseok and Doon Jungbae."

"Blue," the younger of the two said, abruptly.

Miyeon nodded. "Minseok prefers to go by Blue." I gave them all a finger wave, stopping dead at Miyeon's next words. "Lucinda is here to try out."

"I am?" I asked, surprised.

Jimin looked me up and down. She was tall, like Gunpyo, with long blonde hair which had pink streaks throughout, and contacts which made her eyes as blue as mine. She folded her arms, tilting her head. "Do you sing?"

Miyeon sighed. "We're dancers. And she dances."

"Let's see it then," Yeosong shrugged. He walked over to a CD player and held up a wire.

"Now?" I asked. I looked at Miyeon. "You never said anything about an audition. What am I auditioning for?"

Miyeon pursed her lips, thoughtfully. "That's fair. Guys, let's show her what we do."

The next thing I knew, the group had gathered together in the center of the room and were performing their own routine to an Infinite song. I watched with a massive grin on my face: they were good. Blue and Miyeon, in particular, were outstanding. Whatever this group was, I wanted in.

Their dancing seemed effortless: a sign this was something they had spent a lot of time practicing. When they finished, I burst into applause. "You guys are brilliant!" I exclaimed, meaning it.

"Your turn," Miyeon declared.

I chewed at my lip. I wasn't nervous about performing in front of them. I'd done that so many times in competitions and recitals that it was nothing. My hesitation came from the fact I had no training in their style of dance, short of a routine King and I had done last summer at the New York Dance Academy, and that had been a duet.

"Just do anything," Miyeon said, as though she could read my mind.

I nodded, pulling my phone out of my pocket and selecting a song. I kicked my shoes off and moved over to the center of the room. The flooring wasn't ideal, but I hadn't brought the right shoes for dancing in.

I knew as I was dancing that I was a little rusty.

Staying in bed as much as I had, had had a detrimental effect on me. My muscles strained, and my movements weren't as sharp as they should have been. What's more, I was more exhausted by the end of it than I should have been. I was going to be bringing back morning runs to my daily routine.

When I finished, I was breathing heavily, but I felt calmer and happier than I had for weeks. Why on earth had I not continued dancing?

Blue and Jungbae burst into an enthusiastic round of applause, while Jimin turned to Miyeon and Gunpyo. "She's not great," she declared. I wasn't sure if she knew I understood her or not, but I decided not to enlighten her on that.

"We need an extra member, and she's been out of action for the last six weeks," Miyeon told her. "I've seen her dance better than this: she's just a bit rusty."

"We'd be the only group with a foreigner in it," Gunpyo muttered, glancing over at me. "Which might be harder for her."

"Oh, I didn't realize I was trying out for an idol group," I said, joining them. "I know I'm not suitable for that—"

"We're not an idol group," Gunpyo cut me off.

Jimin laughed. "With Jungbae's singing abilities, no, we most certainly are not."

"Bite me," Jungbae squawked. I think he was trying to sing the retort at her, but what left his mouth was definitely closer in sound to a squawk than a note. At least we had that in common.

"Then what is this?" I asked, my curiosity getting the better of me.

"We're a busking group," Miyeon said. "We're the

Iron Street Crew."

I stared at her. Busking, to me, was performing in the street for change. That seemed an odd thing for these guys to be doing. "I don't understand."

"Find out later," Gunpyo told me.

Miyeon looked up at her boyfriend. "Does that mean she's in?"

Gunpyo shrugged. "It means she can come along later and see if it's something that interests her, and if so, yes, she's in."

제13 장

Lucinda

We spent the afternoon in the basement. Underneath the building, it was cool; a much-needed haven while dancing. The time was spent with the Iron Street Crew showing me their routines, most of them being cover dances to popular K-pop songs. They were good and tight. The mirrors lining the room made sense.

By the time we emerged topside, the sun had sunk a little further in the sky, but the heat and humidity remained. "If you like what we do, and you want to be a part of it, next time we'll start teaching you the routines," Gunpyo told me.

I liked Gunpyo. Whether self-elected or nominated by the others, he was a sensible leader who was always looking out for the others. Miyeon and Blue were the creative ones, and Jimin was the slightly bossy perfectionist.

Gunpyo led us to an area of Hongdae that was alive with bustle and tourists. I wasn't sure if it had been designed like that, or if people were taking advantage of the architectural design, but there were lots of areas which could become mini stages. We passed one area where a trio were already performing. I paused to watch the three girls, fascinated.

They'd chosen a 2NE1 song and I recognized enough of the routine to know they were copying it rather than using one of their own. They weren't brilliant: the girl at the back was half a beat behind the two at the front. Yet, they had the crowd around them enraptured. So many people had their phones out, filming them. It was kind of mesmerizing.

A hand wrapped around my arm, tugging me away. "Don't give them any more attention than they are getting," Miyeon hissed at me. "The leader is a manipulative piece of trash."

"OK," I said, hurrying after her. "You want to elaborate?"

"The group is trouble and you should stay away. That's all you need to know."

Because that didn't tug at my curiosity …

"Tonight, just blend in with the crowd," Blue instructed me.

I arched an eyebrow. "Blend in? Blue, have you not noticed how white I am? Because I don't blend."

Blue shrugged. "Just wait until we're set up. Foreigners love Gunpyo."

I glanced over at the tall leader. I'd be lying if I said I couldn't tell why. Gunpyo was good-looking. He reminded me a little bit of one of the vocalists in ASTRO.

It didn't take long for Gunpyo and Jungbae to set the CD player and speaker up, while Jimin and Yeosong (I discovered they were a couple too), set up some banners covered in what had to be the Iron Street Crew's logo.

The crowd began to grow. There were more females around us than there had been with the trio, but the crowd was almost evenly mixed. There were clearly a lot of 'regulars' as the crew would happily chat and interact with them.

I took a seat on a wall, giving myself a good view in the center. Finally, they got started with a BTS cover dance. The moves were complicated, but they made them look as effortless as BTS did. Meanwhile, the crowd were cheering them on, almost everyone on their phones, filming them.

I watched, as entranced as I had been in their basement hideout. They had all put on a bit more makeup before leaving, but otherwise, they all looked the same as they had earlier. Only, now they were in front of a crowd, it was like their energy levels had quadrupled. They were jumping higher, somehow even more in sync, and even more importantly, they looked alive.

By the second song, I had pulled my own phone out to record them myself, mainly because I wanted to look at each member individually, which I couldn't really do now. The crowd seemed to be sharing the same opinion I did. I overheard so many people complimenting their performance, commenting how they needed to record it so they could watch it again and again.

By the second song, I'd also decided I wanted in.

There would be a lot of practice involved, and a lot of different styles of K-pop dancing to learn, but it would be worth it. Combined with the fact that these performances would be regular, and new routines would need to be learned to keep current, to keep the crowd coming back again, and again—because there were several other busking groups about to compete with—it would be a rush and a brilliant learning opportunity.

The group finished up early evening, hanging around to chat with the slowly dispersing crowds, before Miyeon and Gunpyo walked over to me. "What do you think?" Gunpyo asked.

"I have never seen anything like that," I admitted. "And if you still want me, I want in."

"I told you so," Miyeon said to Gunpyo.

"Is that a yes?" I asked. When Miyeon nodded, I let out an excited squeal and wrapped my arms around her. Then I jumped back, apologizing profusely. For half a moment, I had forgotten the importance of personal space for Koreans.

"I am starving," Blue said, coming over and joining us. "Chicken?"

My eyes lit up. "I know it's a bit far from here, but I know a really good chicken place by SLA."

Gunpyo looked at Blue, who shrugged. "I'm escorting Miyeon back anyway," Gunpyo said.

"Count me out, guys. I've got work," Jungbae declared, scooping up the CD player and the portable speaker. "I'll take these back on the way."

"Jimin and I are out too," Yeosong added. He didn't give a reason, but took Jimin's hand in his own, leading her away.

"I guess it's just us," Blue shrugged. The four of us walked to the subway station to head back to Gangnam.

I was tired, but happier than I'd been for a while. I wasn't going to pretend that I wasn't still hurting from our breakup, because I was. But I wasn't going to let that rule my life. Not everyone was lucky enough to find the love of their life on the first try.

"You've gone quiet," Miyeon muttered as we took a seat in Roosters.

"I'm trying to work out what I want to eat," I informed her, looking at the menu hanging on the wall. I don't know why I bothered. I was one of those people who, once I found something I liked, would always get the same thing whenever I went back. "Dakgangjeong," I shrugged, picking the sweet and spicy crispy chicken.

The guy behind the counter turned around: TK. I forgot he worked here. "Oh. It's you," he said, unenthusiastically.

"*Ya!*" Yoo Chaewon called. "I've told you, that's not how you speak to customers."

"It is when the customer's boyfriend punches you in the face," TK grunted. He glowered at me, then stormed into the back.

Miyeon turned, leaning against the counter as she arched an eyebrow. "OK, I thought your ex was back in America. Is he talking about Sungil?"

"Baek Sungil?" Gunpyo repeated in disbelief. "You're dating the chaebol heir of the Baek Group?"

"No, I'm dating ..." I stopped myself from correcting them, sighing. I couldn't even tell them the truth. "We broke up," I said, shortly.

Classes had been a blur to me. I'd turned up, but I had spent the entire time very conscious of the fact that Minhy ... King was sitting in the same room as me. After a few days, I'd realized that if I wanted to pass the year, I needed to pay attention and filter everything else out. After that, I had started taking notes and focusing on assignments—anything but who was in the class with me.

I wanted to slap myself.

Instead, I muttered I would be back, then hurried to the small hatch in the counter. I took half a step through, then remembered where I was. "Would you mind if I went to speak to TK?" I asked Chaewon. He was watching me in amusement but gestured that I could go through.

I gave him a grateful smile and made my way through into the small kitchen. TK wasn't there. He hadn't come back out to the front, which meant the only other option was the back door. I pulled it open and stepped through, outside into an alleyway.

TK was crouched against the wall, drinking from a bottle of banana milk. "What do you want?"

"Sungil and I aren't dating," I told him, firmly. "I have barely spoken to him since the day he hit you, which, for the record, no matter what happened, I don't condone." My sentence was one rambling mess, and the look he gave me made me question whether or not he understood what I had said.

"What do you care anyway? You're one of them."

"One of what?" I shot back at him.

"You know," he shrugged.

I stared at him. "Psychic?" I asked. "Because while I think I need to be to understand whatever you're not telling me, I can assure you, I am not psychic."

TK stood and walked over to me. He was easily as tall as Gunpyo or Sungil and towered over me. There were days when I hated being so short. But today was not one where I was going to let TK know that. I folded my arms and glowered up at him.

"Rich."

I almost choked on my laughter. "Rich?" I repeated.

"Aren't you?" he said, folding his arms and glowering back at me.

"Really?" I said, shaking my head. At the face he pulled, I held up a hand. "I am not going to stand here and pretend my parents aren't well off, and didn't pay for me to come here, because they did. But I'm also not going to stand here without pointing out that I don't judge a person by their bank account."

"Says the girl who is at an obvious advantage and has never had to worry about things as trivial as money," he sneered.

He let out a disgusted sound and started to move past me, but I stepped in front of him, blocking his way. "What I find most interesting here is your hypocrisy. You're there claiming that we're all judging you because of your lack of money yet you can't see the fact you're doing the exact same thing to me. The only thing I'm judging you on is the fact you're a narrowminded jerk."

I was too irritated to give him a chance to respond. Instead, I turned my back to him and stormed back through the kitchen, apologizing to Chaewon as I almost walked into him, then went back into the restaurant.

The others were already seated at a table in the window and I went over to join them. "What was all that about?" Miyeon asked.

"Nothing worth ..." I trailed off when I realized TK was standing over me. "What?"

"It's my break," he said, gruffly.

"So?"

TK rubbed the back of his neck, glancing over his shoulder to where Chaewon was giving him a pointed look from behind the counter. He turned back to me. "I was wondering if I could join you while I took my break."

I stared up at him, contemplating whether I should ask him if he earned enough money to sit with us, and then internally shook myself: there was enough of the Regina George attitude coming from Yerin. It didn't need to come from me too. That was being petty for petty's sake, and I wasn't that kind of person.

But I was the type of person who would check with others first.

"Do any of you have any objections?" I asked the table. I sensed a little unease from Gunpyo and Blue, but as both of them responded with a no, I assumed it was simply because they hadn't met him before.

"Grab a chair," I said, before introducing him to the people sat at the table.

We sat in an awkward silence until Blue tilted his head at TK. "Do you dance?"

TK shook his head. "Not really. I'd rather play computer games."

Blue's eyes lit up. "What?"

TK told him the name I didn't recognize, and Blue did an excited jiggle in his seat. "Me too! Give me your user name?"

I glanced at Miyeon. "Does this mean anything to you?"

"TK has probably made a friend for life?" she offered as we watched TK move around the table, practically draping himself over Blue as they fell into a deep conversation about game tactics. "No one in ISC games."

I ate my chicken, watching in amusement: TK and Blue were passionate about their games. "How often do you, the Iron Street Crew—"

"Call us ISC," Gunpyo cut me off. "It's easier."

"How often do you meet up?"

"Every weekend when it's not exam period," Gunpyo replied. "It gets harder because Miyeon's on this side of the river and she has a stupid curfew."

"We try to learn the dances on the weekend and I practice during the week when I can't get over. Every Friday, Saturday and Sunday evening, we perform in Hongdae. So long as the weather is good enough," Miyeon elaborated. She leaned forward. "Are you really in?"

I nodded.

"Yes!" she hissed. She held her fist up and waited for me to bump it. "Welcome to the family."

제14 장

King

November

I stared at Seungjin, trying to process what I was feeling. We had both been studying at my desk when Seungjin had gotten a text message. "How come you have a phone?" I asked him, deciding that was the easiest of things to start with.

Sungil was sitting beside Jaehoon on my bed when he laughed. It was a dry, dark laugh. "Because his father owns Atlantis Entertainment?"

Seungjin spun and scowled at Sungil. "Because once they said that we were going back to school and acting like everything was normal, I told them if they expected me to act like I would at school, I would be getting my phone back. And it was Oh Seokbeom who gave it me."

"Of course," Sungil muttered, although he clearly didn't believe him. It earned him an elbow to the ribs from Jaehoon.

"What is it with you?" Seungjin demanded. "If I

was getting some form of special treatment from my family, don't you think that I'd be still performing? Not one of us has had a solo project during this time." He stood and kicked at the desk chair. "And why wouldn't we be able to have a phone? We're not in the dorms anymore. We're here, away from Atlantis, where it's not easy for any of them to contact us if they need to. Instead of complaining at me, why don't you go to Atlantis and ask for yours back too?"

Maybe he had a point. I'd gone so long being in Atlantis without a phone that I had forgotten what it was like to have one. If they were going to keep us here, I should think about getting mine back too. Which led to the next point. "Does it say why they want to see us? It's a Sunday."

"As if the music industry ever stops," Seungjin muttered, sitting back down. He glanced at his phone. "Seokbeom said, 'The VC wants to see Bright Boys and King, at six tonight. Make sure you're all there', and nothing else."

"What on earth does Sejin want with us?" Jaehoon grumbled. "I doubt that's going to be good news."

"I doubt it's Sejin," Seungjin said, placing his phone face down on the desk. He looked up and found us staring at him. He sighed. "I guess it's going to come out eventually."

"What?" Sungil demanded. He got up and walked over to the collection of desks, staring down at Seungjin.

"Don't act like you're one of us," Seungjin scoffed. "You gave that up when you quit."

"He's our friend," I cut in, seeing Sungil's dark

expression.

"Just tell them, hyung," Jaehoon muttered.

"You know the new manager H3RO has?" Seungjin said.

I nodded. "The American who got them a number one comeback after a nearly two-year hiatus? Who in Atlantis doesn't know about her? She's saved their career."

"American Korean," Seungjin corrected me.

"Well, I kinda figured that," I shrugged.

Sungil slipped into the chair at the spare desk. "Are they going to have her save your careers?"

"I hope so," Seungjin said. "Although, this will be a case of me using my family connections."

I stared blankly at him. Jaehoon, on the other hand, suddenly found his ripped jeans more interesting. "You know," Sungil said. I looked up and found him staring suspiciously at Jaehoon. "This was the thing you were talking about weeks ago, right?"

Seungjin shot Jaehoon a dark look and he held up his hands in defense. "I didn't tell them anything."

"Them?"

"Sungil and King," he admitted. "All I said was that you might have found something to help us."

"What?" I asked. "This has something to do with that manager? Holly ... Lee ... Holly Lee? Wait, is she related to you too?"

Seungjin nodded. "She's my half-sister. I didn't even know she existed until before the summer."

My eyes widened in hope. "She saved H3RO."

Seungjin let out a long breath, his elbows resting on the desk as he sank his head into his hands. "Don't get too excited. Sejin hates her."

"How is that a problem?" Jaehoon asked.

"Father wants her to join Sejin as Vice Chairwoman, which, obviously, Sejin isn't happy about. He is the one who told her unless she can prove herself by getting H3RO to number one, he was going to disband them. She wants to save them."

"And she doesn't want to save us?" Jaehoon frowned. "Why not?"

"I don't think she doesn't want to save us, I just don't think we're her priority."

"But she is asking to see us," I pointed out. "That's got to be a good sign, right?"

"I guess we'll find out in a couple of hours," he shrugged.

I watched as he chewed his lip, trying to work out if the look on his face was worry or hope. I opted for the latter, wanting to keep optimistic.

For the next few hours, the optimism stayed strong.

Until I walked into Atlantis.

At that point, it began to falter.

Part of the problem was that I was there with them. The other was, when we stepped off the elevator, Hyunseo was in the waiting room already. I knew that his court case was still ongoing, and nothing had been resolved. Much as I wanted to be hopeful at this point, seeing him was like seeing a dark omen.

As we congregated in the waiting area, I spared a glance at the assistant, and then did a double take. "Isn't that Lee Sejin's assistant?" I asked Dongyeol. "Park Inhye?"

Dongyeol nodded. "Yeah, she switched over to Holly's team."

"You can go in now," Inhye said, then stopped when she saw me. "Oh, you're here too?"

"Is that a problem?" I asked, hesitantly. *That* wasn't a good feeling.

"Just wait there a moment," she said, before ducking into Holly's office.

I glanced at Apollo as he happened to be standing next to me. He looked as worried as I felt. Wonderful.

Inhye reappeared a few minutes later. "Holly will speak to you all together, and then a couple of individuals after."

I walked into the office, following the others. Holly's office was similar to Sejin's, but a bit smaller. Being in here, it was clear she wasn't just a manager. None of the managers had offices as big or extravagant as this.

At one side was a desk, at the other were several couches. Holly was sat by them in a chair. She was really pretty. A bit old for me, but still pretty. She was quite tall, slim, and wearing a suit dress. I could also see the resemblance to Seungjin.

Despite being old, she was far too young to be working as the Vice Chairwoman. Where was Sejin, anyway?

"Please, come in," she said. "I think there's enough room for everyone."

We filed in, filling the couches. Except for Hyunseo and Jaehoon who chose to stand behind.

"You're all a bit …" she frowned. "I guess that's understandable," she added before shaking her head. "OK, here goes. I spoke to Lee Woojin, the Chairman," she added, as though we didn't know.

Or maybe to stop anyone from asking who she

was? As far as I was aware, Seungjin, Jaehoon, and I were the only ones who knew. But then, I hadn't been in the Atlantis offices for a while.

"I've looked into what has been happening with you and had a few ideas which I shared with him. Lee Woojin has agreed with me and they're going to happen. Hopefully, you will all be on board with them."

"This doesn't sound good," Yongsik muttered behind me.

"I've given this a lot of thought," she continued. "I've also had some surveys carried out, which I know sounds very American, but I am," she grinned. When none of us grinned back, the smile fell from her face and she cleared her throat. "Yes, well … the results …" she took a deep breath.

"The public think your reputation is damaged beyond repair. Like I said, I've thought long and hard about this, and I think the only way we can salvage any of your careers is to disband Bright Boys."

The room fell into chaos with vocal objections.

"What about me?" I demanded. "I'm not in Bright Boys."

My question was lost in the noise. I could see Holly trying to quieten us, but I was too desperate to know about my own future than to quieten and have the conversation dominated by Bright Boys.

The thing that abruptly ended the conversation was Seungjin. Specifically, Seungjin flipping the glass coffee table over. I knew he worked out, but the table went flying, crashing into the bookcase where the glass shattered everywhere.

We fell silent, staring at him in disbelief. He turned to Holly, panting at the exertion. There was pure rage in his eyes. "I trusted you!" he said, his voice dangerously quiet.

"Seungjin, I promise you, I am doing this with the best intentions," Holly said. I could see she was trying to appear calm, but her voice caught as she spoke.

"Screw you."

Holly let out a long breath. "Please guys, just sit and let me finish, and then I promise you I will sit here for as long as it takes to answer your questions."

"What about me?" I asked, feeling selfish for asking, but still needing to know the answer.

"All of you," Holly said, holding up a hand. She turned to me. "I appreciate you're not in Bright Boys, Minhyuk—"

"King," I said, stubbornly. I was clinging onto my stage name like it was going to save me, but I was going to try anything.

"King, I'm including you in this."

It was like I was sat in a vacuum and someone had sucked out all the air and sound all at once. I sat there, staring dumbly at Holly. I could see her mouth moving, but little of what she was saying was registering.

As though she could sense this, she stood up. "I need you all to listen to me and hear what I'm saying."

I stared at her trying to focus. I felt like I was hanging off the edge of a cliff … No, I felt like I was standing in front of a house I had built, and it was burning down in front of me while my hands were tied, preventing me from doing anything about it.

"I am not going to spend much time speaking ill of how things were run under Sejin," although she kept her tone even, the expression she made when she said the Vice Chairman's name was telling. I took a glimmer of hope at this. "I can't say I agreed with much of it, including how this was handled. Maybe if something had been done differently at the beginning, we wouldn't be here, or maybe we would. The fact is that we can't find out now. We are where we are, and I need to do what I think is best for you, as well as Atlantis. The reputation of Bright Boys has, frankly, been destroyed. That is why I am ending your contracts with Bright Boys, and your solo career, King. I am not going to end your contracts with Atlantis. At least, not until you hear my plan and you can make your own informed decision. OK?"

"What's your plan?" Hyunseo asked.

Holly looked at him. "Park Hyunseo?" Hyunseo nodded. "Your path needs to be a little different. I can't do anything until your court case has been resolved, and I wish to speak to you separately after this. However, I want you to know, and I am saying this in front of everyone, I am not going to abandon you. I will be honest and say opinion of you is split in Atlantis, but I will *not* abandon you."

I glanced at the oldest member of Bright Boys and for the first time, saw a glimmer of hope there. He believed her. Or, at least he wanted to believe her.

"OK," he said, quietly.

Holly gave him a small smile. "Would you mind waiting outside for me? I want to speak to the others now."

That glimmer of hope died in front of me.

With his shoulders slumped, he walked to the door like he was walking to his execution. My stomach churned as I turned back to the woman. Honestly, I couldn't tell if I wanted her or Sejin in front of me right now. A glance at Seungjin told me he certainly wanted his brother there, and I knew he didn't like the man.

"As for the rest of you, or at least, everyone but Yongsik—"

Everyone turned to look at him. He looked terrified. At twenty-two he was the oldest in the room. He wasn't old, but the older you got, the harder it would be to move to another company—especially after coming off the back of a group scandal resulting in a disbandment. That execution wasn't too far of a stretch at the possibility of a career death sentence.

Holly held her hands up. "Just let me finish!" she cried. "It's not …" she shook her head. "Tomorrow morning there will be an announcement being made. Atlantis Entertainment is partnering with the Seoul Leadership Academy, which I believe everyone *but* Yongsik attends."

I glanced at Ryan. I think he was still technically enrolled, but he hadn't been attending. He'd been back in Busan. Did that mean he was coming back?

"The company will be taking an active role in the academic structure of the school, to include performance-based classes," Holly continued. Our vocal and rap coaches, along with the dance teachers will take turns leading classes at SLA. All of you will attend these. They will be an optional route for the students already there as many parents, as well as students, will insist they stick to the academic route, but for you, they will be mandatory. Are you following me so far?"

"You want us to stay in school?" Seungjin asked in disgust.

Holly nodded. "I am trying to repair your

reputations. I need to put some distance between you and the scandal. I need people to forget you."

"The worst thing that can happen to an idol is to become forgotten and irrelevant," Seungjin snapped at her, voicing what all of us were thinking as we nodded our heads in agreement. "This isn't America."

"No," Holly agreed. "In America, pop stars can be in and out of rehab with drug problems. Rappers can go to prison and return to their careers when they're released. Singers can still get number one singles after assault cases. Here, the public, and I include your fandoms in this, they're not as forgiving. That's why most of the disgraced idols head to early enlistment hoping the time away will save them. Or, those who have already served, find their careers disintegrating beneath them. Those of you at SLA are too young for enlistment, and unless Yongsik particularly wants to do that now, I'm not suggesting it as an option for you, to be clear," she added.

"No," Yongsik agreed, quietly.

"And that's why I want the public to forget you. You're all school age, and there's not much I can do with that. I know a lot of people think that education is forgotten about when you're an idol, and I appreciate, in some cases, that is the truth, but that's not going to happen here. I will still expect you to get qualifications when you re-debut."

"You want us to re-debut?" I blurted out.

Holly nodded firmly. "Yes. But I'm not going to *just* re-debut you. Again, with the exception of Yongsik and Hyunseo, I expect you all to attend SLA. You will go to all of your classes, and you will study, and you will do voluntary work on top of that. And while the press is getting bored of watching you being exemplary members of society, you will also be attending those performance classes and improving your singing or rapping, and dancing. At the end of the year, much like when you were trainees, because that's what you're going back to being, you will be tested. If you pass the grade, I will re-debut you."

제15 장

King

Holly folded her arms, taking the time to look us all in the eye. "And let me be absolutely clear, I have plans, and they currently involve every single person in this room, but I need you to prove to me that you still want this. Because what I have planned; it's going to be a hell of a lot harder than anything you've done so far." She sat down, placing her hands in her lap. "Now, if there is anyone who feels they either cannot, or do not, wish to do this, speak now and I will arrange to have your contract terminated."

"What about me?" Yongsik asked. "As you said, I'm too old for the Seoul Leadership Academy."

Holly took a deep breath. "I am not going to lie to you. You are a little harder. You didn't graduate high school, as you were a trainee here, which means getting you into university is next to impossible. Atlantis is only working with the Seoul Leadership Academy, and not the Seoul Leadership University, despite their partnership."

"You don't know what to do with me, do you?"

Yongsik asked.

"No," Holly admitted.

"What good is that?" he demanded.

"I have something that I'm considering, but until I can get any traction with it, I want to keep it to myself because I don't want to get your hopes up."

"Then why did you tell me what you wanted from these guys?" Yongsik asked, quietly.

Holly met his gaze. "Because I wanted you to see that I am trying, and I have every intention of resolving things with you."

"What about H3RO?" Seungjin spoke up.

Holly looked startled as she looked at him. "What about H3RO?"

Seungjin was relentless. "If you're managing H3RO, how can you rescue us?"

"Just to be clear, I'm not rescuing you. You're rescuing yourselves. I also have no intention of managing you: you already have a manager," she trailed off, and it sounded like she was saying something about not taking another job. "The point is, there's enough people at this company who *do* want you to succeed that they will work to help you. You just have to help yourselves first."

Seungjin glowered at her before exploding into a stream of expletives.

"Tell me how you really feel, Seungjin," Holly muttered.

"Really feel?" he repeated. "Oh, I'll tell you: I want nothing to do with you. I came to you asking, no, *begging*, for your help, and you *disband* us? Go to hell!" With that, he stormed out of the room, slamming the door so hard, it bounced open again.

Calmly, Holly walked after him, stopping at the door to close it. She turned back to us. "I will call Seungjin after, but on the off chance he doesn't answer, which seems likely, can you please assure him I'm not ending his contract unless he specifically asks me too. The same goes for all of you," she added. "I want you to succeed, but if you feel this path is no longer right for you, then I shall have your contracts terminated. If you want to take some time to think it over, you can. Atlantis and the SLA are announcing their partnership tomorrow. I would suggest you at least try attending the classes, considering you're already there anyway."

"What about me?" Yongsik asked again. "You said you had an idea."

"I also said it wasn't concrete," Holly pointed out.

"I want to hear."

Holly stared at him, before slowly shrugging. "Very well, but I want to speak to Hyunseo, alone, first. He has been waiting long enough." She looked over at us. "Think about it, guys." She stepped to the side and let us file out.

As we swapped places with Hyunseo, I turned to the others. "What do you think?"

Apollo glanced over at Inhye before looking back to me. "I think we need to have this conversation somewhere else. Not here."

"I think chicken is in order," Dongyeol said. We all looked at him. "Judge all you want, but I am starving, and I think better after I've eaten."

I scratched at the back of my head. "Sure. Let's go back to our room. Seungjin might be there and he should probably be part of this conversation."

Z

Seungjin wasn't in the room when we got back. As far I could tell, he hadn't been back either. I headed over to the couch and sank onto it. One by one, Dongyeol, Apollo, Jaehoon and Ryan came in and sat either beside me on the couch, or on the floor in front of it.

Strangely, we all sat in silence for quite some time before the eldest in the room, Ryan, spoke. "Did I understand that all correctly?" he asked. Ryan was originally from China, moving to Busan in the south with his mother when he was six. Although he was quite fluent in Korean now, he had struggled when he had first come to Seoul, because there was such a difference between the Seoul and Busan dialects.

"She has disbanded us," Jaehoon confirmed, grimly.

"And wants us to keep coming here?" Ryan asked. "But I've been back in Busan until last night. I haven't been attending any classes. I wasn't attending school in Busan either. I'm not clever enough to come to this place."

"I can assure you, hyung," Apollo said, his tone dry. "A fair number of students at this school are here because of their money, not their intelligence."

"What Apollo means," I quickly cut in, seeing Ryan's expression. "Is that you're not stupid, but the classes aren't as advanced as you'd think. Besides, if there are performance-based classes, you'll have absolutely nothing to worry about."

"Are we doing it?" Jaehoon asked. He seemed surprised.

"You don't think we should?" I asked him.

"I don't see why I should trust her. Seungjin doesn't."

"H3RO do," Ryan said. "I've spoken to Dante a few times. He said she works hard and only has their best interest at heart."

"But she also said she was H3RO's manager, not ours," Jaehoon returned. "Don't forget, we've still got Oh Seokbeom as a manager. He hasn't cared until now, so why would he start?"

"Here's how I see it," Dongyeol said suddenly. "I think she's right about our reputation. I've spent a lot of time hiding out in the library, using the computers, and I've seen what the comments about us online are like. Even the rest of you must have noticed that after the initial buzz of us being here, everyone stopped caring. Right or wrong, the public don't like us."

Dongyeol was right about that. At least we were being ignored, rather than getting nasty comments in real life from our classmates. "And you think staying here will help?"

"I know she said that if we wanted to, Atlantis would terminate our contracts, but if the public hates us that much, what other agency will take us? I don't know about her plans for us re-debuting; I don't even know how long she'll stick around at Atlantis. I do think she makes a point about clearing our reputations. If we officially disband, get our heads down, and wait for this to die down, if nothing comes of this re-debut, we might then be able to leave and go elsewhere, but with a cleaner slate."

"I'll stay," Apollo said. He laughed. "At least now I can ditch this stage name."

"Apollo?" I asked, surprised. "I thought you liked

it?"

Apollo pulled a face. "Lee Sejin chose it. It's not that I don't like it, it's that I don't feel like me. I had a stage name from before."

Even though I got on with him, I wasn't close to Apollo. We hadn't had many conversations together and he was older than me. From what I could remember, he was an underground rapper before joining Atlantis.

"Then what do you want us to call you?" Ryan asked.

Apollo got to his feet, pacing back and forth as he rubbed his arms. "She thinks we need to clear up our image?" he asked, referring to Holly. When he received various nods, he sighed. "Joochan. I am Yang Joochan, the student."

"I'm staying," Dongyeol added.

Ryan and I both nodded our agreements before we looked to Jaehoon. He stared back at us, slowly lowering his head so he could rub at the back of his neck. "This had better work."

"What about you?" Joochan asked.

I looked up and found him staring at me. I frowned. "I just said, I'm in."

"No, I mean, your name."

"Oh." I slumped back into the back of the sofa as I thought about it. King was who I was on stage, but Minhyuk was me. I had been Minhyuk longer than King, but I didn't know Minhyuk anymore. There had only been one person who had called me Minhyuk the whole time, and I had been a complete jerk to her.

Lucinda.

If I wasn't King anymore, then I didn't have a

dating restriction anymore.

But I had been a complete jerk to her.

She wouldn't still be interested, and did I even have the right to find out?

"King!"

I looked over at Dongyeol, blinking. "Huh?"

"Well, that answers that," he declared while I stared blankly at him. "I called both names. You answered to King."

"I guess I'm King," I agreed.

제16 장

Lucinda

For the first time since arriving in Seoul, when I stepped outside, it was cold. Not just cool, but cold. "I see fall is finally here," Miyeon said, shivering. "We're up early. We still have time to go get our blazers."

I shook my head. "It's OK. It'll be warm in the classroom."

Miyeon shot me a sideways look. "You know there's a reason why they give us blazers, right? They don't heat the classrooms."

I stopped and turned at her. "Huh?"

Miyeon gave me a grin as she linked her arm through mine and dragged me back up to our dorm rooms to get our blazers from the closet. Baekhee had gone, but Eunbyeol was still in the bathroom, putting her makeup on. "It's cold out," I called to her, feeling surprisingly sympathetic towards her this morning. She had a huge zit on her chin and was desperately trying to cover it.

"Why did you do that?" Miyeon asked as we

walked back to the cafeteria.

I hadn't realized it before, probably because this was the first time wearing it, but the blazer was lined. "I don't know," I said, stopping. Something felt off.

"What's wrong?" Miyeon frowned, staring at me.

I looked around. "Is it me, or is it strangely quiet?"

Miyeon glanced up and down the corridor, her frown matching mine. "Yes."

The uneasy feeling didn't leave me, and as we entered the cafeteria, I could see why. It had been trashed. There was food everywhere, like a food fight had taken place. And yet, there was only one person in the cafeteria: TK.

"What the hell happened?" I blurted out, looking at the mess in confusion. And equally as important, where were the adults?

TK turned, and I saw the state of him. He was covered in a bright orange liquid—there was some form of spicy breakfast soup for breakfast—but even worse, there were tears in his eyes.

I darted over, or started to, until I nearly slipped on a pile of beansprouts. I slowed down but kept moving towards him. "What happ—" My eyes fell on his arms. The soup had been hot when it had been thrown at him. "What are you doing?" I demanded, reaching out for his shirt. He stared dumbly at me as I started unbuttoning it. I could tell it had cooled, but he needed looking at in case he was burned.

"What are you doing?"

I glanced over at the doorway, finding King, Sungil, Seungjin and Jaehoon there. Seungjin was the only one who seemed pleased. There was a smirk and an attitude about him. Jaehoon and Sungil seemed amused, though confused. And King … he looked furious.

From the way he was glaring at me, I knew it wasn't about TK being covered in food, but because I was undressing him.

"Was this something to do with you?" TK asked.

I turned, about to tell him I had no idea about any of it, and then realized he was looking at the four guys in the doorway. I followed his gaze. Jaehoon and Sungil were both staring at him with the same amused expression, but Seungjin looked positively smug. I was willing to bet he *had* had something to do with this.

"Get your hands off her," King growled through gritted teeth.

I arched an eyebrow, staring at him in disbelief. "Excuse me?" I asked, my hands finally leaving TK's opened shirt to sit on my hips. "Who do you think you're talking to?"

It was Seungjin who responded. "The only person responsible for this is you," Seungjin said, coldly, ignoring me and King. "Your family is good at messing up other people's lives. Let's see if your father can clean this up before the principal sees it."

TK suddenly pushed past me, making a beeline for the door. If it hadn't taken me a moment to catch my balance, I would have charged after him. I had fully expected him to punch Seungjin, but he didn't, instead barging between King and Jaehoon, out of the cafeteria and into the corridor.

The irritation set in and I marched towards to the door. As I tried to get past, King grabbed my arm. "Where are you going?" he demanded.

"I'm going to make sure my friend is OK," I told him, shaking my arm free.

"Your friend?" he repeated. "He was all over you."

My eyes narrowed as I glared up at him. I didn't get angry very easily, but right now, I wanted to scoop some of the food up off the floor and fling it in his face. "All over me?" I repeated. "I was undressing him!" King's eyes widened, and I could feel my face heat up. I hated when it did that. There was no need for my embarrassment. The one who should be embarrassed was King. "And it's none of your business anyway."

"Atlantis cancelled me."

I stared up at him, giving him a half-hearted shrug. "So?" I asked, my voice cold. I didn't wait for a response, partly because of the hurt look King gave me, but I was angry too. I stormed out of the cafeteria, then broke out into a jog.

"Wait up!"

I paused, finding Miyeon following me. She quickly caught up. "What on earth was that? Is there something going on between you and King?"

"No," I said, truthfully. I closed my eyes, realizing I was shaking, and took a couple of deep breaths. "What is this place?" I asked, quietly.

"Hell," TK said.

My eyes shot open and I found TK beside me, carrying a brush, mop, and bucket. "What are you doing?"

"Seungjin is right. If the principal comes in and finds the cafeteria like that, she will fire my dad."

"Where is he?"

TK gave me an unimpressed look. "My dad works

through the night and gets all his jobs done before the students and teachers wake up. He went to bed half an hour ago."

"Surely, he won't get in trouble if he's not here," I pointed out. "That cafeteria is a mess. It would have to be obvious to anyone that he was not responsible for that."

TK turned to me, the look of incredulity reappearing. "Are you for real? Did you not notice the lack of adults in there?"

"Yes," I said, slowly.

Miyeon let out a long sigh. "Cha Yerin."

"She has the power to remove adults?" I asked in disbelief. Sure, she had the Queen Bee status at the school, but no one had that much power.

"Her mother is the principal," Miyeon reminded me.

My mouth dropped open. Now that Miyeon had said it, I vaguely remembered her telling me this when I first met her, but even then, could she really have that much power over the kitchen staff and teachers? I glanced over at the cafeteria doors. "What happened in there?"

"I take it you haven't seen the news this morning?" TK said. I shook my head. "Bright Boys was officially disbanded, King was pulled from his solo activities and rejoined Bright Boys as trainees again. Oh, and Hyunseo's court date is set for three weeks' time."

"But why is that your fault?" I asked.

Once more the look TK gave me implied he thought I was an idiot. "Hyunseo assaulted my brother. That's why he's in court, and why they're all trainees."

"That's ridiculous! You're not your brother!"

"I know!" TK roared, flinging the bucket, mop and broom down the corridor. Miyeon and I jumped backwards, out of the way of his rage. "This isn't America, Lucinda. Things don't work the same out here!"

I was aware of that, but I was only just beginning to see how different everything really was.

"OK," I muttered, crouching down. The bucket had been full of cloths instead of water, and I quickly scooped them back into the bucket.

"What are you doing?" he asked as I picked the mop up.

"You're not going to be able to clean that whole cafeteria by yourself," I shrugged, before walking into the cafeteria.

King and his friends had gone, thankfully. I stood near the door, looking at the mess before me. Most of the tables had empty trays on them, the contents all over the floor, tables, and benches. If I had to guess, they had all been dumped, rather than thrown in a food fight like I had first suspected.

Behind me, the door opened. "You're going to be late to homeroom."

"Yes," I agreed. "But if this isn't cleaned and your dad is punished like you think he will be, then you won't be returning to homeroom at all. Your scholarship here is dependent on his job, right?"

Miyeon marched past us both and started stacking trays. "We probably have an hour before they're coming back in to prepare for lunch, so stop standing there and start cleaning."

Z

It took more than an hour. The kitchen staff did return as Miyeon predicted, but there seemed to be an unspoken agreement that they wouldn't acknowledge us.

"We should go get changed," TK muttered as we put the cleaning equipment away.

"Yes. No," I said, quickly changing my mind.

Miyeon looked at me like I was crazy. "Lucinda, you stink."

I glanced down at my uniform, then at the others. We'd tried to keep our uniforms clean, but there was that much food, we had ended up covered. All the scrubbing and mopping had also made us sweaty, and combined with the food … Miyeon wasn't wrong.

"Why should we change?" I asked them.

"Because we stink," Miyeon repeated, dryly.

"We only smell because we've been cleaning up a mess that our class caused," I shrugged. "Instead of being any later for our class, why don't we turn up as we are and let them suffer for it?"

"Isn't that a little petty?" Miyeon asked.

I shrugged again. "We have one shower between us. If we wait for the other to finish, we might as well not bother going to our morning classes. And if I have to sit next to Seungjin making him feel uncomfortable, then so be it."

Miyeon and TK stared at each other. I could see they were both reluctant. I didn't blame them: we really did smell as bad as we looked. I was insane and I knew it. Normally, I wouldn't have even suggested something like this. Then again, I wouldn't have had to clean up like that either.

TK let out a long breath. "I'm not in a dorm

room. I'm in a room with my father. If I go back to that looking like this, he will be upset."

"If you want to come back to our room and use our ..." I trailed off at the mortified expressions on Miyeon and TK's faces. I held my hands up. "Then you and I are returning to the class like this."

Miyeon looked down at her skirt, then at me, shaking her head. "I can't do it."

"Go change. We'll cover for you," I said.

"Get cleaned up and then report to the medical office. You won't be in trouble if you're ill," TK pointed out.

Miyeon gave us a grateful look as she thanked us, then hurried off to the dorm. TK and I started walking to the classroom. "You didn't have to do that," he told me.

I glanced up at him. "I'm not going to force either of you to sit in dirty clothes just to join me in a dirty protest. Our class is—"

"Any of it," TK cut me off.

I frowned. "What do you mean?"

"You stood up to your boyfriend, you helped me clean up, and now you're going to class like that," he gestured to my uniform.

"Min-Kin-*Sungil* is not my boyfriend," I said, stumbling over the name. "And even if he was, I don't agree with any of whatever that was. I don't really know what is going on between Bright Boys and your brother, but you're not your brother."

"What if my brother attacked Hyunseo's sister?" TK asked quietly.

I stopped dead, not sure I'd heard him correctly as I frowned at him. "Your brother attacked Hyunseo's sister?" I repeated. "I thought Hyunseo attacked your brother?"

"He did," TK admitted. "He ended up in the hospital."

Seeing as the common cold seemed to result in a trip to the ER in Korea, that didn't necessarily mean his injuries were that severe, but an injury was an injury. Even if it was possibly justified. "The only thing I know is what was reported in the news," I told him. "And you don't have to tell me the whole story," I assured him.

"There's not a whole lot I can tell. Baek Sungil has told me many times the reason Park Hyunseo hit my brother is because he attacked his sister, Mina. Gukyung was dating Mina, but he says he did nothing wrong and Hyunseo has made it up just because he didn't like the fact he was dating his sister."

"And you believe your brother?"

"He's my brother!" TK snapped.

I held my hands up, saying nothing.

"He's my brother," TK repeated, softer this time. "If he tells me he didn't do it, I have to believe it."

There was something in his voice which had slivers of doubt in me, but I wasn't going to question him further. The whole thing was clearly sensitive. "OK," I muttered, gently.

제17 장

King

Despite the information our teacher was writing on the board, all I could see was the expression Luna had on her face as she had left me in the cafeteria. She hadn't been present in the last-minute assembly the school had called to officially confirm the partnership with Atlantis.

Seungjin, Dongyeol, Joochan, Jaehoon, Ryan, Sungil and I were well aware of what was being proposed, and we had sat at the back of the assembly hall, acting like we couldn't hear the hushed whispers that were flying around, or see all the looks that were being sent in our direction.

Lee Woojin, Chairman of Atlantis Entertainment, had joined Principal Cha on the podium to explain the changes. Not once had he looked in our direction. Holly had been right: if Woojin was unable to look at us, we didn't have many allies within the company.

Although the announcement of our situation hadn't been discussed in the assembly, combined with the press-release that had gone out that morning, I was sure most of the student body had been able to link the partnership with us.

Or maybe Woojin had said something? In all honesty, I was too busy searching the large hall for Luna. She hadn't appeared in class either.

Not until midway through the morning.

At first, I didn't recognize what I was seeing. She was… filthy. Her white shirt was covered in all kinds of food smears, and her skirt looked like it still had a bit of kimchi attached to it. There was definitely an orange streak down her calf that I could only associate with the breakfast soup.

It wasn't until I looked at her face, or rather her hair, that it dawned on me that it was Luna I was looking at. Her long blonde hair, usually kept impeccably straight, had been pulled back into a ponytail with all kinds of stray pieces stuck up haphazardly. It was the familiarity of dancing: all the times we'd danced together, whenever she'd pulled her hair back, this was the result. Dozens of memories flooded my brain, making me inhale sharply.

Beside me, Sungil looked at me, then looked up. "She helped?" he looked at me, pulling a face. "She honestly helped him clean that cafeteria up?"

I chewed at the inside of my lip, my heart torn. On the one hand, she had helped the guy whose brother had ended my career. On the other, it swelled at the fact she was prepared to do that.

And then my heart started hurting.

She was helping someone other than me. This wasn't how this was supposed to go.

Moments after her, TK entered the room, his tall frame taking up the space behind her like an unwanted backdrop. He was standing far too close to her for my liking. Much as I wanted to run up there and push him back, I couldn't. I had to keep my image clean.

"What time do you call this?" Nam Woosung, our teacher, was asking them. "School hours are not the time to be having romantic interludes."

My eyes fixed on Luna as her cheeks went pink, waiting for her answer.

"If I was going to have a romantic interlude, it would be somewhere more romantic than the cafeteria, cleaning up other people's mess," she told him.

"You didn't think to clean yourselves up first?"

Luna shook her head, folding her arms, and then turned, fixing her attention on Seungjin. "If I have to suffer cleaning up other people's mess, then the other people can suffer through this."

"You've got to admit," Sungil muttered at me, keeping his voice low. "That girl is brave. Brave or stupid …"

"Yes, she is," I agreed, watching her walk across the classroom to her seat next to Seungjin.

I knew the moment he caught a whiff of the smell, because he gave her a look of disgust, covered his mouth up, and shot his hand in the air. "Woosung ssaem, she stinks!"

"Then you need to speak to whoever made the mess and have a word with them," Nam Woosung declared with a shrug. If I didn't know any better, I would have sworn he knew what had happened.

It took about ten minutes for the smell to permeate across the room. It wasn't body odor—it was the food. One of the side dishes had had fish in it. "That's nasty," Sungil grumbled, covering his nose.

"Woosung ssaem, this is revolting!" Yerin snapped, suddenly standing. Luna turned to her, her cheeks once again pink in embarrassment, but it didn't stop her from sending a defiant glare back at Yerin.

Woosung turned from the board to face her, arching an eyebrow. "Cha Yerin, what is revolting is the behavior of students who think it is acceptable to throw perfectly good food all over a room and leave it to other individuals to clean up. However, if the individuals who orchestrated and participated in that revolting act were to confess, I would allow your two classmates to go clean up without gaining any demerits. Assuming they want to, because it doesn't look like they are bothered."

Yerin sat down, heavily. "I don't know what you're talking about," she told him, before flipping her hair over her shoulder. She reached into her bag and pulled out a large bottle of perfume, squirting it around her.

Woosung turned to Luna and TK, who sat behind her. "I'm sorry. Lucinda and Taekyung, you will both have to stay in your uniforms until lunchtime."

"That's cool," Luna said. Despite the fact her cheeks remained pink, she really didn't seem bothered. Knowing Luna, she probably wasn't.

After a while, the smell seemed to fade, but my irritation didn't. TK was the reason why my career was nonexistent; why I was sat in a classroom instead of a recording studio; why I was single.

The bell finally rang for lunch and the classroom seemed to evacuate itself. It wasn't until I was in the hallway that I realized the smell *had* been that bad. "Come on," Seungjin said. "I want to see how clean they got that cafeteria for her to stink that much. Honestly, it was like sitting next to the fish market in July."

I watched as Luna started to leave the classroom but was called back in by Nam Woosung. TK was with her too. And then the door was closed.

"Are you coming?" Sungil asked, tugging me along. He leaned in closer. "Leave her be: she's clearly downgraded."

"Who downgraded?" Seungjin was just ahead with Jaehoon, but he turned to look at us. "Oh yeah, you were dating that nutcase, weren't you, Sungil?"

"Something like that," Sungil muttered.

Inside the cafeteria, Ryan, Joochan and Dongyeol were waiting for us. We stood in line, inspecting the area: it was cleaner than expected. We collected our lunch then chose a table at the back of the room.

"It's spotless," Seungjin grumbled, jabbing at his noodles in disappointment.

"What's spotless?" Joochan asked.

"The cafeteria," Seungjin responded, continuing to sulk into his lunch.

At their confused expressions, Jaehoon quickly explained. Dongyeol looked sharply at Seungjin. "Did you have anything to do with this?" he demanded, keeping his voice low. "That's not keeping a low profile. What if a teacher had seen you?"

"How didn't a teacher see what happened?" Joochan added.

"It was not my idea and I took no part in it," Seungjin snapped at them. "And even if I had, so what? I'm back here because of his brother. It's only what he deserves."

"You really think childish pranks are the right way to go about getting us debuted again?" Joochan asked, rolling his eyes.

"It's stupid," Dongyeol agreed.

"It's doing something," Seungjin disagreed. "And I can't stop others from doing something when they acknowledge the injustice."

"Only if you don't know who's behind it." Ryan set his chopsticks down. He was quiet and serious, following the conversation until now. "Let me make this clear to all of you. As far as I'm concerned, you're all still Bright Boys, and you're all still my brothers." He looked at me. "You might not have been in Bright Boys, but you trained with us, and debuted just after us, and this affects you too." He turned back to Seungjin. "But this? This reflects on all of us. I want us all to debut again, together, but not like this. This makes us barely any better than Min Gukyung."

"How can you compare us to Min Gukyung?" Seungjin asked in disgust. "He's spreading lies about Hyunseo. It's nothing like what he did."

I bit my lip. Seungjin hadn't been there. He still didn't know about Mina. I was sure the only reason Ryan did was because he was the closest to Hyunseo.

"Whether it's spreading lies or claiming someone punched them unprovoked, it's bullying," Ryan said, simply.

"Even if you didn't have anything to do with this, when we do manage to debut again, the last thing we're going to need is a new scandal about how you treated someone at school. That kind of thing appears in the news regularly, and other agencies may be supportive of the idols affected, but I don't think Atlantis will. Not again," Dongyeol added.

"I'm not in Atlantis," Sungil pointed out.

Ryan sighed. "It doesn't matter. It doesn't matter if this doesn't affect you directly. I don't even care about that. The fact is, you shouldn't be doing it because I know you're a decent person. It's as simple as that." He looked at Seungjin, then me and Jaehoon. "All of you are decent people. Stop acting like you're not."

"I don't like him!" Seungjin said, slamming his hand on the table, making the metal trays clatter as they bounced.

"Don't talk to your hyung in that tone!" Dongyeol snapped. Usually it was Seungjin who was the strict one about being respectful. It wasn't often that Seungjin had to be reminded of honorifics when addressing his seniors, but he was clearly angry.

"I'm not telling you to like him," Ryan continued as though he hadn't noticed. "I don't care if you like him or not. I'm telling you not to get caught up in this. If you don't want to be his friend, don't be, but don't you dare act like you're anything else. Just ignore him."

"This is a joke," Seungjin grunted before getting up. "And I'll do what I want." Leaving his tray virtually untouched, he walked out of the cafeteria.

"I'll be right back," I muttered before chasing after him. I caught him up in the corridor. "Seungjin!" I called after him.

He stopped and turned. "What's up, King?" he asked.

"You've got to stop it," I told him. Even though it pained me to say so, I knew Ryan was right. This was quite possibly the last chance I would ever get and I didn't need Seungjin ruining it. "I get it. I hate TK too, but I love being an idol more than I hate him."

"Don't you see, if we make his life hard, his

brother might drop the charges!" Seungjin said, running his hand through his hair, the irritation and desperation radiating from him.

"What if it doesn't work?" I asked. "What if Hyunseo gets charged and sent to prison anyway?"

Seungjin tilted his head. "You know something, don't you?" he asked, slowly. "You were there. What really happened, because Hyunseo isn't the type to just attack someone, even when provoked?"

I shook my head. I'd made a promise and I wasn't going to break it. "What happens if we re-debut and then we're back in the papers for bullying?" I pressed.

Seungjin took a step towards me. "What do you know?"

"I know we need to do this properly and try to rebuild our reputations like your sister suggested."

"Half-sister," Seungjin snapped. "And you're not answering my question."

"Nor am I going to," I told him. "It's irrelevant. The fact is we're back here and we're all trying to get out. What you're doing isn't going to help us."

"I'm not doing anything."

"You can't pretend you don't know more than you do," I told him.

Seungjin arched an eyebrow. "If you can, I can," he sneered, before walking off. I let out a long breath, watching him go.

제18 장

Lucinda

My stomach grumbled all the way through until the bell ringing for lunch. I'd been cleaning the cafeteria instead of eating breakfast and now I was starving. If I hurried, I would be able to have a quick shower, and get some ramyun cooking while I did.

I stood, making a beeline for the door when … "Lucinda Williams? Min Taekyung?" Nam Woosung called.

So much for that idea.

I stopped, finding TK right behind me, and Woosung behind him. "Could I speak to you both for a minute, please?"

We walked back to his desk while Nam Woosung hurried to close the door behind us. He turned to face us, and then perched on the desk nearest the door. "What happened this morning?"

I gave him a single shoulder shrug. "We walked into the cafeteria and found it a mess. We decided to clean it," I explained. It wasn't a lie.

Woosung let out a long sigh. "And you both thought it would be appropriate to turn up to class like that?" he asked, gesturing to our stained uniforms.

"Sorry," TK apologized.

I gave him an unimpressed look, before turning my attention to our teacher. "I figured if no one could show some consideration to not leave a public area tidy, and clean up after themselves, why should I show that consideration to those who made the mess in the first place?"

"Lucinda, I don't know how things are done in America—"

"They're not," I cut him off.

"Excuse me?" he asked, looking a little startled that I had interrupted him.

"I can't speak for every school but trashing a cafeteria to get back at someone through their parents would never have happened at my school." I folded my arms. "For a country which is big on respect, it was certainly lacking this morning, and if you want to tell anyone off, it should be those who made the mess in the first place."

"Lucinda!" TK hissed at me.

I rolled my eyes. "Fine, next time, I will make sure I'm even later to class by taking a shower first."

"There shouldn't be a 'next time'," Nam Woosung said.

"Then maybe you should find out who orchestrated this, and make sure they're punished."

Nam Woosung licked his lower lip as he folded his arms, mimicking my own pose. "Lucinda, I am being patient because you went above and beyond to help a friend out, but do not push me."

"I'm not—"

TK's hand clamped down over my mouth. "Thank you, Woosung ssaem. May we go and clean up now?" He refused to remove his hand, despite the face I was glowering at him.

"Go," Woosung agreed.

TK's hand moved, only to grab my wrist and tug me out of the classroom. Then he turned to me. "We should have been in so much trouble, but he was letting us off."

"That's the problem, TK! We shouldn't have been in trouble!" I was getting a little more emotional than I needed to be, but I was equally getting tired of how everyone seemed to be reacting to this.

At first, I figured Nam Woosung had been supportive. He'd let us sit down as we were and stuck up for us with Yerin. His comments then also suggested he knew more than he was letting on, and yet his suggestion was essentially to keep quiet about it.

"I'm going to get a shower," I muttered, stalking off. I got halfway down the corridor when Yerin, flagged by Kareun and Eunbyeol stepped out in front of me. "Oh, my favorite people," I said, dryly, before trying to step around her.

Yerin stepped with me, stopping me. "Lucinda." She paused and took a sip of her drink.

I sighed. "Yerin."

"I always had my suspicions of you."

I stared at her, bored. "Yerin, I have less than an hour of lunch to go back to my dorm and get showered and changed, so unless you move to the side and let me pass, Gandalf, I'm going to spend the afternoon stinking out the classroom too. And that will also be your fault."

"I think you shouldn't make any accusations unless you have the evidence," she said.

"You're not going to move, are you?" I asked with a sigh. I folded my arms. "So be it. What earthshaking news have you got to share with me?"

"News?" she repeated before shaking her head. "No, I'm here to tell you to stay away from Korea's idols."

I stared at her. "I honestly have no idea what you're talking about."

"Lee Seungjin."

I blinked. "Seungjin? Again? Really?"

"Stay away from him," Kareun echoed.

"Let me say this slowly, just in case my Korean pronunciation is off, but I do not like Seungjin—"

"Why?" Kareun demanded. "What's wrong with him?"

I stared at them, wondering if there was a right answer to this at all. "While I do not deny that Seungjin is very attractive, I am not attracted to him. I have no intention of trying to date him. You will find no threat from me."

"And yet you insisted on sitting your dirty self down next to him," Yerin pointed out.

"Yes, well some people decided to trash the cafeteria, so there is that?" I retorted.

"He is too good for you!" At that, Kareun reached out and punched my collar bone. At least, I thought it was a collar bone. I was busy reeling from the pain when I realized she had stuck a note on me. I reached for it, yanking, then wincing in pain as I pulled it free from my hair.

쓰레기—*sseuregi*—quite literally, trash.

I balled the piece of paper up and threw it at Kareun. With a cry of rage, she grabbed Yerin's drink, ripped the lid off it, and threw it at me.

Only it didn't hit my face, where she was aiming.

A hand wrapped around my wrist, jerking me to the side. The drink splashed on my other arm as it was flung into the air when I whirled around straight into a person's chest.

The moment was lost as the pain kicked in. Whatever Yerin had been drinking, it had been hot. I let out a hiss of pain, bringing my hand in to nurse against me as I fought back the tears.

"Are you OK?" King asked me.

"No," I said, trying to pull myself free of his grip.

King hung on. "You and I are going to have words later," he said to Kareun, his voice acidic. Then, ignoring her apologies—at splashing him, not me—he pulled me away from there.

I let him. My eyes were filled with tears and I could barely see. My chest hurt where I'd been hit, and my arm hurt from the drink, but I was also struggling with the fact someone would do that because they thought I liked an idol?

The running water alerted me to the fact we were in the bathroom. Then my arm was being held under the icy flow. I let out a small gasp at the shock, then appreciated the numbing effect.

"Is that better?" King asked.

I nodded, staring down at my arm under the water. King had stuck it straight in, not bothering to roll the sleeve of my shirt up, so I couldn't see what the damage was. I left it there for a few minutes, my fingers beginning to go blue under the cold water and the temperature of the room. If they didn't bother heating the classrooms, they certainly weren't going to bother with the bathrooms.

Finally, I pulled my arm out, and eased the sleeve back. The skin was mostly red, but that seemed to be from the cold and not the burn. "We should get you to the hospital," King said, softly.

I shook my head. "I don't think it's that serious." I prodded at my arm. I couldn't feel much of a burn anymore.

"You should get it checked out."

I shook my head again. "I don't want to go to a hospital," I said.

"You got burned!"

I stepped back. "We broke up," I told him. "You don't get to do this."

"Just because we broke up doesn't mean I stopped caring." King turned and took a few paces back from me, kicking at the corner of the toilet cubicle in frustration. He turned back to me as the door banged against the side. He shook off his anger as he shook his head. "Luna, I'd gotten caught up in a scandal. It wasn't my fault."

I stared at him, unblinking, and then I started laughing, the sound hollow as it echoed around the tiled room. "Not your fault?" I repeated. "King, we had plans that night. If you had stuck to it, you would have been with me. Instead, you blew me off to go *clubbing*!"

"Luna, that's not what happened," King said, his eyes going wide. He moved back in front of me.

"Really?" I demanded. "*Really*? Did we not have plans?"

"Yes, but—"

"Did you not go clubbing instead of meeting me?" I cut him off.

"Yes, but—"

I held my hand up. "No, King. The simple fact is you went clubbing. If you hadn't, if you had met me, you wouldn't have been there. That was the night I was going to tell you I was staying in Seoul. I'd wanted to surprise you." The anger left me as tears threatened to spill again. "I get it. I do. Your life is very different to mine. I never expected us to be attending the same school, and I *never* expected that we would have been able to date normally, but you *dumped* me because you got in trouble when you went clubbing."

"It was a situation I couldn't get myself out of," King said, quietly.

I ignored him, focusing on my hair instead, something catching my attention. There was a wad of white in it, about four inches from the bottom. At first, I thought it was tac, but when I picked at it, I realized it was chewing gum.

OK, so it was only gum, but that was the last thing I needed. I burst into sobs at that, blindly picking at it through the tears.

The next thing I knew, King was pulling me to him, wrapping his arms around me. There was a small voice in the back of my head telling me to break free from his hold, but I ignored it. He felt good and he smelled good. He was familiar and reassuring and the last few months seemed to evaporate.

Finally, I pulled back, regretting it almost at once. The second I was out of his arms, all the hurt—physical and emotional—seemed to hit me again. "Please don't cry," King murmured, reaching up to wipe my tears away.

"What do you care?" I asked. I stepped back out of his reach and looked around. We were in one of the boys' restroom. "What if someone sees us?"

"I don't care if someone sees us, but I do still care about you," King said, quietly.

"Whatever," I sighed. I moved over to the sink and started running the cold water again. My makeup was all over my face anyway, and there was a questionable food stain at my hairline. Lord, I was a mess. I started splashing water in my face, trying to clean myself up as best I could.

"I never stopped caring about you, Luna," King said.

"It's Lucinda, *King*," I said, giving him a pointed look.

King slowly shook his head. "You'll always be my Luna."

"I'm not your anything."

He stepped forward, closing the gap between us, and then wrapped his arms around me, holding me tightly, my back flush against his chest. I closed my eyes, biting down on my lower lip. I thought I had done everything I could to not think of him like I was now. That I had finally gotten over him.

The butterflies in my stomach and my pounding heart told me otherwise.

I pushed myself free, ducking under his arms. "You can't do that," I whispered. I ran out of the bathroom, away from him. The hallway was empty—Yerin, Kareun, and Eunbyeol had disappeared, thankfully. I started walking towards the dorm, then someone was at my side. "What are you doing?" I asked King.

"Escorting you back to the dorm."

"It's the middle of the day, on a school campus," I pointed out.

"And yet you have a burn on your arm."

I paused, staring up at him, then sighed. I hung my head, ashamed that I wanted the company. As soon as we stepped outside, and the wind whipped around us, causing me to shiver, King was draping his jacket over my shoulders. I didn't object. I didn't even tell him he should wear it and keep warm. I just accepted it and pulled it close.

King joined me in the lift, following me to my dorm room. I typed in my code, opening the door, and then stared up at him. "Are you going to join me in the shower too?"

King's eyes went wide as he spluttered out a no. I stepped into the room then handed the jacket back. "Thank you," I muttered, closing the door on him.

Before I even started showering, I attempted to remove the gum from my hair. I tried ice and anything else Google had suggested, but nothing would work. Because the wind had blown it about too, it wasn't just a small lock. I ended up cutting four inches off the bottom of my hair, the ends sitting in the trash can.

I stepped into the shower, using the stream of hot water to wash the fresh tears away. Yes, I was crying at having to cut my hair. I don't care how shallow it was, that was my hair. But it wasn't just about my appearance. It was also because I'd had to do it.

제19 장

Lucinda

Finally, I got out of the shower, wrapping towels around me. The bathroom in the dorm room was marginally warmer than the boy's restroom, but mostly it was steamy from the shower. I opened the door, allowing the steam out and some of the bedroom warmth in. I turned back to the sink, using my hand to wipe away the condensation.

Still wrapped in the towel, I sat on the edge of the toilet and stared at my reflection in the bathroom mirror. With my hair in a towel turban on the top of my head, and my eyes ringed in smudged mascara thanks to the shower (or maybe all of the crying), I looked a mess. I felt a mess too.

On top of that, my wrist still hurt. I'd tried my best to keep it out of the direct stream of the water, but it was still throbbing. It didn't look too bad: I hoped the pain would subside soon.

I hadn't set out to be friends with any of Bright Boys. If I was honest, I wasn't even sure I would class any of them as friends. Dongyeol and Apollo would be friendly enough if we saw each other in the hallway, but they were older than me and didn't hang out with me. Short of Seungjin who only spoke to me because I sat next to him, the rest barely said anything to me. While they were all certainly good looking, I wasn't interested in dating any of them.

Or, I wasn't any more.

It probably wouldn't have mattered to anyone that King wasn't in Bright Boys—he was still an idol. Not that anyone had ever guessed there was anything happening there. But so what if they had? Was it really that bad? Shouldn't fans be happy if they were happy?

I was beginning to suspect I lived a sheltered life. I had never experienced anything like this before.

No one had ever thrown a drink on me: that was something which only happened in the movies. Nor had I ever been attacked like that. The way Kareun had gone for me was a whole new ball game for me ... and I was at a loss for it? Surely it wasn't just because I had helped TK out and gone into the classroom covered in food?

Then again, if it was because she thought I liked Seungjin, that was even more ridiculous. As far as I could tell, Seungjin and Kareun weren't dating. King had previously mentioned that the members of Bright Boys couldn't date either—that it was a clause in the contracts of all idols at Atlantis. If they were dating, didn't she trust him enough not to cheat on her? Didn't she even think to ask him if he liked me?

I stood and moved over to the counter, hunting out my makeup removal wipes and started wiping away at the smeared panda eyes. I wasn't going to waste any more time crying over this. I had done the right thing and acting like this was only going to make me doubt my actions long term.

Once my face was clean, albeit still red and a bit puffy, I moved into the bedroom and over to my closet, pulling out a fresh uniform. The one I had been wearing was still in a small pile on the floor where I had left it, but now I was clean, I could smell it. Wonderful. That would be joining the laundry on my way back to class.

Dressed, I put on some fresh makeup to try to mask the blotchy skin, then I finally turned my attention to my hair. With the towel hanging up, I started to run a brush through the tangles.

I was in the process of finding my parting when the door opened. Through the wet strands, I found Baekhee staring at me, her eyes going wide. "Where's your hair?" she blurted out.

"Bathroom trashcan," I replied, tears threatening to spill again.

"It was true?" Baekhee asked, hesitantly. She looked over at Eunbyeol's bed with fear in her eyes.

With a split-second decision, I marched over to the door, sliding past her, then locked it. I turned back to her and folded my arms. "What's the deal with you and Eunbyeol?" I demanded.

"I …" she hesitated, the fear directed at me.

I pointed at my hair. "I am not part of whatever cliquey group they've got, Baekhee," I told her. "If you ever ventured out of hiding at lunchtime, you would know I spent my time sitting with Miyeon. They don't like me, and I don't like them. The fact I've lost a third of my hair should tell you that."

Baekhee looked over at Eunbyeol's bed, swallowing. "But you and Eunbyeol—"

"Are roommates," I finished for her. "We had

come to an unspoken understanding that if she stays out of my business, I stay out of hers."

Baekhee chewed at her lower lip. I could see a bead of sweat forming at her temple, and she went to wipe it away as she moved over to her desk, sitting down at it. "In middle school, Eunbyeol and I used to be best friends."

I stared at her in disbelief. That was an unlikely combination if ever I heard of one. "What the hell happened?"

"Yerin," Baekhee shrugged. "SLA. To start with, we were all friends, then Yerin started sabotaging my exams and assignments. She couldn't stand the fact I ranked number one. As time went on, she forced me out of the group, and after that, no one wanted to be my friend. Eunbyeol stayed with Yerin. It's why I study in the library. It's safer."

I couldn't fault her for that. I walked over to our bed and perched on her bottom bunk. "Can we be friends?" I asked her, softly.

Tears began to appear in the corner of Baekhee's eyes, but she nodded. "I would like that."

I flopped backwards onto her bed before my own tears started pouring down my face. "Kareun thinks I'm making moves on her boyfriend."

"I don't understand."

"She thinks I like Seungjin," I explained. I stared up at the slats above me. "Actually, I wouldn't be surprised if she thought I was trying to hook up with the whole of Bright Boys too, possibly all the idols in Seoul, from the sounds of things."

"Do you?"

I shifted my weight so that I was propping my

weight up with my elbows. "Do I what?" I asked her with my eyebrow arched.

Baekhee blinked rapidly. "Like Seungjin," she said, quickly. "I mean, I don't think you're trying to 'hook up' with Bright Boys."

"But you think I like Seungjin?" I asked in surprise. I guess King and I had done an excellent job of hiding the fact that we had ever been a couple.

Baekhee caught her lower lip between her teeth, then slowly nodded. "Yes," she whispered. "You're pretty. I bet he likes you too."

I let out a long sigh. "After this morning, I can assure you he doesn't like me. But no, I don't like him."

"But he is smoking hot," Baekhee said, seeming surprised at my comments.

I nodded my agreement. "I think he's exceptionally attractive. Seriously, I don't know how someone can be that good looking, but I don't like him like that." I flopped back down on the bed. "Besides, the fact he's attractive doesn't make him a nice person."

"Seungjin is a nice person!"

I sat back up and fixed Baekhee a look. "Baekhee, do *you* like Seungjin?"

"I, uh … no …" she said, flustered. "I mean, I like Bright Boys, but Seungjin isn't my bias and … even if I did, it would be a waste of time anyway."

"What do you mean by—"

"We're going to be late!" Baekhee yelped before I could finish asking the question. She turned around and swiped a handful of papers off her desk—the previous night's assignment if I had to guess. "The bell will go soon."

I glanced at the clock and realized she was right,

jumping to my feet. All my things were still in my locker, so all I really had to worry about was my hair. I had no time to dry it now, and seeing as it was so cold outside, I hurriedly pulled it back into a messy knot. That would have to do for now.

Baekhee and I charged back to the classroom. I was faster than her so I slowed my pace to match hers, but we made it into the classroom just as the warning bell rang. Almost everyone was already in there, either sat behind their desks or on them. Baekhee, who sat at the front of the class, slipped into her seat in front of me, trying to catch her breath.

I hurried past her, and past my own, to the lockers at the back of the classroom. I pulled the door open and trash fell out, dropping to the tiled floor. I stared at it, then brought my eyes up to the locker itself when I saw the liquid dripping down the side of the locker below.

I could feel my mouth go dry as I licked at my lips, wondering if I was going to scream or cry. My books were covered in a sticky coating of banana milk. I reached for the notebook I needed for this class and pulled it out tentatively with my finger and thumb. More banana milk ran off it, splashing all over the floor. With the amount of milk in there, there had to be several bottles worth. I could count eight empty strange shaped bottles either in the locker or having just fallen out.

I sucked in a deep breath and then blew it out just as slowly. The notebook was unusable. I wasn't sure if it was even recoverable at this stage. The class bell rang, and I looked up, realizing that the class had been watching me in silence.

Well, crying was out of the question.

I stood and turned, finding Kareun and Yerin

watching me. Both had their arms folded, and smug smiles on their faces. Eunbyeol was nowhere in sight. I wasn't surprised.

I cleared my throat as I wafted the notepad in the air with a quick snap or two. My aim was to shake some of the liquid off it, and if that happened to splash on my front row audience, so be it.

The squeal from Kareun was immediate. I looked at her, just in time to see her palm moving towards my face. I flinched, but it never hit me.

When I looked again, TK was holding onto her wrist.

King was just behind him: too far away to have gotten there in time … or part of it all? No. I refused to believe he had any part in this. TK was one thing, but this? Not after he had saved me from Kareun and Yerin earlier.

"Get your hands off me!" Kareun squealed, trying to pull her arm free, but TK hung on.

"What is going on in here?" Our teacher, Nam Woosung, cried, his voice carrying over the strangely quiet classroom. He strode down one of the aisles, the other students moving out of the way.

"Nothing," Kareun said, snatching her hand back as TK let go of it.

Silently, TK moved to his desk, sitting down at it and turned his attention out of the window.

"Nothing?" Woosung repeated, folding his arms as he fixed his attention on me. "Then what is that?"

I glanced down at the still dripping notebook, and the collection of trash around my feet. "Your guess is as good as mine," I said, refusing to cover anything up for anyone. "I opened my locker and found it like this."

Woosung looked at me in surprise. Apparently, people didn't tend to do that here. "Do you know who did it?"

I glanced at Kareun, finding her giving me the most venomous death stare. While I had a very good idea of who did it, I didn't have any proof. "Not for certain," I shrugged. "But you're not getting my history assignment today."

The class remained silent, watching us like we were playing a tied football game and we were coming up for the final whistle. I was certain they all knew who had done it, but none of them were speaking up either.

Nam Woosung looked between Kareun and I, then slowly shook his head. "Please clean up that mess. Lucinda, you can turn in your assignment tomorrow," he added, giving me a sympathetic look. I had a suspicion he had an idea of what had happened too, but unless someone said something, he wouldn't do anything about it. "Everyone else, get back to your seats."

I moved to the end of the lockers where the trash can and cleaning equipment lived and made short work of the mess. My books were ruined. I scooped them out, depositing them in the trash can with everything else.

Empty handed, I returned to my seat, surprised to find some blank sheets of paper and a pen waiting for me. I glanced at Seungjin in confusion—surely they hadn't come from him—but he met my gaze. "That was nothing to do with me," he mumbled. He shifted his textbook closer to me so that we could share.

I continued to stare at him in amazement. Had I just walked into a parallel universe.

"Honestly, that was nothing to do with me," he

repeated.

"OK," I muttered, picking up the pen and turning my attention to Nam Woosung.

I didn't think he had played any part. Not with this, at least. He'd seemed confused when I'd looked at him earlier. I just wasn't sure why he was being nice to me now.

제20 장

King

I spent the whole of the history lesson paying more attention to Luna than I did to Nam Woosung and whatever historical event he was talking about. That was beginning to be the story of my life lately: paying more attention to Luna.

As it was, I could barely take my eyes off her. She was still one of the most beautiful girls I had ever seen. It wasn't just the natural blonde hair and her eyes which could change from gray to blue depending on her mood. It was that she was as nice inside as she was outside. But she wasn't a pushover from it either. That was evident when she had refused to cover for whoever had put all that trash in her locker. She might not have been able to say who it was, but she wasn't ignoring it like so many other people would have done.

I glowered at the back of Kareun's head. Judging from her run in with Luna earlier, I was willing to bet that was something to do with her. I just couldn't prove it. I also wasn't sure I could afford to accuse her of something when all I had to back it up was my gut feeling. Not when I was supposed to be keeping a low profile.

When the class finally ended, my page almost as empty as it had been at the start of the lesson, we all filed out of the classroom, moving to the newest lesson on the timetable: performance. Despite everything, I was looking forward to this one. Until I walked into the classroom.

The classroom we were using was one that had clearly been repurposed over the weekend. I'd walked past it the previous week and it had definitely had desks in it. Now, aside from the whiteboard giving away it's previous life, all the furniture had been moved out, and the one full wall at the back had been replaced with a mirror.

Our class was only about twenty people—just less than in the homeroom class. Clearly, some had opted to stay in their academic classes instead. I wasn't surprised to see any of my classmates. Apart from Sungil. "What are you doing here?" I asked him. "Won't your father kill you?"

Sungil looked at me then nodded. "I'm not doing it because I want to get back in at Atlantis. I know that can't happen." Sadness filled his eyes. "I miss it, King."

I understood that. I just also knew how angry his father would be if he found out. Worse than that, I had an idea of how bad the consequences would be too.

Seungjin and Jaehoon were in the class too—no surprises there—and they caught my eye in the mirror they were warming up in front of.

I could see Luna in the mirror too. She was just behind me with Miyeon and Baekhee. The three of them were chatting, but Luna and Miyeon looked confused. I tried to be subtle as I inched closer to them.

"Where are the desks?" Luna asked, looking around. "What is going on? Is this a TV show thing?"

"I have no idea," Miyeon responded. "I was with you this morning, remember."

They both turned to Baekhee. "There was an assembly this morning," she mumbled, barely audible over the noise in the class.

"Atlantis Entertainment has partnered with the Seoul Leadership Academy," I explained, joining their conversation. I ignored the suspicious look the three girls were giving me. "As of today, SLA will be offering performance classes. From what Principal Cha was saying in the assembly this morning, anyone who missed the assembly would be automatically signed up, but could switch out to the academic classes if they wished."

"You signed up?" Miyeon said, addressing the question to Baekhee, but not hiding her surprise.

At the slight squirm, Luna elbowed Miyeon's side. "This is a cool idea. I love dancing. What about you, Baekhee? Are you a dancer? Or do you prefer singing?"

"Singing," Baekhee mumbled, her eyes fixed on her feet.

The door to the front of the room opened and the teacher walked in.

That was when my heart sank.

The teacher was a choreographer from Atlantis: Ro Chanheon. I'd trained with him when I had previously been at Atlantis. He was a good dancer, but he was blunt, direct, and …

"Oh, look, it's Baek Sungil. Has your father finally decided that you're not too good to dance?"

Case in point.

"And I'm also joined by Bright Boys, King, and…" he trailed off as he scanned the class and his eyes fell on Luna. "What do we have here?" he asked, shooting her a scathing look which instantly got my back up.

Luna turned bright red, but instead of apologizing, she planted her hands on her hips. Given how she had no qualms with talking back to me, I wasn't surprised, but getting on Chanheon's wrong side was not the best way to start this class. "What does that mean?" she demanded, before I could stop her.

Everyone, included Chanheon, looked startled: questioning a teacher like that wasn't normal.

"Don't tell me: Onyx," Chanheon sneered. "They're the flavor of the month."

"What the hell is Onyx?" Luna asked. I couldn't tell if she genuinely hadn't heard of Onyx, another group at Atlantis, or if she was struggling with the Korean—wondering if Onyx translated into something she had yet to learn.

Chanheon was less than sympathetic. "It must be BTS then. Another who thinks they can move to Korea and be an idol."

Luna held her hands up. "Hey!" she objected. "I have just arrived. When did I say I wanted to be an idol?"

"Honorifics," I hissed, aiming the warning at Luna, before I cleared my throat. She was using informal language with Chanheon. The fact she was a foreigner wouldn't garner any sympathy with him.

I knew it was too late when Chanheon licked his lips. "Well, it seems this *sunbae* knows better than I," he said, emphasizing the word to make the point that she was *not* his senior. "Seeing as we were going to start with the singing portion of the class, why don't you show us your talents and seniority?"

Luna blinked rapidly. "I'm sorry," she said quickly, using formal language. "I.." she glanced helplessly at Miyeon and Baekhee.

I had no idea what I could possibly say to help the situation. Chanheon hated quitters almost as much as he hated disrespect. The fact that I had been put back in the Atlantis 'basement' as a trainee, regardless of the circumstances, wouldn't put me in his favor, and it certainly wouldn't help Luna out.

"Yes, let's assess the talent in this class," Chanheon continued before I could work out something to say which wasn't going to upset the situation further. "Come along," he declared, striding out of the classroom.

"We should follow him," someone said.

I leaned over to Luna. "Are you OK?" I asked, giving her a sympathetic smile. She nodded her head, although the confusion seemed to remain. As the class started to filter out of the room, I quickly pulled Luna to one side. "You can't forget to use honorifics with Ro Chanheon. He hates it," I informed her. "He also hates people who give up."

"So, what you're saying is, suck it up and go sing for him?" Luna asked.

I nodded. "And if you don't know the polite way to say something, just don't say it," I added.

"If he hates me now, it's not going to compare to his opinion of me when he hears me sing," she muttered, following the last student in the class out of the room. "And what is Onyx? Are they a group?"

"You really don't know?" I asked, surprised. Luna shook her head. "They are our sunbae group at Atlantis," I explained. "They debuted a few years ago now. I think they're the company's most popular group. Unless you include B.W.B.B. but seeing as how most of their members are inactive due to enlistment, I think Onyx win out."

Luna continued to stare at me in confusion, but she shrugged. "Thank you," she said then started to follow the rest of the class out of the room.

I looked up and found Seungjin watching me, an eyebrow arched. I shrugged at him, then followed the others.

I followed the small crowd of our class to a room three doors down. This room had also been another classroom. Chanheon had us gather in the corner where there was a monitor attached to a laptop, two mics and a half dozen speakers: the setup wasn't much different from at a noraebang. Apart from the fact Chanheon would now be judging us.

He had already loaded a song up for Luna: BoA's Valenti.

As far as song choices went, it wasn't a bad one. It was mid-tempo and not too high …

The perplexed look Luna was giving the screen didn't bode well.

Luna blew out a breath and took the microphone Chanheon was offering her, remembering to bow her head at him as she did so. "This is not going to end well," I heard her mutter under her breath.

"Is this a good idea?" Jaehoon asked me. "Are we all forgetting that time we went to the noraebang after your performance?" He, Sungil and Seungjin had joined my side as Chanheon had started the music.

"I'm not sure you could class that as singing," Sungil muttered. "Lucinda was awful."

"That's not a nice thing to say about your girlfriend," Seungjin said, though his eyes were on me.

Sungil looked between the two of us, frowning. "She's not my girlfriend anymore."

"Chanheon is going to destroy her. He seems to think she's over here to be an idol," Jaehoon added.

"Is she?" Seungjin directed the question at me.

I looked at him, trying to read the guarded expression. Why did I feel like there was more to that question than it sounded. "I don't know," I said.

And then Luna started singing. I couldn't stop myself from wincing: Sungil's description had been an understatement. She was off-key, completely out of time with the lyrics, she was … terrible.

"How do we make it stop?" Jaehoon asked me, although he looked like he felt sorry for Luna.

I know I did: her face was flushed with embarrassment. She knew she wasn't good, but she was continuing to try. I had to give her points for that. She was determined not to quit.

After forcing her to sing (or attempt) two verses and a chorus, Chanheon finally killed the music. There was some awkward applause, but for the most part, we stared at her in silence. Everyone in the room was there because they wanted to be an idol. Ruthless as the industry was, no one wanted to be the one to be negative.

"Thank god!" Yerin exclaimed. "My vacuum cleaner sucks less than that. It also makes less noise."

I gave the girl a sharp look. Yerin made her

opinions clear on her future as an idol: never going to happen. She had told me on more than one occasion that her goal was to go to an Ivy League college in America, before returning back to Seoul where she would marry a rich man. She wasn't the first girl to think this way, but it left me wondering what the hell was she doing in this class?

"That's uncalled for, Yerin," I snapped at her. True, it hadn't been the best performance, but Luna didn't know the song and there had been no sheet music provided for her to follow. Combined with not knowing the lyrics, she hadn't been given much of a chance.

"She's not wrong," Luna shrugged, setting the microphone down. "I was bad."

"You were bad because you were asked to sing an unfamiliar song."

"Is that so?" Chanheon asked. The look he gave me had me regretting saying anything. My attempt to defend Luna had inadvertently insulted Chanheon and now she would suffer. "Seeing as you feel a western song would be more appropriate for this idol class, you should sing one."

"Oh, I never said that!" Luna objected, then looked horrified as she clamped her hands over her mouth. *Honorifics!*

"Pick a song and sing it," Chanheon growled at her.

Chewing at her nails—something I'd never seen her do before—she moved over to the computer, looking at the library. Finally, she settled on an old Taylor Swift song ...

It was better. I mean, it was in time, and not off-key ... for the most part, at least ... but Luna was simply not a singer.

This time, Chanheon allowed her to get half way through the first chorus before cutting the music. "Enlighten us as to why you're in this class?"

"Let her rap."

I turned to Jaehoon in surprise. "What are you doing?" I hissed at him as Chanheon turned and glared at him.

"She can't sing," Jaehoon agreed. "But I've heard her rap. Let her show you that."

Chanheon turned back to Luna, tilting his head. "You're a rapper?"

Luna opened her mouth, then, pausing, closed it. I sent a silent prayer of thanks out for that. "If I had to choose between singing and rapping, yes, sir," she said, instead.

"Then, by all means, please show us."

Having witnessed her rapping skills, I was surprised at how reluctant Luna seemed as she scanned the computer's library. When it seemed like she was taking longer than needed, I hurried over. "Are you OK?" I asked her, ignoring the look of venom Chanheon was giving me.

"I'm not a rapper," Luna told me in a low voice.

"I've seen you: I disagree."

Luna shook her head. "No, you've seen me rapping. Covering another artist's song does not make me a rapper. I don't write my own lyrics or even alter some to fit me."

"Just being able to rap is half the battle," I assured her. "Chanheon is a dancer; a choreographer. He's not a vocal coach. He won't be able to pick up on any mistakes or really be able to judge. He just thinks he can."

"I'm not sure how that's going to help me," she mumbled, finally selecting a song.

"It will help you for today. Tomorrow, in front of a vocal coach, they can make their own decision. For now, rap. Chanheon will move on and let this drop."

Luna shrugged as she hit play. This time, she had gone for a song by Nicki Minaj.

I stepped back and watched her perform. She might have doubted herself, but she wasn't bad. She just needed some help and guidance to polish it.

Frankly, Chanheon needed to watch her dance. It wouldn't matter how good or bad her vocals were once he saw her talent.

Instead Chanheon watched her rap, his expression stoic. He allowed her to perform the whole song and when she finished, he clapped. Not as loudly or with as much enthusiasm as most of the class, but I knew she had passed his approval.

"Interesting," was his only response. He turned to the rest of the class. "You," he pointed at Kareun. "You're up. Let's see what you've got."

With his attention no longer on her, Luna joined my side. "Now what?" she asked me, wearily.

제21 장

Lucinda

The second class had been as nerve-wracking as the first. Although Chanheon had said there would be vocal coaches, none had appeared. Instead, Chanheon had split us up into groups.

We had walked into the class and found four pieces of paper stuck to the mirror, each of them had five names on them. I lingered at the back of the crowd while excited chatter erupted as my classmates sought out their names.

I had already spotted mine. Most Korean names, when written in Hangeul, took up three-character blocks. My first name alone was three: 루신다. With my surname included, it was easy to find my name on the lists without getting too close.

As people started to split off, I finally got close to the papers, looking at the one with my name—and the four that were listed with it. On the list was Yerin's name.

"How do you feel about that?" King said, quietly, joining my side.

"I don't know," I admitted. "Not particularly

thrilled."

"What about you?" I asked, trying to find his name. "Who is in your group."

King sighed. "My group." He pointed over to where Sungil, Jaehoon, and Seungjin were standing, sending him a questioning look.

"I thought you were friends?" I asked, surprised. Instead of responding, King folded his arms. I was about to question what that meant when TK joined the three looking both uncomfortable and miserable. "Oh."

A heavy sigh escaped King as he stepped in front of me, blocking my view of TK. He stared down at me, fixing me a solemn look. "I don't like him." Before the scoff had fully escaped my lips, he had shaken his head. "But I will be civil to him."

I bit my tongue, deciding against commenting. I would give him the benefit of the doubt on that. Instead, I gave him a small smile. "OK," I agreed, softly. I glanced over at the other sheet of paper with my name on it. My heart sank.

Both Baekhee and Miyeon were in my group, thankfully. Unfortunately, the other two names were Cha Yerin and Han Eunbyeol. "Wonderful," I muttered under my breath as Chanheon's voice boomed over the chatter, demanding we get into our groups.

I made my way over to Miyeon, already wondering if it was too late to bail on the class. "Where is Baekhee?" I asked, looking around for the girl in question. She wasn't here.

"Why haven't you transferred out of this class?" Yerin asked, joining us.

"I don't know," I sighed. "Why haven't you developed a personality yet?"

"Oh, that's right, you want to be an idol," she continued.

I rolled my eyes, crossing my arms. "Yerin, I thought it was made clear yesterday that I don't want to be an idol."

"And yet you're in this class," she sneered.

"What has that got to do with anything?" I asked her, frowning. "I'm a dancer. If there's an option to dance I'm going to take it, especially if it means I don't have to take any more classes in Korean," I added. It wasn't that I didn't understand the Korean, but sometimes it still exhausted me, especially when reading textbooks.

"Because the partnership SLA has with Atlantis Entertainment means the end of year showcase is essentially an audition," she explained, looking at me like I should have known that.

Well, I'd missed that piece of information. But it didn't change anything. "I don't want to be an idol, Yerin," I said, firmly. "The only thing I really want from this class is to take up the opportunity to learn a different style of dance under the tutelage of an expert."

"I've heard your singing," Kareun declared, suddenly appearing like a wasp at a picnic. "Passing is setting your expectations too high."

I barely gave Kareun a second look as I marched over to Chanheon. "Excuse me, but how set are these groups?" I asked him. "It's no secret that I suck, so can I just do this as a solo effort so as not to pull everyone else's grade down?"

Chanheon made a weird movement, where, instead of tilting his head, he seemed to slant his whole body. "Did we become equals?" he asked me.

I stared at him, taking a moment to process his question, then replayed what I had said. I lowered my head with a sigh, realizing I had spoken to him far too informally. "I am sorry," I mumbled.

Chanheon clapped his hands, drawing everyone's attention to him. "I am not going to tolerate any disrespect in this class. Whether you want to be an idol or you signed up because you thought it would be an easy grade," he shot me a pointed look. "This is *my* class and you will treat it and me with respect. The groups have been created based on the strengths and weaknesses of you as individuals, so you can work together. If you are lucky enough to pass the Atlantis audition requirements, joining an idol group is a likely possibility and you will need to be able to work together and hide each other's weaknesses if you wish to succeed. You will not be judged only as individuals, but as groups as well."

I wanted to tell him that wasn't what I had intended, but I stayed quiet, knowing that would only upset him further. I started to turn, to return to my group, but his next words stopped me dead in my tracks.

"For the lack of respect, that will be ten laps."

"Laps?" I repeated. Surely, he didn't mean around the track outside? This was a performance class, not gym.

"Twenty," Chanheon snapped, glowering at me. "Each."

I was about to object, but Miyeon was at my side, dragging me out of the room. "Shhh," she hushed me.

"What the hell?" I demanded, angry at Chanheon, not her.

"I think we need to have some Korean lessons so we can work on your formal speech," she grunted at me as she continued to pull me down the corridor.

"Miyeon, where are we going?" I asked her.

"Thanks to you, our group has to run laps around the field," Yerin yelled as she marched towards me.

"What?" I repeated. "Why? It's not gym." Yerin stopped in front of me and I folded my arms to glower back at her. "Personal space, Yerin. You might want to learn what that is."

"And you might want to learn how to correctly speak to people who are more important than you. Like me."

"Or what?" I asked her. "Are you going to throw a drink over me? Or will you go running to mommy?"

I didn't think there was any space left between us, but somehow, she got closer. "I don't understand how this is such a difficult concept for you to comprehend. You are a nobody."

"Do you want my number?" I asked her, arching an eyebrow.

The question surprised her, and she took a step back. "What?"

"My number?" I repeated. "Usually, people only want to get this close to me if they want to kiss me, but I need at least one date before that. Call me old-fashioned."

"What? Yuck! Gross!" Yerin exclaimed, her expression looked like she had taken a large bite of something rotting. "Just … just learn your manners because I am not going to run around a field for you ever again." Still shaking her head in disgust, she turned and stormed off. Eunbyeol shot me an uneasy look before running after her.

I let out a sigh, closing my eyes as I slumped back against the wall. There was something about Yerin that refused to let me back down to her, but that didn't mean my heart wasn't pounding as I did so.

"You're insane," Miyeon muttered, joining my side.

"What was that about?" Baekhee asked as she seemed to appear from nowhere.

"Where have you been?" I asked her.

"Lucinda has no fear," Miyeon responded.

"Why are we out here?" Baekhee asked, growing even more confused.

"Honorifics, or lack thereof," Miyeon explained. "Luna upset Ro Chanheon and our group must run twenty laps around the field."

"Have fun," Baekhee shrugged, starting to head to the studio.

"Miyeon is including you in that," I called after her, feeling guilty.

Z

The afternoon didn't get any better for Baekhee. Not only did it start raining by lap four, but Baekhee was not an athletic girl. Although I encouraged her to not run all twenty laps, she was paranoid that Chanheon would be watching from the window. I was sure he had better things to do than count our laps, like teach the class, but I couldn't convince Baekhee. Instead, I slowed my speed and jogged around with her so that she wasn't running alone.

By the time we made it back into the classroom,

all five of us were drenched. Yerin, annoyingly, was the kind of girl who managed to not only look good soaked through, but damnit, she somehow oozed sex appeal.

Eunbyeol, Miyeon and myself looked wet and a little weary. Baekhee, on the other hand, looked like she was about to keel over. I'd noticed that Koreans didn't tend to go red in the face very often, but Baekhee looked like a stop sign. If she wasn't soaked from the rain, she was most certainly soaked from sweat. Worst of all, she was still trying to catch her breath.

Hard as it would be for me, I was going to take King's advice and stay quiet unless I knew for absolute certainty what I was saying was not going to offend Chanheon. I felt terrible for how much Baekhee was suffering.

Thankfully, when we arrived back in the studio, it was empty. According to Miyeon who had seen a few students in other studios, the class had broken off into their groups to practice by themselves.

"I hope that will serve to teach you a lesson," Chanheon told us, although I knew his comment was directed at me. He handed Eunbyeol an envelope with 'Team Yellow' on the front. "You have five weeks." He marched away, going to check on another group.

Before I could ask Eunbyeol what was in the envelope, Yerin had snatched it off her and ripped it open. "4-Minute, Crazy," she read.

I blinked. "I don't understand."

"4-minute is a group, idiot," Yerin snipped at me. "This is the song Ro Chanheon expects us to learn."

"I've never heard of it," I shrugged.

"Have you been living under a rock?" Yerin asked with a sneer.

"New York," I responded dryly. "This may come as a surprise to you, but I don't know all the groups yet."

"I'll find the video," Eunbyeol offered, helpfully. She pulled out her phone and started typing away on it. The video quickly loaded and I joined Eunbyeol's side to watch, wondering what I had signed up for.

Until Yerin snatched the phone from Eunbyeol's hands. "Just to be clear, I will be taking Jiyoon's part," she declared. "Lucinda, your rapping is acceptable. You might be able to pull off Hyuna's lines."

I raised a shoulder. I'd probably care if I knew who that was … no, that was a lie. I was doing this to pass a class, not to become an idol. Yerin could take all the parts she wanted. Plus, something told me this wasn't the battle worth fighting. "Fine," I accepted.

Yerin looked surprised. She'd probably been waiting for me to argue with her. She handed the phone back to Eunbyeol so we could all watch the video.

I'd not heard the song before, but I liked it. I was also pleasantly surprised. Girl groups, like boy groups, had rappers. Or this group did, at least. Which meant nobody would be subjected to my singing. I wasn't sure who was who of the rappers, but I had my fingers crossed Hyuna was the first one. In English, I could rap fast. In Korean … not so much. The first rapper had a slower rhythm and less Korean lyrics.

After watching the video a couple of times, we split up the parts. And by 'we', I mean Yerin split them up. My luck had held out: Hyuna was who I needed her to be.

"We're going to start with the dance first. Tomorrow, come with your lines learned," Yerin declared, taking charge. I stood back and let her.

"Which of you know the choreography?" she asked, turning to Eunbyeol, Miyeon and Baekhee.

Baekhee took a step back, lowering her head as she moved behind me.

"I do," Miyeon and Eunbyeol both said.

Yerin folded her arms. "Why are we still waiting?"

Chanheon said we had 5 weeks and I could tell this was going to feel like five months ...

제 22 장

Lucinda

"D on't mess this up," Yerin growled at me and Baekhee.

I slowly licked my lips, then chose to ignore her. The girl was driving me mad. I didn't like her to start with, but the last two weeks had been enough to make me, a non-violent person, want to slap her. She was becoming unbearable.

King had told me that Yerin's goal in life was to go to an Ivy League college in America, before returning home to Seoul to find her husband, where her aspirations were to become a housewife and look after him. It wasn't my choice in career path, and considering she was going to all the effort to get into one of those colleges made little sense to me, but each to her own. What I did object to was how much nastier she was getting every day. If I didn't know better, I would have sworn she wanted to be an idol.

"I think I'm going to be sick," Baekhee whispered

at me.

Baekhee had a beautiful voice and could hit some high notes I could only dream about. Only, she wasn't a dancer. It also appeared that she suffered from stage fright. "Just pretend we're dancing in front of the mirror," I whispered back. "The audience are just your reflection."

"I don't think I can do this."

"You will do this, or so help me, I will make your life here hell," Yerin threatened her.

When Baekhee flinched like she had been slapped, I stepped between the two of them, despite myself. "Yerin, backup, or so help me, *I* will walk out of this room and you can try to do this routine with four people, and then we'll see how well this goes."

Yerin narrowed her eyes. "You wouldn't dare."

I shrugged. "Are you stupid enough to find out?"

Yerin backed off. I turned to Baekhee. "Are you OK?" I asked her.

"You are insane," Miyeon muttered, joining us. "But Baekhee, you're going to be fine. You know this. We've been practicing all week."

Miyeon was half-right. For the last three nights, the three of us had stayed up long past curfew going over the lyrics and the routine, again and again. Baekhee knew it, until she thought she had gotten something wrong, and then she would freeze.

And the thing that usually made her mess up was Yerin.

To make matters worse, for this performance, as well as Chanheon, we also had Atlantis' vocal trainer, and a rapper; Sa Hyesun and Ruzt. Until now, none of the three trainers had been actively participating in our practices. Chanheon was always lingering, making notes on his iPad, but he had never once offered any form of constructive feedback.

"I think I'm going to be sick," Baekhee repeated again.

I stepped in front of her, placing my hands on her shoulders. "Baekhee, you've got this," I told her firmly. "If you make a mistake, it's completely OK, just keep on going. And remember, as you told me, you don't want to be an idol."

"No, but I still need to pass the class," she mumbled.

"Class!" Chanheon called, clapping his hands to gather our attention. "Enough. I want to finish up with the boys' performances, and then move onto the girls'. I don't care if you are happy to be here all night, but we're not, so if we don't get this done, you will be getting fail marks. Team Blue, get into positions."

I moved with my team to the back of the room and sat down on the floor as King, Jaehoon, Sungil, Seungjin, and TK moved into position.

The past two weeks hadn't been going well with me and King. In between classes, homework, and practicing for the group dance, I'd had to try hard to avoid him. Whatever had happened the other week had stirred up something in me which I thought I'd buried good and deep. Just when I'd managed to bury it again, he'd give me a look … then promptly ignore me.

Whatever was going on with him, I wasn't going to get caught up in it again.

Team Blue were performing an EXO song. So far, we'd seen the other group, and this was the best by far. There was no doubt that three of them had debuted because their singing and dancing skills were leagues above most people in the class. Sungil was also good. I could see why he had been snatched up by Atlantis once upon a time. Even TK wasn't bad—he just wasn't as refined as the others. I was sure they were going to get top marks.

Until Chanheon opened his mouth.

"Three of you are former rookies at Atlantis," he said. It wasn't a question, but they nodded anyway. "And you," he pointed at Sungil. "You were a trainee there." Sungil nodded. "Then why the hell was that performance so bad? If EXO had seen it, *they* would have been embarrassed at that attempt of copying their song."

There was no way it was that bad. Sure, I wasn't an expert when it came to singing or rapping, but I couldn't fault it. Even their dancing was good. They had made the other group look amateur, and honestly, I wasn't looking forward to going after them.

"We're not rookies anymore," Seungjin responded, not bothering to hide the contempt from his voice. "We're not because that jerk," he pointed an accusatory finger at TK, "That jerk's brother ruined everything for us. You're still at Atlantis. I know you know this. So why would you put him in a group with us? He wants to destroy us like he has Hyunseo."

"How dare you?" Chanheon cried.

"Seungjin, let it go," I heard King mutter.

Seungjin whirled on the spot and sent him a murderous look which I was becoming all too familiar with. "Don't you dare stick up for him." Seungjin turned again, knocking TK with his shoulder on his way out of the classroom.

"And what about you?"

"Me?" King asked, caught off guard at the question.

"You debuted too," Chanheon stated, bluntly. "Now you're back here."

My eyes slid to King. Much as I was trying to avoid him, I had watched the performance with him drawing my gaze the entire time. Although he was a good singer, it was his dancing that had me mesmerized—nothing had changed there.

As though he caught me staring, he turned his gaze to me, briefly, before looking back at Chanheon. "I want to be here," he responded, simply. "I want to be an idol and re-debut more than anything."

"You do?" The question came from Hyesun, the female vocal trainer.

King just nodded. It was still enough for me to feel the dig.

"You couldn't tell from that performance," Hyesun muttered, loud enough for everyone to hear. She made a few notes, then looked back at King. "I saw you when you were a trainee. You had talent. I saw you when you debuted. I thought you were going to go far. Yet, here we are, more than a year later, and whatever I saw back then, I no longer see. If you want to redebut with Atlantis—assuming you've not already burned your bridges there—you are a long, long way from being at the level you need to be."

"I think it's clear, this was an abysmal performance." Chanheon added, dismissing them. "I think you should sit down and let Team Yellow up there.

King and Jaehoon shared a look, but my attention

was on Chanheon. There was a vein in his temple and it was pulsing so hard, I was sure it was about to explode.

Great. That meant he was going to be in a bad mood for our performance.

"Let's finish up with Team Yellow," Ruzt announced before Chanheon could yell at anyone.

Our group stood, swapping places with Team Blue. I glanced over at Baekhee, giving her a thumbs up and what I was hoping was an assuring smile. After saying she was going to throw up so many times, she finally looked like it.

I sucked in a breath, sent a silent prayer that we would all succeed, and then waited for the music to start.

The performance went … OK.

Compared to our practices, it was one of the better performances. For me, I didn't completely stuff up my lines … I did manage to mispronounce something, but I was taking that as a win.

Even so, the performance was far from perfect. I'd been busy trying to dance around Baekhee and then Eunbyeol, as Baekhee took a left instead of a right. Baekhee had frozen. "Keep going!" I'd hissed at her. At that point, I moved to the opposite side, so when she'd started dancing, I wasn't able to help her find her beat again. She had managed to finish the dance but she had been a few beats behind and moving faster to try to catch up, rather than skipping a move to get there.

"What was that?" Chanheon demanded, aiming his question at Baekhee.

She stared at him like a deer caught in headlights, breathing heavily at her exertion, unable to answer him.

I raised my head, meeting Chanheon's gaze. "The

best we could do," I told him. "I know it wasn't perfect, and I certainly wouldn't debut *me* based on that, but we did our best."

"Debut you?" Chanheon repeated, appalled at that prospect. "If this wasn't a school class, I wouldn't keep you in it."

I frowned at him, crossing my arms. "That's a little unfair."

"The K-pop industry is unfair," he snapped back at me. At that moment, I could see that vein pulsing again, and I knew I should have kept quiet. Even King was signaling at me to keep quiet, but Baekhee looked like she was going to burst into tears beside me.

"Why are you even in this class?" Hyesun asked. I looked at her in surprise at the tone full of disdain she was directing at me. Until now, she had been pleasant with the girls, and even Eunbyeol had been excited when she'd learned she was coming in as a vocal teacher: apparently, female idols at Atlantis had always claimed she was the sweetest trainer and was always patient with them, but there was a sharpness to her words. "Everyone here is here for the opportunity to sign to Atlantis Entertainment, and yet you are here making a mockery of this process."

I blinked in surprise, forgetting my honorifics once again. "Excuse me?" I asked, also momentarily forgetting my Korean. I shook my head then returned to the correct language. "How am I making a mockery of this process?"

"You and Hong Baekhee have no right to be in a class if you're not going to put one hundred and fifty percent into it," she clarified. "If the both of you don't want to be here, leave."

"Excuse me?" I said again, outraged. "I want to be in this class, I just don't want to be an idol: I know I don't tick any of the boxes for that. I am a dancer and I want to learn as much as possible. This class may incorporate all aspects of being an idol, and if I could take it without the singing or rapping, I would, because I know I'm nowhere near the level that is expected of me, but that doesn't mean I'm not taking this seriously." I glanced over at my team, then back to Hyesun. "I am and *will* work as hard as I can, but I don't want my efforts to reflect badly on the people you have me working with."

My words were met with a stony silence from both Hyesun and Chanheon. Then the vocal teacher turned to me. "I don't really remember your performance: it wasn't bad. It wasn't good. You made mistakes on both your lyrics and your dancing."

"I was paying attention," Ruzt said. It was one of the first things he had said all afternoon. He was softly spoken, with a thick accent that told me he wasn't from Seoul but had the ability to command attention. Everyone looked at him. "It's far from perfect, but your rapping is quite good. Raw, but good." I stared at him in surprise. "There's a lot of work to be done," he continued. "But I think you have the potential."

"A lot of work?" Chanheon scoffed. "There isn't enough time for that."

"There is if someone is prepared to put in the time," Ruzt argued. He turned back to me. "I have an idea for your rapping. I'm prepared to put in the time if you are?"

"You know I'm not Korean, right?" I blurted out. My hands clamped over my mouth in horror, but Ruzt laughed.

"I had guessed. Is that a problem?"

I slowly shook my head, feeling my cheeks heat up as more than one pair of eyes landed on me. "Thank you," I said, bobbing my head.

"And now it is time to address the elephant in the room," Hyesun interjected. "Hong Baekhee."

"Literally."

I turned and shot a murderous look at Yerin's comment, turning back to the girl beside me. Baekhee looked like she wanted the floor to open up beneath her. My hands curled into fists as I fought back the urge to leap across the room and shake Yerin.

"Hong Baekhee," Hyesun continued, ignoring the remark. "I am going to be blunt with you. While your voice is good enough for an idol, your dancing is not. More importantly, neither is your look. You are not a pretty girl. You also need to lose at least thirty kilograms before you should even consider auditioning for an idol company. You also need to seriously consider plastic surgery."

"Now, that's just rude!" I growled at the senior woman.

"That is simply stating the facts," Hyesun retorted. "There is a standard in this industry and Baekhee is not close to meeting that. Frankly, I'm surprised Baekhee is even enrolled in this class."

"Sa Hyesun is correct," Chanheon said, turning his attention back to Baekhee. "Until you can lose the weight, you will not be permitted to join the audition. Instead, you can …" he shrugged and waved his arm dismissively. "Who cares? Do something with the organization of the auditions. Something which keeps you behind the scenes."

"Thank. God." Yerin muttered, enunciating each word.

I looked back at Baekhee. Her head was hung, her hair hiding her face, but I could see the tears dripping from the end of her chin.

"It's a class," I snapped. "We're not auditioning. Maybe, just maybe, some of us are here to learn, to do something we enjoy, and have no motive other than that." My anger was making me forget everything as I alternated between English and Korean, and anything resembling formalities had gone. "Why don't you teach instead of put people down?"

"Excuse me?" Hyesun demanded, outraged.

I knew I couldn't speak to them like this and not expect some form of consequence, but they had no right to speak to Baekhee like that. Even if there was an element of truth to what they were saying, she didn't deserve to hear it in front of everyone.

"One hundred laps around the playing field, between you," Chanheon snapped. "Then, when you've done them, you can come back in here and sweep and mop all the dance studios. Once you've completed that, I want a hand-written letter of apology."

My jaw tightened as I finally saw sense to keep quiet. I turned to Baekhee to apologize, but found her running from the room, slamming the door behind her.

제23 장

King

C hanheon dismissed the class moments later, and I hurried out, trying to catch up to Luna. She really needed to learn when to be quiet. Ro Chanheon was an excellent choreographer, but he was not a nice person, and he held grudges.

Unfortunately, someone else got to her first.

"Why must you always open your stupid mouth?" Yerin demanded, shoving Luna into the wall.

I was about to step in, but Luna whirled around and shoved Yerin back, hard. Yerin stumbled backwards with a small squeal. "Quit shoving me, Yerin, because I'm not going to hold back anymore!"

"What is going on out here?" Chanheon yelled down the hallway.

"She started it!" Yerin cried, before realizing who was speaking, then she solemnly hung her head.

Luna's mouth dropped open as she turned to look at Yerin. "Are you kidding me, right now?"

"I don't care who started it, but I want two hundred and fifty laps out of your team."

Yerin waited for Chanheon to leave before turning to Luna. "Have fun with that."

"What the hell does that mean?" Luna demanded.

"First of all, I told you once, I wasn't going to run laps because of you ever again. Second of all, it's raining." Yerin turned to Eunbyeol, linking her arm through hers. "Let's go."

"I hate her," Luna muttered in disbelief.

I started to walk over to her again, but once more, someone else beat me to it.

"I'll help," TK told her.

Luna looked up at him, tilting her head. "Help with what?"

"The laps." When she tilted her head in the other direction, he shrugged. "I agreed with what you said. Chanheon and Hyesun weren't nice to Baekhee. Plus, I was going to go for a run anyway."

"I'm not abandoning you: I'll run," Miyeon said, though she sighed loudly. "I hate running in the rain."

"Eighty-four laps," TK sighed. "It's going to take us all night. Though, I guess I might sleep tonight if I run enough."

"Sixty-two," I said, finally joining them, though I refused to look at TK.

"What?" Luna asked, confused.

"It's only sixty-two, well, sixty-two and a half, when split between four people."

Luna stared at me. "Who's the fourth?"

"Me."

The blank expression remained. "Why?"

"Because I don't agree with what Chanheon and Hyesun said either."

Beside me, TK snorted.

I chose to ignore him.

"Let's get this over with," Luna muttered. Without waiting for me, she started walking towards the door.

It was late, it was dark, it was cold, and as Yerin had stated, it was also raining. Although the track had lights, Chanheon hadn't turned them on, so we were running in the dim light from the school and the university. It was a good thing the track was even, otherwise we might have tripped and really hurt ourselves.

Back when I was an Atlantis trainee, we'd had to run up and down the bank of the River Han every morning—five miles each way. This was closer to fifteen. If it wasn't raining, it would have been infinitely easier than it was, but the rain didn't let up once. Between us, it took nearly two hours to complete the laps, and I was ready to drop.

By the time we had finished, we were all red faced, exhausted, and cold. "I can't feel my fingers," Miyeon mumbled through chattering teeth.

"Who does this as punishment?" Luna asked. She'd been asking the same question for the last thirty laps, as if it was her mantra, keeping her going. "I need a shower."

We stumbled back to the dorms. Inside, although the lobby wasn't heated, was much warmer than outside. Ignoring the yells of the security guard as we dripped water everywhere, we hurried to the elevator.

"I could sleep for a week," Luna muttered, wringing out the bottom of her sweater. Like that was going to do any good at this point. She let out a long deep sigh. "I don't want to clean the dance studios," she added, miserably.

TK let out a long moan as the elevator pinged open. "I had forgotten about that."

As we got in, Luna looked at him, the bewildered expression returning. "TK, you don't have to clean the studios too. That was our punishment." She shook her head. "It was *my* punishment. I'm the one who doesn't know when to shut her mouth."

"You were standing up for your friend." I snorted before I could stop myself, and three sets of eyes looked at me. "What does that mean?" TK demanded.

I looked at TK, about to shake my head and let it drop, but then I remembered what was happening tomorrow. The thing I'd been trying not to think about all day, considering we were being evaluated: Hyunseo's court case. "It's OK for Luna to stick up for someone, but not Hyunseo?"

"Luna?" TK looked at Luna, pulling a face. "*Lucinda* didn't attack someone unprovoked."

"Neither did Hyunseo!" I snapped at him. I nearly blurted out the truth then, but I remembered my promise at the last moment and instead stalked away to the stairs before I could say anything I regretted.

Taking the stairs in soaking wet clothing was something I did regret, but I had climbed three of the four floors before the anger wore off enough to realize. Instead, I stalked the rest of the distance to the dorm room.

Despite the late hour, the dorm room was empty. We still had some time before curfew and I suspected the others were with Hyunseo. I possibly should have been there too, to show my support, but despite everything, I wasn't a member of Bright Boys. Instead,

I peeled off my soaked clothing, wringing them out in the sink before depositing them in the laundry basket. Then I took a long, hot shower, trying to chase off the chill that had set in.

The room was still empty by the time I got out. I pulled on some sweatpants and a hoodie. I was exhausted and the thought of crawling into bed was appealing. I could get a powernap in while I waited for takeout; we'd missed dinner by running, and I'd run a lot this evening.

Until I remembered that Luna still had to clean the studios.

The idea of cleaning with how I currently felt didn't appeal to me in the slightest. The thought that Luna would be doing it by herself appealed to me less. I got out of bed, pulling on my duffel coat and shoes and hurrying back over to the school. Thankfully there was a covered walkway between the dorm and the school, so I didn't get soaked through a second time, but it was still cold.

I wasn't surprised to find Miyeon with Luna. I was surprised to find TK there too. "What are you doing here?" I demanded as I walked in.

"Helping," he said shortly, as though that was obvious. Given the fact he was cleaning the mirror, it probably should have been, but I didn't like the fact he was here.

"I have a headache and I'm tired," Luna said, stepping in front of me before I could tell TK to go away. I looked down at her. Her eyes were more gray than usual. "I'm not going to turn down help when all I want to do is go to bed, but if you're just going to argue with each other, I will do this alone." Miyeon cleared her throat. "Us girls will do this alone. I don't care that you don't like each other, and I don't care if you think you've got a good enough reason for that. I'm too tired for arguments and bickering tonight."

I glanced over at TK, my eyes narrowing. I didn't like him being here. I didn't like the fact he thought he was a good enough friend that he could be here, but that could be addressed tomorrow. Silently, I went and grabbed one of the brushes propped up in the corner.

Between the four of us, we made short work of the dance studios.

"Can I ask you something?" TK asked, suddenly.

I looked up from the corner I was sweeping, assuming he was talking to me, then realized he was talking to Luna.

"What do you want to do?"

"Finish cleaning," she replied, wearily. "I'm really grateful for the help, because I would have been here all night and I'm tired."

"No," TK said, shaking his head. "I mean, Sa Hyesun was right about one thing: people are in this class because they want to be an idol."

"Do you?" I asked, surprised.

"Why?" TK asked, his expression going dark. "Do you have something to say about that too?"

I laughed harshly. "No, I'll let Atlantis do the talking on that, considering your brother is the reason they've had to disband a group which was making them money. Good luck with that."

"Some people need to be aware of the fact that attacking someone, unprovoked, needs consequences," TK shot back.

"I wouldn't mind being an idol," Miyeon

declared. "I like dancing, though I'm not sure I'm good enough at singing. I'm only here because of a scholarship. I need to work for my family, and until I start earning as an idol, I won't be able to do that."

"You're here on a scholarship too?" TK asked, his eyes widening, this time with panic as he shot a sideways glance at me.

As though realizing that I was there, fear also filled Miyeon's eyes. From the other side of the room, Luna folded her arms and arched an eyebrow at me. "Really?"

"I didn't say anything!" I objected angrily.

"Apparently you don't need to," she pointed out. "Why is everyone in this school so terrified of being here on a scholarship?"

"Because this school prides itself on being elitist," TK snapped at her.

"Why?" Luna demanded. "Look at it: it's falling apart." She pointed at a crack in one of the walls, and at the ceiling where three of the lights were out. "They may have given this room a lick of paint and hidden a wall with some mirrors, but they can't even afford to replace a lightbulb. The school should be grateful that someone is paying for a student's education, even if it's not their parents. And let's not forget this school went from academic to performance over the space of a weekend. I spend more time in a studio than I do in a classroom these days and I've not even been taught anything by one of these teachers. I've learned more from you teaching me a routine, than I have from the supposed professionals. I've had no vocal class or dance class: we might as well get our lessons from YouTube. At least they don't bitch you out when you get something wrong."

"Do you really think I care if someone is here on a scholarship or not?" I asked Luna, surprised that she would even think that. "I've told you before: the reason I don't like TK isn't because he's here on a scholarship. It's because his brother is the reason my friends are back here. Hyunseo is in court *tomorrow*. Min Gukyung has not only ruined Hyunseo's career, he's also about to ruin his life."

"Hyunseo hit my brother!" TK cried.

"Your brother *attacked* his girlfriend!" I yelled at him. The promise I'd made was forgotten about as I finally decided I'd had enough of the lies TK was spreading, especially when they were now affecting the way people—Luna—was thinking of me.

I took a couple of steps towards TK before I realized what I was doing, but Luna threw down her mop and jumped between the two of us. "OK, if we're going to do this, let's do this. Sit down, both of you."

TK stared at her, his eyebrows shooting up behind his fringe. "What?"

"What?" I said, echoing his words.

"Sit," she instructed us. "You two are going to talk it out and get it off your chests, but you are not doing it standing up, because there is too much aggression radiating from you."

"Lucinda, are you sure that's a good idea?" Miyeon asked, hesitantly.

"Yes." She folded her arms and gave me a pointed look as TK sat down, albeit while shooting me a murderous look. The glower Luna gave me wasn't much better as she continued to stand between the two of us like a referee.

"I am not responsible for my brother's actions," TK told me.

I shrugged at him. "He's your brother."

"Your father voted to pass a law that meant a canning company in Incheon was sold up into parts because it couldn't pay the new tariff. In the end, everyone who worked there lost their job there," TK shot at me.

"What has that got to do with anything?" I demanded, pulling a face.

TK shrugged. "That was your father's fault."

I stared at him. "So?"

"By your logic, you're responsible for that."

"What?" I scoffed. "How am *I* responsible for my *father's* actions? He passed a vote—one of many people who also voted the same way as he did."

"Then how am I supposed to be responsible for my brother's actions?" TK demanded. "I didn't even know he had a girlfriend. School sucks enough when people find out you're here on a scholarship, but when everyone, from the group to their annoying fandom is constantly blaming you for their favorite group disbanding, it sucks even worse. It's not my fault."

TK got up, but walked away, rubbing at the back of his neck. Luna turned to me, tilting her head as she gave me a pointed look.

"Fine," I mumbled. "OK, fine," I called, louder. "You're right: you can't be blamed for your brother's actions. But that doesn't mean you can't tell him to drop the charges."

TK whirled around. "You think I haven't tried? We're not close, King. He doesn't even like me, never mind listen to me."

"Oh."

The room fell into an awkward silence and for once, I had no idea what to say. Miyeon, fortunately, did. "You never said what it is that you want to do?" she said to Luna. She had been following the conversation, so I was grateful for the pause. "What do you want to do when you graduate?"

The look Luna gave Miyeon told me that the two of them had already had this conversation, but then Luna's eyes went wide. "The same thing I always wanted to do: I want to be a dancer."

"Then why are you here?" TK asked, frowning.

She shrugged, refusing to look at me. "My world changed. Then it changed again."

"Is that supposed to make sense?" Miyeon asked.

Luna slowly blew out a breath. "Probably not," she admitted. "But that's OK. All you need to know is that many things have changed for me this last year, but the one thing that hasn't has been my dream to be on the stage. I don't want to be an idol. I don't even want to go back to America to be a singer. I'd be quite happy being a backup dancer in a music video or a tour, but my dream is Broadway." She yawned, glancing at the clock. "We should finish up. We're nearly done and I need to have something to eat before I start writing apology letters."

We finished up in silence. My head was full of the conversation on repeat. Luna had come out here because of me, but she still wanted to dance? And TK wasn't close to his brother, but had tried talking to him anyway? Everything was a mess.

I flicked the lights off as we left the classroom. We had about ten minutes to get back to the dorm before curfew, when Luna suddenly stopped in front of me. I barely avoided walking into her. "What's the matter?" I asked.

"Baekhee," she said, suddenly. "I forgot all about her."

"She will be back in our room," Miyeon said. "We can check up on her."

Slowly, Luna shook her head. "No, she doesn't like Eunbyeol. She won't be with her by herself," she said, glancing back down the corridor.

"If you're caught out of the dorms after curfew, you'll be in trouble again," TK pointed out. "And I'm not going to run laps for you for something that could easily be avoided like that."

"I wouldn't expect you to," Luna assured him. She took another step towards the dorm, before stopping again and sighing. "I'm going to the library. I'm sure that's where she will be. You guys go back. I'll sneak in." Miyeon bit her lip, looking torn, but Luna shook her head again. "I'll go. You go back."

Miyeon and TK nodded, before hurrying away, wanting to get back before curfew. Luna turned around, then seemed surprised to see me. "I'm going with you," I told her.

"There's no sense in you getting in trouble," she said, rolling her eyes. "You go back to your dorm. Don't you have to keep a low profile anyway?"

That question was a small dig, but I chose to ignore it. "I'm going with you," I repeated.

"Fine," she shrugged. "But you can't blame it on me if you get in trouble."

Once again, I chose to ignore the dig as I walked with her. "Where are we going?" I asked, eventually.

"The library," Luna replied, shortly. "Like I just said."

"Are you mad at me?" I stopped and folded my arms.

Luna looked up at me with an arched eyebrow. "Is there a reason why I should be mad at you?"

I rolled my eyes. "I am not playing this game," I said, continuing to walk to the library.

When we reached the door, Luna grabbed my arm. "Wait here," she said.

"Why?" I demanded.

Luna looked up at me and sighed. "For Baekhee, not me. I don't know what state she's going to be in and I don't want her to feel embarrassed. She has been embarrassed enough today."

"I'm not going to say anything insulting to her!" I objected.

Luna gave me a sad smile, and I finally saw the Luna I'd missed. "I know," she agreed. "But you're a gorgeous idol, and she has terrible self-confidence, which I'm willing to bet is at rock-bottom today. Having you see her today isn't going to help her. Let me check on her first."

I stared at her. Her eyes had softened and looked bluer than they had earlier. That was somehow reassuring. "I'll wait here," I conceded.

Luna disappeared inside, leaving me in the cold hallway. I stuffed my hands into my coat pockets and started pacing back and forth down the corridor. It was now too late to order food. I'd have to raid the emergency ramyun stash when I got back to the room. My stomach grumbled in agreement. Tteokbokki … there were some instant spicy rice cakes too: a portion of those wouldn't go amiss either.

The door behind me opened, much quicker than I expected. "Is everything OK?"

Luna was grinning. "Yes."

I gave her a questioning look. "Is Baekhee not coming with us?"

The grin grew. "No, I think she's OK in there tonight," she added mysteriously before setting off back towards the dorms.

"Are you not going to tell me any more than that?" I asked, hurrying after her.

Luna looked up at me and the smile suddenly vanished. "No. I'm good at keeping secrets."

Yet another dig.

This time, I grabbed her arm and stopped her from walking off. "Enough with the digs, Luna. Just say what you need to say."

"Luna?" she repeated, surprised. "I've asked you not to call me Luna."

The look she gave me made me uncomfortable, like I was sharing an intimate secret. I suppose I was. "You're still my Luna; my Moon Princess," I said, quietly.

Luna wrapped her arms around herself and I didn't fail to notice the small shudder. "You can't call me that, King," she muttered.

I stepped closer, reaching for her. She'd pulled her hair back into a high bun, but during the course of our cleaning, strands had worked free. I avoided them as I cupped her cheek in my palm. Her face was cold. "You'll always be my Moon Princess," I admitted.

She stared up at me, her eyes wide. They'd gone back to seeming more gray than blue. "You broke up with me, King. You can't call me that anymore."

"Are you kidding me?"

I jerked away from Luna like she had a current pass through her and we turned to find Seungjin and Yerin a few paces from us. Both were standing there, staring at us like we had committed a crime.

I suppose, in some ways, we had.

"What are you two doing here?" I asked, trying to divert the attention from us.

Seungjin marched up to me. "Are you kidding me?" he repeated, growing close. "We've been sent back to this hell hole to clean up our images and you're here fooling around with a fan?"

"What about you?" Luna snapped back before I could deny the accusation. "You're out with Yerin. What's your story?"

"Seungjin and I are just friends," Yerin cried. I glanced at Seungjin, not missing the surprise and hurt flash through him at that statement. I knew it!

"That's more than what me and King are," Luna told her.

It probably would have hurt less if she had punched me in the face. We weren't where we used to be, but after this evening, after running around a track for hours then helping her clean, I would have thought she might have considered us to be friends, even if it was a messy friendship.

Seungjin snorted. "If you go around touching fans like that, you're going to get into even more trouble than you're already in." The statement was clearly aimed at me.

I turned to Seungjin, the anger taking hold. "Don't you dare accuse me of touching fans inappropriately."

"I never said that, but if the shoe fits …"

Before I could hit him, a new voice boomed down the corridor. "What is going on here?"

The four of us froze. I recognized Ro Chanheon in an instant. "Nothing sir," we all replied, almost in unison.

"Curfew was more than thirty minutes ago. Would any of you care to explain why you're not in your rooms?"

"We were just returning from cleaning the classroom," Luna hurriedly supplied. "Sir."

"Really?" Chanheon asked, looking at the rest of us. When we all nodded and the small smile appeared on his face, I knew we had said the wrong thing. "Which classrooms were you cleaning?"

I glanced at the others. There was nothing down here but the library and some offices. "Aw hell," Luna muttered under her breath.

The small smile grew into a grin that would rival the Cheshire Cat's. "I want you all to report to the front of the school at 5 am sharp," he said. "Dress warm."

"Is that not outside of curfew?" Luna asked, cocking her head.

Chanheon's smile turned smug. "I am going to enjoy this."

I had a horrible feeling we wouldn't.

제24 장

Lucinda

5 am was a sucky time in the morning. Even if I was going out for a morning run, I wouldn't normally set my alarm until 6 am. Reporting to Ro Chanheon this early meant I had gotten up ten minutes ago, doing as he suggested and dressing warmly, and making sure I had stuffed some food in my pockets. The cafeteria wouldn't open for another two hours so I had filled my coat pockets with the kimbap triangles that Miyeon didn't approve of.

I was exhausted, and it was only a Tuesday. Hopefully, whatever this was would be over by homeroom and I could get a quick powernap in.

King, Seungjin and Yerin were already waiting when I arrived. I wasn't late, but they were clearly better risers than I was.

Chanheon, on the other hand, had us waiting in the cold for fifteen minutes longer than what he had said; at least it wasn't raining this time. When he did appear, it was in one of those small cars which only had two doors and you had to push down a seat in the front to get in the back. I was fairly certain it would fit in the back of one of my dad's pickup trucks.

The four of us looked at it uncertainly.

"Get in," Chanheon instructed us without getting out of the car.

"I'm sitting in the front," Yerin decided.

I rolled my eyes. "Yerin, you're the shortest one here. Let Seungjin sit in the front."

"I am sitting in the front," Yerin repeated, gritting her teeth together.

"Let her sit in the front," Seungjin sighed, moving to the passenger side. "We won't be in here long."

An hour later, we were still in the car, sitting in an awkward silence. I was in the middle, sandwiched between King and Seungjin. Both of them were slim, but there wasn't much space back there. The three of us all had our knees under our chins.

"Where are we going?" I asked Chanheon, before quickly adding a hasty "sir," to my question.

"You four are going to learn the importance of teamwork."

I stared out of the window, trying to work out where we were. It was still dark, and it was getting darker. We weren't in the city anymore and the further we traveled, the less streetlights and shop lights there were illuminating the area. "Where are we?" I asked King.

"I think we're heading to Bukhansan," he said.

I had done no exploring outside of Seoul and I didn't recognize it as one of the areas in Seoul. "Where is that?" I asked.

"More of a what," King muttered. "Bukhan Mountain."

"We're going up a mountain?" I asked in alarm. The road had become narrowed and steeper, but it never crossed my mind that Chanheon would take us up a *mountain*!

"Shhh!" Seungjin hissed at me, shooting Chanheon a nervous look.

I stared at the back of Chanheon's head, biting my lip. What were we doing up a mountain? What did this have to do with learning to work together? Why was I being shushed by Seungjin? What kind of punishment was this?

After a long drive up the winding road, we drove through a gate in a wall. Chanheon finally stopped the car and got out. "Thank god," Seungjin muttered, flicking the switch to lower the seat in front of him so he could escape. When I finally got out, I thought I was going to fall over, my legs were so stiff.

An artic-like breeze whipped around me, taking advantage of the coat I had unzipped from being too hot and stuffy in the car, and it somehow managed to find all the gaps in my clothing. Judging from Yerin's squeal, she was experiencing the same blast. I hurried to fasten my coat up as I looked around, trying to work out where we were.

As far as I could tell, the wall with the gate completely encircled an old fashioned looking house. It was a one-story building with a small porch running around, and a tiled roof which curled up at the ends. I knew nothing about Korean architecture, but it looked like the buildings in the history books I had been studying of the Joseon Dynasty—which could be eight hundred years old. I didn't think it was that old, but it wasn't like any of the modern buildings I was used to in

Seoul. What was this place?

Chanheon led us around to the back of the building, completely unperturbed despite how cold it was. He pointed over to a fallen tree. "That needs chopping up into firewood."

The four of us looked at the tree, then back to Chanheon. "We'll never get that done before class," Seungjin pointed out.

Chanheon shrugged. "You will be here for however long it takes."

Yerin's mouth dropped open. "Are you expecting me to chop a tree up?" she asked, outraged. Chanheon simply nodded. "Do you know how expensive this coat is?"

"Take the coat off," Chanheon shrugged again as he started to retreat back to the other side of the building behind us.

"Wait, does my mother know where we are?" Yerin demanded.

Chanheon waved his hand dismissively as he disappeared around the corner.

I let out a long sigh. "Korean punishment is weird."

"Let's just get this over with," King muttered, moving over to the tree.

I followed. It was probably only three meters tall with a trunk about sixty centimeters wide. I placed my hands on my hips and eyed it up. There had to be a catch with this.

I was sure the catch was the tools. There wasn't a chainsaw in sight, only two axes and one large saw which would need two people to use it. I turned to the others. "Out of curiosity, have any of you chopped wood before?" I was met with three blank expressions. I sighed. "Me neither."

"Are we really doing this?" Yerin asked in disbelief.

"I'm the foreigner here, so you tell me: how serious is Chanheon?"

"I think using the ax would be harder for you girls," King said. "Seungjin and I should use those."

"I'm not doing this," Yerin said.

"Just shut up and grab the other end of the saw," I told her reaching for the long tool. Yerin glowered at me, folding her arms and tapping her toe. "I can't do this by myself," I pointed out.

"I'll saw with Luna," King sighed.

"My name is Lucinda," I snapped at him.

"Of course you will," Seungjin added almost at the same time.

"What does that mean?" King demanded.

"Any excuse to work with your girlfriend, right?"

"She's not my girlfriend!"

At almost the exact time, I chimed in with, "He's not my boyfriend."

"Will you two just get a room," Yerin muttered, rolling her eyes at us.

I looked over at her and pulled a face. "I sincerely hope you break all your nails today."

"Go to hell!"

"You're here. I must already be in it," I snapped back.

"If it's such an issue, Luna and I will use the ax," King told Seungjin. "You two can saw."

I whirled around to King. "I've told you; my name is Lucinda!"

"Great, now we're in the middle of a lover's quarrel," Yerin muttered.

I spun back to her. "Then why don't you and Seungjin explain why you two were wandering the halls after curfew too?"

"That's a good point," King chimed in.

"Don't deflect your relationship on us," Seungjin said, shaking his head.

I stopped then, taking an actual step back as the three continued to argue around me. This was ridiculous. It was also too cold to want to stay out here with them for any longer than I needed to. Instead, I moved over to the tree and picked up an ax. I'd never used an ax before. We had a wood fire at home which we used all the time in the winter, but the wood was delivered already chopped. Axes were a lot heavier than I assumed they would be.

Regardless, I didn't want to stay here. I was already regretting not bringing my phone and headphones to drown them out. I moved over to the top of the tree, picked up the ax and swung it down at a branch.

It went in and refused to come out.

"What are you doing?" King asked.

"What I can to get home," I said, grunting as I tried to pull the ax free.

"Let me," King muttered, waiting for me to move to the side. He stuck a foot beside the ax and heaved, pulling it free. He turned back to the others. "Yerin and Luna—Lucinda—need to use the saw."

"I'm not using anything," Yerin said. She moved over to what was left of the tree stump and sat down on top of it. "You all might be used to manual labor, but

I'm not."

"What does that even mean?" I asked her, scowling. "Other than you're saying you're lazy."

"I'm saying that my mother pays for people to do that work for me, so why should I do it?" Yerin snapped. "You, on the other hand, are probably used to working manual labor considering your background."

I folded my arms. "My background being I'm American?" I asked her. "Or a dancer?"

Yerin shrugged. "All the scholarship kids have crappy jobs like that."

"Yerin," I said, surprisingly calmly. "I have never had a job. Instead of working, I went dancing. I practiced at least eight hours every day during the week before and after school, and more over the weekends when I wasn't in competitions. Dancing isn't a cheap hobby. There are registration fees, competition fees, I pay the dance school fees, and I have different competition outfits."

Yerin stared at me, her eyes narrowing as though finally doing some math in her head. "You're a dancer."

I nodded, even though it wasn't a question. "I am not here on a scholarship. The fees I'm paying—my parents are paying—are similar to what the fees were for the private school I attended in New York." I sighed. "State, not city, because there is a difference."

"Then what do your parents do?" she asked.

"Why does it matter?" I asked her. "Will knowing their occupation suddenly make me eligible to be your friend?"

"Yes," she shrugged.

I couldn't help the dry bark of a laugh that escaped me at that. "I can assure you that, if that's all your friendship criteria consists of, then we won't be friends. This weird Disneyesque making us work together to become friends *thing* that Ro Chanheon is scheming is more likely to work on me. And this is not going to work on me either." I moved back to the saw and picked up one side of it. "How about we just suck it up, get this tree chopped up, and then we can go back to school where we only have to talk to each other in our performance classes?"

"I don't do manual labor," Yerin repeated.

I swallowed the urge to slap her and turned back to King and Seungjin. "I can't cut this by myself."

"I'll help," King muttered, thrusting the ax towards Seungjin as he moved past him to get to me.

Z

Chopping up a tree is not a quick job. By late morning, Yerin had finally decided to help, albeit by moving the chopped wood into a neat pile. It was nearing eleven when I could smell something that had my stomach grumbling. I stopped and looked around, sniffing the air. "You can smell that too, right?" I asked King.

He did the same as me, then nodded. "I wish I couldn't, because I've just realized how hungry I am."

I abandoned the saw and moved to the front of the house, the others behind me. Outside, Chanheon was stirring a big pot of something that was already making my mouth water. I hurried over. "What is that and can I have some?"

Chanheon nodded his head at a pile of bowls and we hurried to collect them, lining up for the food. Chanheon merely filled his own bowl back up, before moving over to a spot on the porch and sitting to eat.

I grabbed at the ladle, filling up everyone's bowl. Greedily, we stood, eating the stew. Like most other dishes in Korea, it was spicy, but this one seemed to have meat in it, which seemed rather generous for the grouchy choreographer. "What is it?" I asked between mouthfuls.

"Yukgaejang," King replied. "It's basically a beef stew."

"It's delicious," I muttered. Spicy also felt like an understatement. The process of sawing the wood up meant that I had shed my thick coat and still worked up a sweat despite the cold weather. This stew was creating a different kind of sweat as it made my mouth tingle. Nonetheless, I gobbled it down, filling my empty stomach.

Afterwards, again, under Chanheon's supervision, we washed up using the outside tap we'd been using to sip from during the morning. It was icy cold—great for drinking, but not so much for washing up in.

Chanheon glanced over at the tree. "You still have a lot to do. You want to be quick, otherwise you'll be cutting in the dark." He glanced at Yerin. "It might be faster if all four of you helped."

"How long do we have to stay out here?" Yerin whined.

"How long does it take to chop up a tree?" Chanheon shrugged, before disappearing around to the front of the house.

"I really don't like him," Seungjin muttered under his breath.

"He has a point," I said, looking at Yerin. My legs were still aching from the run the night before, and my arms were aching from the morning sawing. The last thing I wanted to do was be out here longer than we had to be, especially if the reason for that was Yerin.

"I don't do manual labor," Yerin said, stubbornly.

"So I've heard," I muttered, angrily.

"You two get started," Seungjin said to me and King, suddenly. "Yerin and I will be right there."

I was not in the mood to deal with whatever drama they had going on. Instead, I rolled my eyes and returned to the tree. "What is Yerin's problem?" I grumbled, more to myself than King.

"Which one?" he muttered back.

Whether he intended to or not, that made me smile. With food in me, I felt a lot better; energized. I still didn't want to be chopping up a stupid tree, but I at least didn't feel quite as tired as I had before lunch.

For the most part, I really did enjoy being at school out here, but this was just weird. Who on earth thought chopping up firewood was reasonable punishment for breaking curfew? Curfew, which, thinking about it, was broken because Chanheon was being mean to start with.

It took nearly an hour for Seungjin and Yerin to rejoin us and it was already starting to get dark. "What took you so long?" I asked, straightening to stretch my back. "If we're out here all night, I'm blaming you. We've probably got an hour of daylight left, and more than that needed to finish."

"Will you relax?" Yerin scoffed, resuming her previous job of moving wood around. "Ro Chanheon is not going to make us stay out here all night. My mother would never allow that anyway."

"It doesn't mean I want to be back out here

tomorrow, either," I pointed out. Yerin ignored me, which was probably for the best. And we continued on until finally, the sun dipped behind the mountain.

Aside from the lack of light, the temperature seemed to dip ten degrees all at once, and despite the heat the sawing had generated, I found myself reaching for my jacket.

"We need to stop now," Yerin said. "I can't see anything and it's cold."

It was a good thing she couldn't see the look I was giving her. I did, however, agree. I was also hungry once more and we still had the drive home to contend with. Wearily, the four of us traipsed around to the front of the building.

Seungjin stopped suddenly. I had been right behind him and only avoided walking into him because King pulled me back. I couldn't work out if I was feeling more irritated at Seungjin or feeling more awkward at being in King's arms. The latter won out and I pulled myself free of his grip. "What's the matter, Seungjin?"

"Where is the car?"

"Where's what …?" I trailed off as my brain translated his question and I looked for Ro Chanheon's car. "Where's the car?" I repeated. It wasn't there. "Where's Ro Chanheon?"

"Did he forget us?" Yerin asked.

I shot her a scathing look. "How do you 'forget' four students?"

"Maybe he has gone to get food?" King suggested. As he did so, the moon came out from behind the clouds. It wasn't as bright as a building light would have been, but it was enough to illuminate the area and confirm there was no car there anymore. It was also enough for us to see that the gates were shut.

"What the hell?" I asked the empty grounds.

Seungjin ran over to the gates and tried to open them, but they wouldn't budge. "I think they're locked," he called.

I looked at King, the hunger in my stomach being replaced with anxiety. "Please tell me this is a normal thing for teachers to do out here?"

제25 장

King

“This is not normal teacher behavior,” I replied to Luna.

“This is ridiculous teacher behavior,” Yerin declared. “And when my mother finds out, Ro Chanheon will not be employed at Seoul Leadership Academy anymore.” She pulled her phone out of her pocket and unlocked it before calling her mother.

Or at least trying.

After several attempts, she held it up in the air, cursing it. “Why is there no signal?”

“Probably because we’re in the middle of the boonies,” Luna snorted. I looked at the American and arched an eyebrow. “Countryside; the middle of nowhere,” she clarified. She looked at me and I could see she was worried. “Now what?”

“What about you three?” Yerin asked. “Where are your phones?”

“In my room, charging,” Luna replied.

Yerin looked at me.

“I don’t have one,” I told her.

"Who doesn't have a phone?" she snorted.

"A lot of trainees, actually," I pointed out.

Yerin rolled her eyes. "Seungjin has a phone." Her eyes widened as she looked to him. "Where is your phone?"

"The dorm."

I rubbed at the back of my neck as I looked around, my eyes falling on the oldest person here: Seungjin. He looked as clueless as I felt. In fact, he was looking expectantly at *me*.

"As irritating as Chanheon is, he would have done this intentionally, not accidentally. He's probably still trying to teach us a lesson."

"What is it with Koreans and weird lessons and punishments?" Luna huffed. She stalked over to the house. I hurried after her; the ground was small rocks and pebbles, loose under our feet, and I didn't want her to slip and hurt herself.

"What are you doing?" Yerin asked, following us.

"If he has done this intentionally, he's probably left us a note somewhere," Luna explained. "Use the light on your phone to see if you can see anything."

Yerin did as she said, turning the flashlight on. I spotted the note straight away, pinned to the door. We hurried over.

As I said, if you hadn't finished by the time the sun set, you would stay here.

"That's it?" Yerin said, tearing the note from the door and turning it over. The back was blank.

"Hold up," Luna said. "I'm a little slow at reading."

"It said if we hadn't finished we would stay here," I told her.

"Until when?"

I shook my head. "It didn't say."

"I am not going to become a mountain woman," Yerin snapped at me, like it was my fault we were here.

"You wouldn't survive as a mountain woman," Luna said, dryly. I had to bite back my smile. She wasn't wrong.

"OK," said Seungjin, stepping in between the two of them. "Ro Chanheon is not going to leave us here forever. He is probably going to leave us here overnight."

"Can teachers really do this?" Luna asked in surprise.

"Oh. My. God!" Yerin snapped. "You're not in Oz anymore. Get over it already."

"Kansas," Luna said with a sigh. "We're not in Kansas anymore."

I cleared my throat. "We have two options: we can either spend the night here, or we can make our way back to the school by ourselves."

"It took us over an hour to drive here," Luna pointed out. "It will take most of the night to walk back."

"We don't have to walk all the way back," Yerin said, her eyes lighting up. She held her phone up. "We only have to go as far down as we need to find civilization and signal."

"Then let's go," Luna agreed.

Dropping the note, Yerin turned and led us over to the gate. Seungjin and I tried it once more, but it was definitely locked. "We're going to have to climb over the wall," Seungjin said. The gate was one which sat under an archway, the stone wall stretching out either side. It was at least six feet tall. "Do you girls want to stay here?"

Yerin and Luna looked at each other and then instantly shook their heads. "This is the perfect setting for a horror movie," Luna muttered.

I smiled despite the situation. "I don't think there are ax murderers walking around out here."

Luna looked at me and grinned. "I don't know: there are two axes over there and if Yerin continues to be annoying, there might be."

"Ya!" Yerin objected over both mine and Seungjin's laughter. Yerin turned to Seungjin and swiped at him. "And you're supposed to be on my side."

"I'm sorry," he said, trying to stop laughing.

An irritated sound escaped Yerin and she stalked over to the wall. "Someone is going to need to give me a hand up."

"Don't break a nail, will you," Luna snorted.

"Let me go over first," I told Yerin. "I can help you both down on the other side, and Seungjin can help you up." I turned to him. "Do you think you can get up by yourself?"

Seungjin, several inches taller than me, tilted his head and gave me a less than impressed look. "I'm not the one who needs to worry about that."

I nodded, then took a running leap at the wall, hoisting myself up. The other side was earth and soft when I landed. "OK!" I called.

One by one, the others came over. Out of the safety of the enclosed grounds, the woodland was quiet and eerie. I wasn't going to admit it aloud, but I was grateful that all of us were going together.

"How far down do you think we need to go?"

Luna asked after we'd been walking a while.

Yerin held her phone in the air as though it would help, and then shook her head. "Still nothing."

"How on earth did Chanheon find this place?" Seungjin muttered.

Luna looked at him, then at Yerin before finally settling her gaze on me. She promptly burst out laughing. "What's so funny, Lucinda?" Yerin demanded.

"Look at us," she said, still laughing. "We are four kids who grew up in households with money in the city. We are the four worst people to put alone in the countryside. If this was a post-apocalyptic movie where all technology suddenly died, we'd be useless. We'd be the first to die."

My eyes scanned the three of them, before looking down at me. In the light of Yerin's phone I could tell we all had at least one item of designer clothing on. Seungjin and I had spent the last number of years being idols where we were monitored twenty-four seven, and both Seungjin and Yerin came from a home with a butler. Luna was right.

As though we were all recognizing that fact at the same time, we all joined in the laughter. Which was when things started to go wrong.

Yerin was laughing so hard that she somehow slipped before any of us had the chance to catch her. She fell down heavily, landing with a shriek of pain.

"Are you OK?" Luna cried, dropping down beside her.

"My phone!" Yerin yelled.

"Your phone isn't as important as your leg," Luna informed her as she tried to help Yerin.

Yerin batted Luna's hands away. "It is when we need it to call for help!"

The four of us stopped, looking to the ground. Wherever it was, the torch wasn't facing upwards. "Everybody just stay still," Seungjin said, scanning the ground in the near darkness. "I think I see it!" He took two steps forward. The second step made a crunching sound I didn't like.

"Please tell me that wasn't my phone," Yerin muttered.

Seungjin bent down, picking something up, then swore loudly.

"Great!" Yerin screamed.

"OK," I said, holding my hands out. "It was an accident. This didn't happen intentionally."

"We're still screwed," Yerin snapped, angrily.

"We are not screwed," Luna told her, firmly. "We just need to walk a little further." She stood and then offered her hand to Yerin.

Yerin took it, allowing Luna to help her up, and then Yerin let out another scream before crumpling back to the ground.

"What's the matter?" I asked, alarmed.

"My ankle!"

"Let me look," Seungjin said, dropping down beside her. Gently, he ran his hands over her ankle. Yerin hissed in pain. Slowly, he lifted her leg. "I'm going to move this a little. Be honest and let me know how much it hurts."

He had barely moved it before Yerin was yelling again.

"Enough," Luna snapped. "He's trying to see if it's broken, sprained or twisted. He's not trying to pull your foot off. Unless you've got the most ridiculously low pain-threshold, suck it up and let us know how it really hurts."

"It hurts," Yerin said through gritted teeth. I could see tears glinting in her eyes in the moonlight.

"I don't think it's broken," Seungjin told her. "Equally, I don't think you should be walking on it."

"What do we do then?" Luna asked, looking down the road. "Do we split up?"

I shook my head. "There's no way that Chanheon would have left us without the intention of coming back first thing tomorrow to pick us up. If we try to carry Yerin down the mountain in no light, we run the risk of hurting ourselves. Our best bet is to go back to the house."

"How do we get back over the wall?" Yerin asked.

"We'll figure that out when we get there."

Seungjin crouched down in front of her and together, we helped her onto his back. We walked slowly up the hill, taking our time on the uneven ground as we now had even less light. Around us, despite the cover from the trees, the ground was starting to cover in frost.

"On the plus side," Luna muttered, her teeth chattering. "At least we have plenty of firewood."

"I'm going to burn that whole damn tree," Yerin declared.

We finally encountered our next problem: getting back over the wall. "Do we walk around and see if there's a lower section?" Luna asked.

I shook my head. "We're only going to run the risk of hurting ourselves. The ground is even more uneven."

Before I could tell Seungjin to set Yerin down, he was taking a running leap at the wall, Yerin squealing as they went flying. Somehow, he managed to pull himself up. He was wiry, but stronger than he looked.

On top of the wall, Yerin smacked the back of his head. "Give me a warning before you do something like that," she hissed at him as he dropped off the other side.

"Are you OK?" I called.

"We're fine!" Seungjin called back. "We're going inside."

I let out a long sigh then turned to Luna. "Your turn." I held my hands together for her to use as a step up. "Just wait on the top so I can help you down."

She nodded, stepping onto me. I pushed her up, and she scrambled up, doing as I requested and waiting for me. I quickly joined her, finding her watching me. in the moonlight, her hair looked silver. Despite how much I wanted to deny it, she was still my Moon Princess. "What?" she asked.

I gave her a sad smile. "Just thinking."

She chewed at her lip before shaking her head. "Whatever you're thinking, you probably shouldn't."

"I know," I agreed. "But I'm still thinking it."

Kissing her.

That's what I was thinking of.

Running my hands through that silken hair as I let myself remember how her lips felt beneath mine. I could almost taste her again.

She was right: I shouldn't be thinking it.

With more effort than running sixty laps had taken, I lowered myself off the wall. I turned back to the wall, holding my hands up to help her down, and once more, the image of a Disney princess came to my mind.

I was an idiot.

I was an idiot who had been in love.

I was an idiot who was still in love.

Luna turned and lowered herself, and in the moment that she jumped I made an executive decision: I caught her, but stumbled, falling backward so she landed on me.

Unlike a drama, I stumbled intentionally, wanting her to fall on me.

I succeeded.

I stared up at her molten eyes and knew that she still felt the same way about me. "What are you doing?" she whispered, though making no effort to move from on top of me.

"Honestly, I'm praying that it's not too late."

Luna's breath hitched in her throat as she stared down at me, then she slowly sucked in a breath. "This isn't fair," she said, still whispering, like the loud sound might spoil the moment. She might have been right about that. "You can't say things like this when we're up a mountain, only for things to return to normal when we get back down. You hurt me, King. If I'm going to let you hurt me again, it sure as hell won't be for one night up a mountain."

We were lying in a stupid place, on the icy cold ground, but for some reason it seemed like now was the only opportunity we would get to talk about this. Whether Luna felt this way, or I was holding too tightly to her, she didn't try to wiggle away.

"I still love you," I told her.

She stared at me, then slowly shook her head. "You can't say things like that."

"Like what?" I asked. "The truth? Because it is.

People might say I'm too young to have found my dream career, but I did, and I lost it. The same people might say I'm too young to have found love, but I did, and I don't want to lose it too."

"I don't think you've lost it," Luna said, her voice a whisper once more. I looked up at her, my heart pounding in my chest. "Atlantis seems to want you to re-debut."

"And what about us?"

"What are you two doing?" Seungjin bellowed across the grounds, his voice seeming much louder than it probably was.

Of course …

Luna leaped off me like I had electrocuted her. Grumbling curses at Seungjin under my breath, I got to my feet. "We're coming!" I called back. I waited for Seungjin to disappear back inside the house before grabbing Luna's hand. "What about us?"

"What about us?" Luna asked with a sigh.

"Have I lost that too?"

She stared at me, chewing her lip. "I don't know," she admitted. "But I think that before I consider it, you need to work out what you really want. You could be picked to be in this new group Atlantis is looking to create, and that would be amazing. But have you considered where I would fit in that? If I *could* fit in that? We thought it could work, and it hasn't so far. Only now, I'm here, and I'm finishing our school here whether you're my boyfriend or not."

She hurried off before I could respond.

Not that I knew how to respond.

제26 장

Lucinda

The building was as modern as I expected it to be: it wasn't. I'd never been in anything like it since being here. Although the walls were made of stone and there were tiles on the roof, the door was a sliding door and paper thin. I wasn't sure it offered much in the way of security or warmth.

What I hadn't noticed earlier was that each of the rooms led out onto the small porch, almost like a row of cupboards. None of them were much bigger than a double bed, apart from the one which had had the note stuck on the door. That one could probably fit two double beds in it.

There were no lights, only candles, which Seungjin had set around the room on the floor. There wasn't even a fireplace. In all honestly, it didn't seem much different from camping. At least, with the door closed, the room was warmer than it was standing outside.

"How is your ankle?" I asked Yerin.

One of them, I was assuming Seungjin, had found

some blankets and spread them over the floor. Yerin was sat in the middle of it, her shoe off and her ankle bound up in a bright white bandage. At least Chanheon had left a first aid kit.

"It hurts. I'm cold. I'm hungry."

I nodded. "Me too." I shoved my hands into my pockets and pulled out several slightly squashed kimbap. I tossed one over to her, then one to Seungjin and King.

"You have food?" Seungjin asked in surprise, tearing the wrapping off it and devouring it in two bites.

"That's all I have," I told him. I glanced around the room. There was very little in it. "Have you looked in the other rooms? Is there any food in them?"

Seungjin shook his head. "I was binding up Yerin's ankle."

"I'm going to check them out," I told them, stepping past King to go back outside.

"I'll come with you," King said, following me.

Outside I arched an eyebrow at him. "There's three doors. I'm not going to get lost."

"I want to talk to you," he said.

I turned and shook my head. "Not about us, or the lack of us," I told him. "I've said what I've had to say on that, and until you've thought about—which you have not done in three minutes—we're not going further with this conversation."

"How long do you think I need to know how I feel about you?"

"It's not me," I told him, tapping at my chest. "It's not me you need to think about. It's your future." I shook my head. "Christmas," I said, deciding to give him a definitive deadline. "By then you will know the outcome of this audition. When you've passed and you're being told what is expected of you for King 2.0, then you can work out what you feel."

"And what about you?" he asked.

I shrugged. "I guess it's the same for me."

"You don't want to be an idol," he said, clearly confused.

"No," I agreed. "But when you can work out where I fit into your world, I will be able to work out if I still want to be in it, or at least, in what capacity."

I pushed open the door to the next room and peered in. It was, unsurprisingly, dark, but my eyes had been growing accustomed to the darkness and I was able to walk around without worrying about tripping over anything. There was nothing in there, so I moved onto the next room. This one proved more fruitful. "What's that?" I said, pointing at a sack in the corner.

King walked over, pulling it open and putting his hand in. With a handful of the contents, he walked back to the doorway and the marginally better light. "Rice."

"Rice, water and firewood," I said. "We can eat something warm tonight."

While King dragged the sack towards the door, I hurried around the back of the building, bringing an armful of chopped logs with me. It wasn't until I was close to the stove—like contraption that Chanheon had been using earlier that I realized there was wood next to it. Wood which was dryer than the wood in my hands.

I knew enough about fires from lighting the one in our living room to know the dryer the wood, the better. The fire had long since extinguished itself, and I scraped the dead embers out to replace with the dry wood. Stealing one of the candles from inside, I managed to get the wood to light. The flames were soon licking at the bottom of the pot King had filled with water.

I sat on the porch next to it, my eyes closed as I appreciated the heat on me.

"Are you dating King?"

I opened my eyes and found Seungjin standing in front of me, his arms folded, but his expression wasn't completely hostile. I shook my head. "No," I said, truthfully.

"And what about me?"

I cocked my head in amusement. "Wouldn't you know if we were dating?"

"No, that's not what I meant," he said, flustered. "Kareun said you liked me."

"We had fun at karaoke," I told him. "But the most I liked you was as a friend."

"Liked?"

I nodded. "I know you think you have your reasons, but the way you've been treating TK is cruel."

"His brother—"

"His *brother*," I repeated, cutting him off. "Exactly: his brother, has done questionable things. Not TK. TK's actually a nice person. He has his faults, like we all do, but he helped out with Baekhee when he didn't need to."

"You don't know what happened. You weren't there."

I shrugged. "From all accounts, neither were you."

All of a sudden, Seungjin's eyes went wide and he swore loudly, kicking at a stone and sending it soaring against the side of the house with a loud bang. There was a muffled squeal from inside and then King came running out. "What's the matter?" he demanded.

"It's Hyunseo's court date and we're stuck up a mountain," Seungjin grunted angrily.

"He's going to be fine, hyung," King told him.

"Is he, though?" Seungjin demanded. "You read the news stories. No one believed in him. No one believed in us. That's why Holly disbanded us."

Holly, I was assuming, was someone at Atlantis. "From what you've said, she sent you back to SLA," I chimed in. "I don't think she would have done that if she didn't think you were worth the second chance she's giving you."

"What would you know?" Seungjin sneered.

"I know very little," I admitted. "This … *life* of yours is … crazy. It's crazy and it's competitive, and people either seem to love you or hate you to the extreme. You keep acting like it's not fair that you were disbanded and you have to start again, but the fact you *can* start again shows someone at Atlantis has faith in you." I stood and peered over at the rice. It looked done. I reached for a spoon and took a bit out, blowing softly on it. I looked up and found Seungjin and King staring at me. "What?"

"You really think that?" Seungjin asked.

"It's not like there have been many other groups who have been through the same scandal as you guys have, but your company still has your back."

"They sent us back to school."

"They could have just sent you home," I pointed out. I tried the rice. It was ready. "If they weren't on your side, they wouldn't have kept you at Atlantis. I mean, I know you have rules and everything, but when it comes to someone breaking the law—" at Seungjin and King's protests, I held my hands up. "I didn't say he was guilty or not, but the fact is, Hyunseo was arrested, and it seems like the only reason others weren't was because Hyunseo kept quiet. Either way, there is a court case. If Atlantis really wanted to get you gone, they didn't need to look far for an excuse. Instead, they kept you." I started dishing out the rice as best I could. "I'd take that as a win." I picked up two bowls and started towards the room Yerin was in, before turning and looking back at them. "TK had nothing to do with this. The ones bringing him into it are you, and honestly, it makes you look like jerks."

Ignoring their objections, I stepped inside and handed Yerin a steaming bowl. "I'm warning you now, I am not a great cook when I have more to work with than just one ingredient, so don't be expecting a Michelin starred meal, because it's just rice."

"Thank you," Yerin muttered, taking the bowl from me. She started eating it greedily as I sat down beside her. She paused to look at me. "This doesn't make us friends, you know."

"Of course not," I agreed. "Because you still haven't given me approval on my parent's occupations."

The door opened and King and Seungjin walking in, sitting down with their own bowls of rice.

"Well, from this cooking, I can tell they're not chefs or restaurateurs," Yerin continued, oblivious.

"No," I agreed.

She paused in her eating again as she narrowed her eyes at me. "What do they do that's so embarrassing you can't tell me."

"Embarrassing?" I repeated with a chuckle. "Oh,

no, Yerin, I'm proud of both of my parents. The only reason I'm not telling you is because it's more amusing not to." I yawned and stretched out my muscles. "I really want a hot bath right about now," I moaned, before finishing my rice off. It was bland, but it had filled a hole and warmed me considerably. Now all we had to do was get through the night.

Although it was early, we all lay down not long after we had finished eating. "We might as well try to get some sleep," Seungjin had said. "The sooner we sleep, the sooner we wake up and it's tomorrow."

I was tired enough that I thought I would be able to sleep through the night. Instead I woke up with a freezing cold nose. I reached up, cupping it.

"Cold?" King's hand was suddenly over mine and I nodded against it.

"If there's one thing I miss about home, it's the central heating," I murmured. "And now I miss beds. I know sleeping on the floor like this is quite normal over here, but I'm just so cold." The more I spoke, the more my teeth chattered.

King nodded, then moved his hand, reaching for the blanket we had been sharing. Gently, he tugged it up and over our heads. Then, he snaked his arms around me, pulling me to him.

"King," I sighed.

"I really want to kiss you right now," he whispered. "But I know that's not what you want. Instead, I'm just going to keep you warm."

I relaxed, allowing him to hold me as tightly as I was clinging on to him. It didn't take long for it to become warm and stuffy under that blanket, but I didn't want to leave the security of his arms or the cotton cocoon.

"Are you OK?" he asked.

I looked up, forgetting how close we were, and my lips brushed his.

King froze. "I need to let go of you now," he whispered. "Because I'm going to end up breaking my word."

Oh, how I wanted him to break his word.

I really, *really* wanted him to break his word.

But that wasn't fair—not after the strict instructions I had given him earlier. "I think that's for the best," I agreed, mentally kicking myself as I rolled over.

It took a long time before we both fell back to sleep.

Z

The sound of an engine woke me up. I was aware of how cold I was, but it took a moment for my fuzzy brain to recognize the sound for what it was. Then I sat bolt upright. "Ro Chanheon is here!" I cried, waking the others.

King and I darted outside, Seungjin helping Yerin just behind us. Ro Chanheon was standing behind his toy car, the open trunk blocking our view of him. "What the hell were you thinking?" Yerin demanded. "My mother will have you fired."

"Your mother agreed to the punishment," Chanheon responded, stepping out from behind the trunk. He looked at us and folded his arms. "I went back to help you."

"How did abandoning us on the top of a freezing

mountain help us?" Yerin asked, incredulously.

To be fair, she took the words out of my mouth.

"To get this," Chanheon reached into the trunk and pulled out a chainsaw. "I told you we weren't leaving until you had finished cutting the tree up."

"I think I hate him," I muttered under my breath, in English—just in case.

"Me too," King agreed.

"Me three," Seungjin added, stepping off the small porch and walking over to our dance teacher to collect the power tool. "Let the girls wait in the car where it's warm," he said to Chanheon. "King and I will finish up."

Chanheon shrugged, gesturing to us that we could do as Seungjin had said. While King followed Seungjin, I helped Yerin over to the car and into the front seat. "How is your ankle?" I asked.

"Better," she responded. I hurried to the other side of the car, squeezing into the back seat, instantly appreciating the warmth. From the front seat, Yerin turned to look at me. "Are you going to tell me what your parents do now?"

I stared back, then grinned. "Nope," I said, shaking my head.

제27 장

Lucinda

Annoyingly, things were different after the night on the mountain. After taking a long, hot shower and finally feeling less like an iceman and more like a human, I had gone to my classes like nothing had happened. Aside from Miyeon and Baekhee, no one had said anything to me about my disappearance. Of course, I wasn't as popular as the other three who had had dozens of people come up to them all day long.

We'd finished the dance class early. With Yerin having a twisted ankle (and she'd needed a hospital trip to confirm that …), Chanheon had decided to go easy on us and let us finish up early.

Miyeon, Baekhee and I had decided chicken was in order, so we had gone to Roosters and found TK working. Which was when we discovered his brother had dropped the assault charges against Hyunseo.

"What does that mean?" Baekhee asked, watching TK. He had taken his break and was eating his dinner with us.

"That Hyunseo isn't going to prison," Miyeon responded for her.

"Is your brother going to get into trouble?" I asked him.

TK, keeping his gaze purposefully on his chicken, shrugged. "They wouldn't let me in the court. The Atlantis lawyer somehow managed to get the judge to agree to a closed session. All I know is Hyunseo's sister turned up at some point."

"Have you managed to speak to your brother?" I asked. "Is he OK? Are *you* OK?"

TK looked up at me and frowned. "You're the only person who has asked me that."

I shrugged back at him. "People suck."

TK puffed out his cheeks, setting his piece of chicken down. "He won't speak to me. I don't know why he dropped the charges, but he hasn't gone home. Dad had to turn his phone off because of all the calls we're getting. The fans went from hating on Hyunseo and Bright Boys to loving them again. Which means they hate Gukyung, and by default, me and my dad."

"I'm sorry," I said, genuinely feeling bad for him. Not that I wasn't happy to hear things had been cleared up, because now positive things might happen for Bright Boys and King, but I didn't want TK to keep suffering for something that was never his fault to begin with.

"Do you want to join us later?" Miyeon asked, pointing at me and her. "We're heading to Hongdae for some dancing."

TK shook his head. "Once I finish here, I'm going to a PC café." He tilted his head, frowning. "Wait, dancing? In Hongdae?"

I nodded. "I'm part of the Iron Street Crew," I explained, with a quick fist bump with Miyeon. "It's a busking group."

"Busking? You?" TK's voice was laced with disbelief.

"I like dancing," I told him. "And I'm pretty good."

"You're pretty white."

My mouth fell open in mock shock. "Wait … I'm white?" I leaned forward. "How did I not notice this before?"

TK stared at me, then started sniggering into his chicken. I reached over and, even though I had already eaten my food, stole some of a wing. "I can get you more, you know?" I shook my head. "In which case, do you want to tell us why you were at Bukhansan?"

"I was caught out of the dorm after curfew," I responded. "I had gone to check on Baekhee in the library."

"You did?" Baekhee asked in alarm.

Huh … so she didn't want anyone to know what she was up to in the library? OK … "I got caught before I found you," I told her, turning to face her. "Are you OK, Baekhee?"

Miyeon nodded. "Ro Chanheon and Sa Hyesun were unnecessarily mean the other day."

"They weren't saying anything that wasn't true," Baekhee said, dismissively. "Besides, I think my mother would kill me if I was doing performance-based classes anyway."

"But what do you want to do?" I asked in concern.

"If you like dancing, come to Hongdae with us,"

Miyeon offered. "We care about talent, not looks, and you've got talent."

"At singing," Baekhee disagreed. "Not dancing. But it's OK. I need to go to the library." She gave the three of us pointed looks. "I realize you all opted for performances classes, but you also have your normal classes too. Exams are coming up. You should be studying, not busking."

She had a point … I looked at Miyeon, who instantly broke out into a huge grin. "We still have three weeks before we have to worry about exams."

"And you have three hours before you have to worry about curfew. It's not a weekend." Baekhee turned to me. "Or do you want to spend another night up a mountain?"

Miyeon sat back in her chair, folding her arms. "I knew we should have had the chicken to go." She cocked her head. "We could still get an hour in?"

I shook my head at her. "You and I know full well your boyfriend would keep us there longer."

"Ugh," Miyeon pouted. "They go to a normal school. They don't have a curfew to worry about."

"They still have exams," Baekhee pointed out.

Miyeon and I shared a look before Miyeon chuckled. "We need to introduce you to the rest of the crew."

"I don't have time to go to Hongdae," Baekhee told her, getting to her feet. "I need to study. *You* need to study," she added over her shoulder as she walked to the door.

"She has a point," TK said, also standing.

I looked up at him in disbelief. "I thought you were going to the PC café?"

"I am," TK agreed. He gathered all our empty boxes, clearing the table.

I laughed and looked at Miyeon. "Want to practice at school?"

We hurried to catch up with Baekhee and the three of us returned to the school. As Baekhee disappeared to the library, Miyeon and I returned to the dance studios, much to Baekhee's disapproval.

"You know, I think we should get the crew to come here to practice," Miyeon mused as we walked down the corridor. "We're the ones with the curfew, but they expect us to cross the city to them. If they came here, we could get much more practice in. I also bet I could set Baekhee up with Blue."

I gave Miyeon the side eye. "Blue and Baekhee? How do you even come up with that pairing?" The two would wind each other up more than Yerin wound me up. Besides, from what I had seen in the library, there was another romance brewing with a former member of Bright Boys …

"Lucinda!" a voice called.

I turned, half recognizing it, and found Ruzt walking behind us. We stopped so he could catch up. "Hello," I greeted him with a respectful bow of my head. "Is everything OK?"

"I had been hoping to catch you in class yesterday, but you weren't there."

I nodded. Ruzt and Hyesun didn't attend all the classes, and they hadn't been in today, which was why I was surprised to see him here now. "I was with Ro Chanheon," I told him.

"I heard," Ruzt agreed. He indicated to the studio Miyeon and I had been about to walk past, and the three of us went in. I was surprised to see Yerin and Eunbyeol there. Given the fact he was rewarded with four looks of confusion, Ruzt closed the door, then moved over to the mirrored wall where he leaned against it. "I wanted to speak to all of you about your team performance."

"Now?" I asked before I could stop myself from blurting the question out.

I was, unsurprisingly, rewarded with a jab to the rib from Miyeon. "At least stick a *sunbae* on the end," she hissed at me.

"I'm sorry, sunbae" I said to Ruzt, mentally kicking myself. Korean was tricky. There were different levels of respect to use when talking, and I knew I should play it safe by being the most respectful, but I spent most of my time speaking to Miyeon and Baekhee—both of whom I was older than, that it felt unnatural. Using sunbae, or senior, was a more respectful way of addressing him, even if the way I was phrasing the question wasn't right. Unfortunately, while Ruzt was only a few years older than me, Ro Chanheon was much older and sunbae wouldn't cut it with him ...

"Lucinda, you have skills as a rapper," Ruzt said as though I hadn't slipped up. I decided I liked him. "As does Yerin." I looked over at Yerin and found her watching us with narrowed eyes. "But both of you are rapping the wrong parts."

I pulled a face. "I mean it when I say I don't want to be an idol. Yerin does, sunbae. She has a bigger part which will put her in the spotlight she needs. Besides, I am reasonably comfortable at rapping in Korean, but Yerin's part is faster than mine and I won't be able to pull that off. I know my limitations."

"Maybe," Ruzt said, although he didn't look

convinced. "But I think with you both rapping the parts you are doing, you are hurting yourself and the rest of the team. Now that Baekhee has left your team, you have an opportunity to change your song."

"We can do that?" I asked.

"Ro Chanheon hasn't announced this yet, so consider yourself at an advantage. You will be expected to learn a second group song. You will also be graded as though this is a real audition … because it is."

I glanced at the alarmed expressions on the faces of the other three girls, feeling a knot of worry appear in my stomach. I didn't know what the audition process was. It wasn't something I had wanted to do, so I had never looked into it. The fact that *they* were worried was what had me concerned. "What does that entail?" I asked.

It was Eunbyeol who replied. "A solo audition. You'll need to sing and dance by yourself. Or rap," she added with a shrug.

"That doesn't sound …" I trailed off as the implications dawned on me. "Aren't the auditions in three weeks?" I'd learned routines in less time, but two group work pieces, a solo dance and rap performance, *and* classes and exams. I was beginning to think Baekhee might have had a point.

Z

December

I work hard. When you spend as much of your life in dance classes and competitions as I do, you have to.

However, while I was in America doing this, I was pulling in a C+ at best in most of my classes. My 2.63 GPA was acceptable back home. Here, it wasn't.

When I'd told Baekhee that, she'd almost fainted, saying that if she ever went home with anything less than a 3.9, her mother would probably disown her. At first, I had thought she was joking, then on the one occasion I had briefly met her mother (and wished I hadn't), I realized it was probably a true statement.

Ever since quitting the performance class, I had barely seen Baekhee. She spent all her free time in the library. I hadn't been worried, figuring she was spending the time with someone, until she started having nosebleeds.

She wasn't the only one.

The closer it got to the week before Christmas, the week all the exams were scheduled, the more nosebleeds seemed to be a common occurrence. It got to the point that I was no longer shocked at seeing all the blood. It's a strange quirk that seemed to effect my Korean classmates, but the less sleep and food they had, combined with the rising stress levels, the more nosebleeds they seemed to have.

Even Miyeon who was pretty laidback was stressed. We had to cut back on our busking too, and by default, she was seeing less of Gunpyo. Apparently not seeing her boyfriend made her grumpy.

Yerin was back to being a bitch. I caught slip of a conversation that something was going on at home for her. I'd tried to be nice and ask, and she'd told me to get lost. I'd tolerated it until I had caught Baekhee in tears, running away from Yerin. After that, I refused to talk to Yerin unless it involved arguing with her about our performance.

Meanwhile, Eunbyeol was acting plain weird. I swear she was either going to have a Miley Cyrus style meltdown or she was going to turn into the girl from The Grudge.

And that was just the girls.

The guys … or at least the Atlantis trainees yoyoed between incredibly focused and tension so thick you could reach out and touch it.

And just when I thought it couldn't get any worse, one week before the first performance exam, and two days before the first academic exam, Ro Chanheon announced we would also be graded on a duet. Thankfully, someone other than me, had pointed out that it wasn't fair and there wasn't enough notice.

"Enough notice?" Chanheon had repeated, incredulously. "How much notice do you think you will have when you're an idol? How much time do you think you will get to learn a change to a routine when you debut?"

"We've not debuted yet," the girl had added.

"If you become an idol, you will be working so hard, you won't know what your bed looks like. In the lead up to promotions, you will spend all your time learning your song and its routine to perfection. During promotions you will go from show to interview to any other number of filming activities. Sleep will become a word you are unfamiliar with. During this, you may, and will, be expected to change that schedule depending on what the company had arranged for you, and that can involve anything from another performance to learning a new song overnight."

"Why would we learn a new song?"

"What if you had the opportunity to sing for a drama sound track?" Chanheon shot back at her. She fell silent. "What if one of your members falls ill and they are forced to drop out of a performance only hours before and you all have to relearn your routine, your positioning and their lyrics?" Chanheon looked at us all, folding his arms. "I am giving you a week, which is more than you'll ever see in this industry. If you can't handle that, you seriously need to reconsider if this is the career for you."

He had a point, and I had to agree with him on that, but he was also forgetting we were still kids. We were still at school and we didn't have all the time in the world to drop everything and focus on learning a new song.

I knew before it was announced that I was going to be paired with either Yerin or King. When Chanheon declared Yerin would be with Seungjin, I sighed and slumped back against the wall, waiting for Chanheon to tell me what I already knew.

Somehow, King seemed to look surprised when it happened.

After our conversation in the mountains, I had been successfully continuing to avoid him.

I still liked him.

I wanted to go back to being his girlfriend—even if it was his secret girlfriend.

I hated myself for that.

I had been secretly hoping that he would realize he wanted to be with me at the end of all this, and I had been allowing myself to raise my hopes over it. It was worse than waiting for a judge to place me at a competition—because I wanted this more.

And I hated myself for it.

"I guess it's you and me," King said. He was standing over me, rubbing awkwardly at the back of his neck, but I didn't miss the eagerness in his eyes.

I opened my mouth, ready to remind him that this didn't mean anything, but then I remembered we were still in a room with twenty other people. Instead I sighed. "I guess it is," I agreed.

He sat down in front of me, frowning. "You don't look thrilled at that prospect."

I shook my head. "It's just that we have a week to learn this," I told him. It wasn't completely untrue, but I wasn't going to admit the truth. I stretched out my back then sat upright. "We have our group practice now. Shall we meet up later and discuss what we're going to do?"

"Sure," King agreed. I felt him watching me as I got up and joined my team.

Was it Christmas yet?

제28 장

King

Chanheon's goal when abandoning us at the top of the mountain had been to get us to work together. Somehow, it had worked. Yerin and Lucinda had managed to remain almost friendly with each other for nearly three whole days before they had resumed wanting to scratch each other's eyes out. Strangely, they were still able to work together.

I'd heard a rumor that Ruzt had been to their group to help them out, which a few other people weren't happy about; why should they be getting the extra attention? There was no evidence, but they had changed their song choice.

Our group was doing better, although I wasn't sure if that was due to Seungjin and I going to Bukhansan, or if it was due to the fact Hyunseo's charges had been dropped and the animosity towards TK had eased off. Perhaps the others were just doing the same thing as Yerin and Lucinda.

We finished up our group practice and I gathered my things. I left the classroom, heading downstairs.

Luna had left before me and I wanted to speak to her about our performance piece. We didn't have long to work on it. I walked outside and spotted Luna and Miyeon. They weren't going to the dorm. They were saying goodbye to Baekhee. Baekhee gave them a disapproving look before she walked off in the direction of the library. Luna and Miyeon, however, were heading for the gates.

There was still a couple of hours until curfew. Maybe they were going for food? That was a tempting idea. I was starving.

I walked after them, trying to come up with a convincing argument for me to join them, when they veered off down into the subway. Curious, I followed them. It wasn't until I was on the train, unnoticed in the next car that I realized that this was verging on creepy stalker behavior.

I got up, about to join them, when the train pulled into a station and they got off. I hurried after them, almost losing them when they went topside in Hongdae. Then I spotted Luna's blonde hair. Even in a sea of people, she stood out to me. It was like my heart always knew which way to tell my eyes to look.

Once more, I was stopped from announcing my presence, this time from the group of guys she was meeting. I didn't recognize any of them, but I automatically hated the one who draped his arm around her shoulders and said something that made her smile at him. Yup. I hated him.

I was curious as to why she was in Hongdae too. I checked my phone: it would have to be a flying visit in order for us to get back to school before curfew. But this was Hongdae and it came alive at this time of night, rather than wind down.

My curiosity was still getting the better of me, and I continued to follow them. In a small area which had been designed like a stage and already had a crowd gathered, they joined a few more people. Thankfully, the one who'd had his arms around Luna was spared a black eye when he kissed another of the girls. They were a dance crew.

That made sense now. Miyeon was a talented dancer: Luna would have come with her to watch.

And then Luna started dancing.

It wasn't just Luna, it was all of them. Whatever dance crew this was, Luna was part of it, and judging from how flawless their cover of BTS' 'Fake Love' was, they had spent a *lot* of time practicing together.

I pushed myself further forward, watching both in awe and surprise. This group had one of the biggest crowds. They were good—excellent, in fact—but I was sure an added part of this was Luna's presence. The only white girl in a Korean street dance crew was going to attract attention. It simply wasn't something you saw every day here.

She was earning more than a few curious stares, but it all seemed positive.

"She can dance," I heard one girl say to her friend.

The friend nodded. "She's also beautiful. I wish I had hair like that."

"I wish I had legs like that! Her dancing skills are amazing. BTS is a boy group and she can keep up with it."

My heart swelled with pride at that. Miyeon was in the group, as was another girl, but they only noticed Luna. I could understand why. It was like watching music. Visual music. Her movements flowed from one move to the next; fluid, graceful … mesmerizing. Despite the conversation, I hadn't taken my eyes off her for longer than it took to hit record and make sure my phone was angled at her correctly.

Or at least, they didn't until I realized my phone was recording the guy who had hugged her. Then I turned my attention to watching her through the screen to make sure I was capturing it all.

I lost track of time as I watched her. BTS turned into Seventeen, then into KNK, then onto BAP. Grace, power and emotion—she had it all.

I loved everything about her.

And damn, that twisted my heart. I really had been an idiot. I knew what I was getting into back then. I'd just panicked because instead of going back to New York, she'd stayed. I should have just explained everything and asked if she would have … it was too late not for 'should haves'.

The song ended and once more the crowd clapped and cheered. I went to stop the recording when I found her staring straight at me through the camera. I looked up, locking eyes with her. Her cheeks were pink, and she was breathing heavily from the last performance, but there was also annoyance in her eyes.

I stayed where I was, refusing to run away. Instead, I watched while she had a conversation with the others, before she made her way to me. Her path was slow as people would stop her and compliment her, some getting surprised when she spoke to them in Korean, but her attention was rarely away from me for long.

Finally, she was in front of me, her hands on her

hips. "What are you doing here, King?" she hissed at me, but only after making sure no one was paying attention to me. "I thought you had to keep a clean image. Being out after curfew isn't doing that."

"I'd wanted to speak to you about our performance piece," I explained. "You left the school and I went to follow you, and then we ended up here before I knew it." I shook my head. "You're in a dance crew?"

"Is that the important thing here?" she asked me. She glanced around again and sighed. "We should probably get back to school before anyone recognizes you."

"You're still thinking of me?" I asked, before I could stop the words coming out of my mouth. We hadn't spoken much since Bukhansan. I couldn't stop my smile, either.

She let out a long sigh. "King, we talked about this."

"Come with me," I said, suddenly.

Luna shook her head. "We're out past curfew. We should get back."

"We're already out past curfew," I pointed out. "It will make no difference if we go back now or later. Come with me."

The crowds had thinned out around us, but her dance crew were watching us, suspiciously. Especially Miyeon, who was arching an eyebrow at me. When she saw us looking, she walked over. "King? Why are you here?" she asked, shooting the both of us a look.

"Luna is my partner for the duets. I need to speak to her."

"And that couldn't wait until tomorrow?"

"No," I said, shortly. "Not when my future is riding on this audition."

Luna let out another exaggerated sigh. "Miyeon, I need to speak to King. Can Gunpyo take you home?"

"Sure," Miyeon said, slowly, drawing out the word more than was necessary.

I didn't stick around long enough for any further conversation, instead taking Luna's wrist and leading her away from the main area of Hongdae. I found a park, empty because of how late it was, and we walked over to the swings.

While she went and sat on one, scuffing her toes in the dirt as she swung back and forth, I took a gamble and ordered takeout for me and Luna, to be delivered to the park. She looked up with a sigh when I walked over. "Is being around me that bad?" I asked her. "I thought we were OK?"

"Yes, we're OK," she muttered.

I took the swing next to her. It was cold and I could see my breath in the air. Luna was wearing a hoodie over a thin top, and the same athletic pants she had been wearing in class. I stood back up, shook my jacket off, and then draped it over her shoulders. "I'm not cold," she told me.

"Liar."

"Are you nervous?" she asked me.

I took a step back and leaned against the frame as I folded my arms and looked down at her. "Not of the audition, but I am of their decision," I admitted.

She turned to me and gave me a sad smile. "What do you want to sing?"

I blinked. "What do you mean?"

"For our duet. This is your audition, not mine.

What do you want to perform that will play to your strengths? And don't think about me; I will learn the choreography so that your dancing won't be criticized, and I will do my best with whatever rap or vocals you choose. But you make sure you pick something that will make you look good for them."

"You would do that?" I stepped in front of her holding onto the chains as I stared at her.

Luna shrugged. "I've said this countless times and I'm seriously considering getting it printed on a T-shirt: I don't want to be an idol."

"That's not …" I shook my head. To hell with it. I leaned down and pressed my lips against hers. She sat there, staring at me, then slowly, closed her eyes. When she didn't pull away, I gently started moving my lips against hers.

There was the briefest pause.

And then she started kissing me back.

My heart soared.

Time stopped.

All was well in the world.

OK, that's a slight exaggeration: our kiss certainly didn't cause world peace. But it did bring me peace.

And a few other feelings.

I let go of the chain with one hand, allowing my fingertips to skim her cold face, before I pulled back. It took a moment for Luna to open her eyes and look at me. "Runaway," I whispered.

"It's probably a bit late for that," she muttered, frowning.

"No," I said, shaking my head. "The song."

She stared at me, still confused. "That still doesn't make any sense."

I stepped back. "The song that we should sing for our duet. 'Runaway' by Pentagon."

"That makes a little more sense," Luna agreed, pulling her phone out of her pocket and opening up YouTube. "Although it's possibly not the best first word to pick after kissing someone."

"That's fair," I agreed.

Luna paused in typing and set the phone down in her lap. She sucked in a breath and turned to face me, planting her feet firmly in the dirt below her. "You kissed me." Her tone was very matter-of-fact, but I could see that pink blush start to creep across her cheeks, despite the dim lighting in the area.

"I did," I agreed.

She folded her arms. "We had a conversation a couple of weeks ago where we agreed you wouldn't be doing anything like that unless you'd made up your mind."

"We did," I agreed.

"Have you made up your mind?"

"Why does it need to be a one or the other?" I asked.

Luna gave me a look of incredulity, grabbing her phone and getting to her feet. I shot after her. "You're the one who decided it had to be one or the other in the summer," she reminded me. "*That's* why I wanted you to work out what you want. You still want to be an idol. You're still going to be with Atlantis. That side of things haven't changed."

"I want both," I told her.

"It doesn't work that way," Luna told me. "Yes, you want both now, but you wanted both before you debuted too. And I know it was unfair of me to just show up here, though I honestly didn't think it would be an issue, but I apologize for that." She took a few paces away from the swings, using her arm to gesture around her. "The only difference between then and now is the country we're standing in. And hindsight. You say you want to be with me now, but in quite literally one week, you could be finding out that you're debuting again. So, yes, you may want both now, but you wanted both last time too."

"Have your feelings for me changed?" I asked, carefully.

Luna's eyes seemed to flash as she glowered at me, her hands coming to rest on her hips. "Have you not heard anything I just said?"

I took a couple of paces towards her. "Yes," I said, softly. "But all of this is a moot point if you don't feel the same way as I do. If you don't, and I understand why you wouldn't, then I will back off." I stared at her, daring her to say otherwise: she had kissed me back, and I *knew* that she still felt the same way about me.

Her hands slipped off her hips, hanging by her sides as she half turned away. She stood there, chewing at her lip before turning back to me. "No," she admitted, quietly. "Which is precisely why I want you to work out what you want because I'm not going through that again."

From behind us, someone cleared their throat. I whirled around and found Hyunseo staring at us. "What are you doing here, hyung?" I asked him, hurrying over to the edge of the play area.

It was the first time I'd seen him since Bright Boys had been disbanded. He looked like he had lost a lot of weight. "You ordered chicken?" he said, holding up the carrier bag he had been holding, but his attention was switching between myself and Luna.

"You work at Roosters?" I asked in surprise. He shrugged, his gaze still drifting to Luna. "Hyung, this is Luna."

"Lucinda," Luna growled at me. Nonetheless, she walked over and smiled politely at Hyunseo. "Lucinda Williams. We met once before in the summer at one of King's performances. We went to a noraebang together."

"I remember," Hyunseo grunted, depositing the chicken on the ground by my feet. He turned and started walking down the path towards the gate and the road behind where a scooter was parked.

I hurried after him. "Hyung!"

"It's none of my business," he said, shortly.

I pulled my wallet out of my pocket and waved it in front of his face. "I still need to pay."

The transaction was completed in an awkward silence. Hyunseo handed back the card and started to leave but paused once more. "Just be careful," he said before leaving the park.

He probably meant with Atlantis, rather than Luna, but he had a point. So did Luna. Somehow, it was like I'd had my epiphany over something so simple. I walked back to her, where she had been watching us with her head cocked. "I ordered us chicken."

"I can see," she agreed with a nod of her head, before laughing. When I gave her a questioning look, she smiled. "I eat a lot of chicken."

"You're right," I said, suddenly.

Luna arched an eyebrow. "That only sounds vaguely stalkerish."

"I'm not being fair to you, nor have I been fair to you. When Atlantis stopped me performing, I panicked. I'm sorry about that. I'm also sorry that I have been a jerk and spent a lot of time avoiding you." I sucked in a deep breath. "And I can wait a week. I can wait as long as it takes."

She stared at me, running a finger over her lower lip absentmindedly. "Let's eat, and then we should head back to school." Luna moved back to the swing, picking up the bag as she did, and sank onto the swing. "There is a giant pile of revision I still need to do."

Z

I was certain, as I hurried out of my last exam, that I had barely scraped a pass overall. If my parents knew just how much I was putting into being an idol and how little effort I was making to study, I was sure they would be disappointed. They'd been supportive of everything until now—including what had happened with Hyunseo—because they trusted me. Yet, if they knew just how little I had studied for my other classes, I knew it would have been a different story.

I got changed into my outfit for the first of the performances. At midday, the performance pieces were going to start for our class and they were going to run until we were finished. I'd heard a rumor that Seungjin's sister was going to be on the panel of judges, along with Ro Chanheon, Sa Hyesun, and Ruzt. Thankfully, it was a closed audition and the only people who were going to watch us was the rest of our class.

It was the group performances first. My group, Team Blue, were performing EXO's 'Ko Ko Bop' for the first group song, and H3RO's 'Who is Your Hero?'. We had practiced so hard, and for so long, that I knew the performance inside out. We just had to make sure we held it together.

The lights dimmed and we got into position. As soon as the music started, everything else melted away. It was an audience of less than twenty, but I knew with every cell in my body this was what I wanted to do—what I was born to do.

By the end of both group performances, I was breathing heavily, sweat was running down my back from dancing under the hot stage lights, but my blood was thrumming. Not at the fact my heart was pounding, but from the thrill. This is what I was born to do.

"Thank you," Ro Chanheon said.

That was it. I glanced at Sungil and Jaehoon, then at TK and Seungjin. We were the first group up and from our last experience with Atlantis, we, or at least Sungil and Jaehoon and I, had been expecting feedback there and then. With little other option, we bowed our heads then hurried off stage.

"What do you think that means?" Jaehoon asked.

I shrugged and then looked at Seungjin. "Why would I know?" he snorted. "She's only the half-sister who disbanded us."

"Maybe we're getting the feedback after all our audition pieces?" TK offered, quietly.

"Maybe," Sungil agreed, gruffly.

It was nearly midnight—long after curfew—that Luna and I were up for both of our final performances; our duet. We were in the wings, waiting for the current performance to finish. I glanced down at Luna who was peering out, watching. "Are you OK?" I asked her.

She looked up at me, chewing at her lip, and then nodded.

"Liar."

"I'm just nervous," she shrugged.

I watched her carefully: I still didn't think that was it. Or, at least, I didn't think it was just that. I turned her to face me, setting my hands on her shoulders. "We're going to be fine."

"It's not ..." She shook her head. "Never mind. We're up."

Before I could get her to elaborate, she had already started marching onto the stage.

Pentagon had been a ten-member group when the song had been released. In the space of a week, we had converted the song into a duet. Luna had taken over all the rap parts, and I had taken the vocals. I hadn't changed anything. Luna had. There were a couple of parts she had changed to English, then realizing the translation hadn't completely fit, had rewritten the lyrics.

I had almost completely rechoreographed our dance: needless to say, something originally made for ten people wouldn't work for two.

Despite this, I was confident with our performance. For the last two days, we had been working on our angles in front of a mirror. Much to Luna's amusement, I had filmed our practices and we'd started watching them back to make sure we were turning our bodies the same or lifting our limbs to the same height.

Luna had laughed at first, until I had informed her this was completely normal; that a lot of idol groups did it. Until now, she had only ever focused on if all the dancers were moving at the same time, on the right beat.

As soon as she'd realized she wasn't raising an arm as high as I was, our overall routine had become tight. She had also put in a lot of extra hours of practice. I was almost certain her grades were going to be as bad as mine because I had dominated her time in a dance studio. I'd protested and her response had been dismissive until the one time she'd snapped, "I can re-sit. You might not get another chance."

I'd performed with Luna many times before, back at the various New York Dance Academy programs we had attended together. Like every other time beforehand, it was like everything else melted away and the only ones in the room were the two of us.

Just us, dancing.

Or in this case, dancing *and* singing.

Only, this time, I felt I was singing for my life. Even the lyrics were appropriate.

Luna didn't put a foot wrong or mess up a lyric. She was perfect. I'd seen enough girl groups to know she had the talent to debut.

By the time the song finished, I knew we had both given it our all. I had nothing left to give, and if this didn't work … I knew I wanted this more than anything, so if I had to leave Atlantis, I would.

제29 장

Lucinda

The group performance hadn't been a train wreck. We'd been at a disadvantage with Yerin unable to dance for a week because of her twisted ankle, then having to learn two songs from scratch, rather than just one like everyone else.

We'd replaced the 4Minute song with EXID's 'DDD' and also taken a Cupcake song called 'Could This Be Love'. The first was designed to show off our dancing, and the second for our vocals.

I was the only one in the room not auditioning, but I was still treating it as such. The group performances might not have been important to me, but they were to the rest of my group. The first performance went well. The second, not so much; for Yerin anyway. It wasn't bad, but she stumbled over her lyrics, and instead of carrying on and acting like everything was as it should be, she panicked.

I probably should have helped her out. I knew the lyrics well enough, but I didn't. I couldn't help but feel she would think I was trying to steal her limelight or something. "She would have lynched you on stage," Miyeon had whispered at me when I had asked her. "The girl is crazy."

It wasn't just Yerin. Because Yerin had messed up her rap, it had thrown Miyeon, who missed her timing on her bridge.

My screwup came after my solo performance. I had been first up and they had asked me to free style a rap. I swear Ro Chanheon was doing it intentionally. "I'm sorry," I said, blanking. "I'm not a rapper. I'm just a person who can cover someone else's rap," I said, fumbling over my words, embarrassed.

"It's OK," the female had said to me. I think she was a manager at Atlantis, but she was also American. "We wanted to give people the opportunity to shine in a freestyle."

"If I had to pick one, my strength is dancing, ma'am," I quickly told her. She nodded and the next thing I knew, a K-pop song I vaguely recognized was being played through the speakers.

All in all, the whole process, while a lot more elaborate than a dance audition, wasn't completely unfamiliar. I was enjoying myself. Which was more than could be said for most people in the room.

By the time the duets had rolled around it was very late and we were all running off fumes. Sandwiches had been provided earlier, but all the dancing had quickly burnt that off.

I had been watching King carefully. Despite everything, I really wanted him to succeed. Until now, he had done well. Of the two boy groups, it was clear that the one with him in, and two other Atlantis trainees, was at an advantage. They were much more skilled and it looked like they had picked up more than a few good habits at Atlantis.

King had made me watch our performance back, recording every single practice. At first, I thought he was a combination of insane and egotistical, the latter of which making no sense, because the last thing King was, was egotistical. Then, after a few viewings, I could see the point, and was watching for cues when I was dancing so we were as sharp as possible.

OK, I might have been a little biased, but I still thought he was the best dancer up there. He wasn't the best vocalist. That was Sungil. Oh my lord, I had never heard him sing like that, but he was knocking it out of the park with those vocals.

King had once told me Sungil had been a trainee with them, but his father had put an end to that. I wasn't sure what had changed, but if I was going to hand a contract over there and then, it would have been to Sungil.

When it came to the first set of duets, I hadn't really been paying all that much attention. It wasn't until the sixth pair that I noticed the pattern.

The pairs had been mixed. Some were male and female, but some were also two males or two females. Everyone's name had gone in a bowl and Chanheon had picked them at random. However, they were all singing either ballads, or songs originally performed by a male and female artist.

It wasn't until we were waiting in the wings for our own performance, watching the pair in front of us, that I confirmed King and I were the only ones who were singing a song that not only originally belonged to a group, but was also not a ballad. It was a great song, and once I'd heard it once, I knew exactly why King had chosen it.

The problem was, it didn't follow what anyone else had done.

"Are you OK?"

I looked up at King, not really wanting to answer that. I gave him a nod.

"Liar."

It took everything in me not to react at that. I wasn't the best when it came to hiding what I felt, and King had always been able to see that, but now wasn't the time for him to work that out. "I'm just nervous." Strictly, that wasn't untrue. But I was more nervous about this performance because of the song choice than doing it.

I started to turn back to the couple on stage. This was Kareun's duet. Annoyingly, she was a good singer. She had no rhythm when it came to dancing, but she could sing. Before I could focus my attention on Kareun, King's hands were on me, pulling me back to him. "We're going to be fine," he assured me.

He *could* tell I was hiding something, but he thought it was my performance? "No, it's not …" I shook my head, stopping myself. He did not need to know, not seconds before we went out there. Thankfully, timing was on my side. "Never mind. We're up." Before he could stop me, I darted out onto the stage.

I took a deep breath as I took my position. Maybe the fact we were different would work out for us. It would only work, if I did my best. I cleared my mind and let the music take over.

Z

Everyone had seemed surprised that we hadn't received our feedback after King and I had finished, but it had been past midnight. Audition or not, it was still a school. It wasn't until we had gone to the rooms we had been using as changing rooms that we had found the notices pinned to the wall. Starting after lunch the following day, we each had a twenty-minute slot, back in the auditorium, with the judges, only this time, there would be no audience allowed for the feedback.

Once again, I was the only one not worried. I only needed a mark good enough to pass a class, not one to get me into Atlantis Entertainment. That didn't mean I didn't have my fingers crossed for everyone else. Or, almost everyone else.

Miyeon had spent many, many hours with the Iron Street Crew saying she didn't want to be in an idol group, because girl groups didn't dance with the same power as boy groups. Yet, I'd witnessed firsthand how hard she had practiced, and I was sure she was only saying that because the rest of the crew thought being an idol was being a sellout.

I also desperately wanted Bright Boys to pass and go back to being Bright Boys. I had downplayed it a lot in class, but I was a Dazzle and I did have Bright Boys posters and albums back in New York. They were talented and they had been punished for something completely out of their control.

And then there was King.

I sat with Miyeon at lunch, wolfing down a giant sandwich, while Miyeon picked at hers. Yeah, she wanted to do well. "Where's Baekhee?" she asked, absently.

"I guess she's in the library. I think she still has a couple of exams left." We'd been so busy practicing over the last few weeks, I had barely seen Baekhee. "I think this weekend, before you all go home for Christmas, we should do something together."

"That's a good idea," Miyeon nodded. "When do you fly home?"

I shook my head. "I don't." Christmas in Seoul was very different to back home in America. Whereas all my friends back home were breaking for Christmas with nearly two weeks off school, SLA, and most other schools here, only closed for Christmas day. It would take me almost two days to travel home: by the time I got there, I would only need to turn around and come back.

The warning bell rang, so we deposited our trays in the hatch and then made our way to the auditorium. The corridor was full with our class, lingering, waiting. Despite the fact I had the last appointment, I still had to wait with them. We all had to wait around, and our homeroom teacher, Nam Woosung was there to monitor us.

I decided to use my time productively: I leaned back and napped.

"Lucinda?"

I shot up, blinking the sleep from my eyes as I tried to focus on Woosung. "Sorry, sir. I was just resting my eyes." I glanced down the corridor. I was the last one there.

"Don't worry, you weren't the only one," Woosung said, helping me up. "You students worked hard." He nodded towards the door. "It's your turn now."

I flashed him a grateful smile, and then hurried into the auditorium. Inside, it was just the female Vice Chairwoman. She was perched on the table she had been sat behind for the judging the day before, sipping at a bottle of water.

I hurried down the aisle, apologizing profusely, worried that I had kept them waiting so long that Ro Chanheon, Sa Hyesun and Ruzt had all gone.

The woman got up, smiling. "Hi, Lucinda," she said, greeting me in English.

"Hi," I said, awkwardly. I had forgotten her name. Helen, Heidi, Hannah.

"Holly," she supplied as though reading my mind. "I hope you don't mind, but I let the others go. I wanted to talk to you myself."

She indicated to the front row of seats, and I took one hesitantly. "OK," I said, drawing out the word.

Holly was a pretty American Korean. She had on a woolen dress and a white winter coat, and her long dark hair was framing her face. I don't know if it was the setting, or her appearance, or both, but she didn't look old enough to be a Vice Chairwoman of a music company. She pulled her coat around her. "I swear, the only thing I can't get used to out here is the lack of heating," she muttered with a shiver. "How are you finding it?"

I shrugged. It was different, but it wasn't that bad.

"I wanted to have a conversation with you, without the others," Holly continued, unperturbed at my lack of audible response. "Lucinda, you are an excellent dancer, and Ruzt tells me with training, you would be a good rapper. In fact, you would make a good member of an idol group."

"If it wasn't for the fact I was a WASP?" White, Anglo-Saxon, Protestant. AKA, not the face of a K-pop girl group member.

"To be blunt, yes," she nodded, with a small sigh. "I'm sorry: I don't want to be the one to crush your dreams, and there's a possibility that another company will—"

"I don't want to be an idol," I cut her off.

Holly cocked her head, her eyes growing wide in surprise. "Really?"

"I really don't," I promised her.

She looked skeptical. "Then why are you here?"

I sank back into my seat and stared up at the stage. "I guess that's the question," I sighed. Then, remembering this was King's boss I was talking to, gave her a smile. "I came out, partly for a guy," I admitted, vaguely.

"Lucinda, you're in high school," she blurted out. "Aren't you a little young to be moving across the world for a guy?"

"Does love have an age limit?" I retorted.

Holly opened her mouth, paused, then closed it. "Huh …" she frowned. "OK, you have a point there."

"It was partly for a guy, and partly for dancing," I told her. "I want to go to Julliard and I want so spend my life dancing. Then, when I'm older, I want to open up a dance school and teach kids. Julliard is incredibly competitive and difficult to get into. I'm great, but being great isn't always enough. I came out here to learn different styles of dancing. I want to learn K-pop dancing, but I don't want to be an idol. I also wanted to learn some traditional styles of dancing like

Buchaaechum fan dancing, but I think I overestimated just how much free time I would have coming to school out here." I leaned forward, suddenly, making her jump. "Actually, that's what I can't get used to out here: do you know how long we spend in a classroom? And then to have all the dancing on top of it? After this, I'm sure Julliard would be a breeze."

Holly nodded, absently, "They do take their education seriously out here."

"So, I'm really OK when you tell me I didn't pass your audition. I didn't realize I would automatically have to audition when I took the class, and I didn't want to drop out or let my team down. I'm sorry if that wasted your time."

"Not at all," Holly said, relaxing back. "It makes this conversation a whole lot less awkward. I thought there would be tears and I really couldn't handle more tears today." She sucked in a breath and then stood up. "Well, in that case, I'm sorry, Lucinda, you didn't pass the audition, but you did pass your class. I believe all the official grade announcements will be shared after Christmas." As I stood, she tilted her head. "A dancer?"

I nodded. "Since I was a kid."

"I can't make you an idol, but I can have you as a backup dancer, if that's something that would interest you."

I let out an excited squeal and then launched myself at her. "Yes!"

제30 장

King

W hen I was a trainee the first time around, we would have weekly assessments. Most of the time it was judged as a solo effort on my vocals and my dancing. Occasionally, it was judged as a group effort. Atlantis wanted to keep an eye on my development and see if I was ready for debut. Every week, I would take part then wait with an uneasy stomach as they made their decision as to whether we passed or not.

When I had auditioned for Atlantis the first time around, I had been nervous.

This? This was making me want to throw up. I'd not been able to eat breakfast, and lunch was a carton of strawberry milk.

I was grateful for that as my stomach churned when I pushed open the door to the auditorium. Jaehoon had gone in before me, but I hadn't seen him come out. Once the verdict had been delivered, we were to exit through the back and not talk to anyone else. There were rumors floating that there were limited places from the school, meaning, if there were ten spots, it was ten spots for the school, not my class.

My class already had twenty of us in the performance class. If I took Luna out of the equation, that was eighteen people I was competing against, in my class alone. Joochan had said there were fourteen people in his year, and I think there were the same number in the year below me. That was a lot of competition.

The four judges were sat behind the table, facing the stage like they had been the day before. Nam Woosung had said we needed to go on the stage, so I did as instructed, spotting a black tape cross in the center and stood on that.

"Lee Minhyuk?" Holly asked, glancing up from her notes. I nodded. "You had previously debuted as King, correct?" I nodded again. "OK, so here's how this is going to work. Chanheon, Hyesun and Ruzt will give you your feedback, and then I'll let you know where we stand going forward."

I'd rather she'd just said yes or no, but this was exactly how it was with our weekly assessments, so I wasn't surprised. I nodded again, waiting patiently. Or, rather, waiting impatiently, but trying my best to hide it.

"You and Lucinda were the only duet to perform a group piece," Hyesun declared. "What made you decide to do that, a song designed for ten people, no less, and turn it into a duet?"

"A song for two people is written with two people in mind, whereas a song for ten is written for ten. I wanted to show more versatility, that we were able to perform more than just one role each," I explained, choosing to leave out that the lyrics also held some importance to me.

"But what about the choreography?" Chanheon asked. "There is very little similarity between your performance and the choreography of the original version."

I nodded my head in agreement. "That choreography worked for ten dancers, but not for two."

"So now you presume to rework a song by a group more successful than you?" Chanheon asked.

My heart felt like it had dropped into my stomach. Had I called this wrong? "That was not my intention," I said, hurriedly.

I caught Ruzt rolling his eyes. "You don't rap, which is what I have been brought in here to judge, but from a spectator's point of view, and from the position of someone who has worked for a few years in this industry, I think you performed well in all your assessments. Your dancing is tight, and your choreography is interesting, if not a little safe."

"Safe, sunbae?" I questioned, surprised when Chanheon and Hyesun were just calling me out on daring to change it for our duet.

"You changed the choreography," he shrugged. "Yes, that was bold, but you changed it to a routine which was safe. Given the stakes and what you're working towards, I understand that, but at the same time, you are capable of much more. You just have to challenge yourself."

"I've seen your choreography before, and Ruzt is right," Chanheon agreed. "There was nothing memorable about your dancing yesterday."

"I agree," Hyesun chimed in. "You have to stand out. You have to make people remember you. I remember the song choice, and I remember your vocals, but the overall performance?" She tapped the side of her head. "Nothing."

My heart sank further. I felt my dream slipping away and I couldn't get hold of it.

"Minhyuk, please come down here," Holly called up.

I blinked, rubbing at my nose as I did my best to discreetly fight back the tears I could feel, and walked over to the side of the stage and the steps down. In front of it, hidden by the edge, was another chair. I sat as requested, trying hard not to fidget.

"You have talent," Holly said. "But I think it was a mistake that you were debuted as you were."

The tear escaped from the corner of my eye before I could stop it. "Yes," I agreed, politely, lowering my head.

"I think you belong in a group," she continued.

My head shot up. "I'm sorry?"

Holly leaned forward, her expression solemn. "I am no longer managing H3RO. My job, as Vice Chairwoman, is to look after all the idols and actors on the Atlantis Roster. I have spent a lot of time trying to work out what to do with you, and Bright Boys—or the former members of Bright Boys. And I have a plan. It's going to be hard work, Minhyuk."

"I'm not afraid of hard work," I responded instantly.

"There are still some things I need to clear up, but this will involve a year-long project, and it will start in February," she added.

"I'm not afraid of hard work," I repeated, firmly.

"That's good," she nodded. "Because it's going to

be hard work. Chanheon and Hyesun will continue to work with you. Ruzt has helped me out for this, but he has a comeback in the new year and will need to prepare for that, so there will be someone else coming to help out with the rapping."

"What is it?" I asked.

"It's an idol group," Holly replied. "A brand-new idol group. It is not Bright Boys, but something else. I still haven't confirmed everything, and that includes the members, so this information cannot be discussed yet."

"Will you be managing us?"

Holly quickly shook her head. "Being a manager is a very hands on job." Her eyes suddenly went wide and she cleared her throat, looking flustered as she shook her head again. "I have to look after all of Atlantis. You will have a different manager. However, I will be overseeing this project personally, so you will see a lot of me, and if you don't, you will always be welcome in my office." She sucked in a breath and slid a pile of papers towards me. "This is a contract. Take it, read it over, get your parents to co-sign it with you, and then return it to me after Christmas if you're happy. We're going to get started December 26th. I hope you'll be a part of it."

I took the contract, almost too scared to touch it. "I really get a second chance?"

Holly nodded. "You do."

"Thank you," I said. "Thank you, thank you, thank you."

I stood, bowed at them, and then practically ran out of the rear exit before they could change their mind.

Z

Christmas Day

I knocked on the door in front of me, feeling almost as nervous as I had going into the audition. I'd found out by chance that Luna wasn't going home. Given the time it took to get to New York, it made sense, but I hadn't thought about it until I had overheard Miyeon and Luna talking.

There was also the small matter of being completely preoccupied with telling my parents that I had a new contract with Atlantis, and going through it section by section. I'd gone back to school on Monday, Christmas Eve, and my first goal was to find Luna. That was when I'd overheard their conversation.

I'd phoned my parents straight away and told them I would be staying in the dorms (although not specifying which ones) and not coming home for Christmas. Now it was Christmas Day, and I was knocking on Luna's door. Maybe it was too early in the morning.

I knocked again.

Finally, the door opened and a sleep riddled Luna stood in the doorway, yawning. Her hair was falling haphazardly out of her topknot, her feet were bare, and she was wearing nothing but an oversized shirt. She looked adorable.

And then she realized it was me, squealed and slammed the door shut in my face.

I sighed and rapped on the door. "Luna?"

"Go away, I'm not cute!"

"You're always cute," I called back.

The door opened a crack. "Liar," she hissed at me, slamming the door shut again.

I laughed, leaning against the door frame. "I'm not going anywhere."

The door opened again. "This is the girl's floor."

I turned, showing her the backpack on my shoulder. "I have chicken."

"It's not even lunchtime."

"Is that going to stop you?" I asked, laughing. Luna glowered at me, then stuck her hand out through the gap. I shook my head. "Oh no, I come with the chicken."

Luna looked at me, her eyes narrowed. "Wait there," she instructed me, like I was going to run away. She shut the door.

It reopened ten minutes later. Luna's topknot had been brushed out and replaced with a pony tail. She'd washed her face, and unfortunately, dressed. "I miss the Little Mermaid," I told her, referring to the character that had been on her nightshirt. It had the affect I wanted, sending pink flooding to her cheeks.

"Why are you here?" she asked me.

I looked around. Although their belongings were still there, the room was empty of other occupants. I looked at her with a sheepish smile. "I heard you'd be here and wanted to spend the day with you. I didn't want you to spend Christmas Day alone."

Luna shrugged, walking over to a bunk and sitting on the bottom one, bringing her legs up under her. "Well, you came with chicken."

I rubbed at the back of my neck. "Actually, I didn't," I admitted. "I came with cereal and milk."

"What?" Luna asked, her mouth falling open. "You mean you made me get dressed for *cereal?*"

I pulled the bag off my shoulder and pulled a box

out. "You're more than welcome to get back into your nightshirt if you like?" I suggested.

She threw a teddy bear at my head.

"I also brought some Christmas movies," I continued. "I wasn't sure what you had planned, but I didn't want you to spend it alone. Plus, it's too early for Roosters to be open, but I will buy you chicken later. I couldn't find anywhere that was doing an American Christmas dinner."

Luna chewed at her lip, then sat up, trying to see in the bag. "What Christmas movies?"

I pulled out a handful and handed them over. "Any good?"

"I guess," she said, begrudgingly.

"I also brought you this." From the bag, I pulled out a small, pre-decorated Christmas tree. It was a cheap decoration from a convenience store I had bought last minute. It was ugly!

Luna took one look at it and burst out laughing. "What is that supposed to be?"

"An offended Christmas tree!"

Luna nodded. "I'd be offended too." She stood up, taking the tree off me, setting it down in the center of the desks. "It's perfect," she said, smiling at it. She grabbed her laptop from her desk and took it back over to the bed. She set it down, sat down beside it, and nodded her head at the other side. "You brought a stack of DVDs. We should probably get started on them, or you'll be here all night."

"I'm not against that," I said as I sat down.

She looked at me, scratching at her temple. "King," she said, softly.

"I did it," I told her.

It took her four seconds to work out what I meant, and then she let out an excited squeal, all but flinging herself at me as she wrapped her arms around me. "Congratulations, King!" she yelled in my ear. "I knew you would do it! I'm so happy for you."

I pulled back. "Really?" She nodded at me, her eyes shining.

"But what about the others?"

I caught my lower lip between my teeth. The truth was the contract was vague. Several former members had been given one, and a couple had been told Atlantis was still making a decision. The only real similarities between those of us with contracts were that there was no group name, and it seemed to imply that we weren't all in the same group.

I'd spoken to Jaehoon and Joochan and they had both been given contracts. All three of us had found a Post It note in the middle of the document. It was hand written by Holly and told us to trust her. That was it.

It was a hard thing to do, but I was going to do that.

"Is the news that bad?" Luna asked. "Miyeon was offered a contract."

"The only person I've seen dance better than Miyeon is you," I pointed out. "You should have been given one too."

"King," she said, patiently. "How many Caucasians do you know in K-pop groups? Besides, it's not my dream. I just want to dance. And Holly did say that if they needed backup dancers, she would give me a call."

Luna might not want to be an idol, but the idea of her potentially being a dancer in a video with me? I'd do everything in my power to make sure that happened at least once! I leaned in and kissed her again.

Only, this time, she pushed me away almost straight away. "King."

"Luna."

"That's not my name."

"It's my name for you," I told her. "You've always been my Moon Princess."

Her face wrinkled up in confusion. "That doesn't even make sense. The only thing on the moon is a bunch of robots."

I laughed.

"What?" she exclaimed. "The moon is literally a robot graveyard and you're calling me the princess of that?"

"You remind me of a Disney princess," I admitted.

She pulled the end of her ponytail to her. "Rapunzel? Elsa?"

"One that doesn't exist yet."

She shook her head, laughing. "*You* make no sense."

"Your name," I pressed. "Luna."

"Your name for me," she returned.

I shrugged. "I know Luna is associated with the moon in English, and you are like a Disney princess, so you are my Moon Princess."

"I thought you liked space," she said, softly, then she sat upright, her eyes wide. "Oh!" she exclaimed before bounding off the bed. I watched in amused confusion as she hurried to her closet, her head disappearing inside it. She rummaged around, before eventually reappearing with a small box. She came back to the bed and held it out to me. "Merry Christmas, I guess."

It was a black box, tied with a silver ribbon, about the size of an apple. I took it from her, surprised at how heavy it was. She sat back down and I tugged the bow loose. I pulled off the lid and found … "A rock?"

"Not just any rock!" she exclaimed.

I looked at her, then at it, then back at her. "Is this a moon rock?"

"I wish," she snorted. Then she pouted. "I actually did try to find you a piece of the moon, but it turns out that unless you're pretty much NASA, no one owns any moon rock. That's a piece of an asteroid."

I stared at it, feeling my mouth quirk up in amusement.

Luna groaned. "I knew it was stupid at the time, and now it makes even less sense." She leaned over, trying to take it from me, but I moved my arm behind me. "King, give it back. It's lame."

"No way!" I exclaimed. "I'm keeping it."

"Seriously, let me have it!" she whined, reaching further.

"You can't take a gift back once you've given it," I objected. "I'm keeping my piece of the moon."

"It's an asteroid!" she cried, lunging for it.

She slipped on the laptop and fell on me. I wrapped my arm around her, pinning her to me. "It's *my* asteroid," I corrected her, gently. Luna fell still. I could feel her breathing heavily against me. "I love it," I added. "I love you."

"Atlantis picked you," she said, her voice muffled slightly by my shoulder.

"But I pick you too."

She looked up at me. "Being an idol is your dream."

"I want both. I want you." Leaving the asteroid behind me, I reached for her face, gently tracing my fingers over her pink cheeks. "However hard I have to work to be an idol, I will work twice as hard to be the best boyfriend I can, to make up for the fact that I'll not be able to see you all the time. I'll make sure that no matter what, you will always know how much I love you."

Luna stared at me, gently shook her head, then suddenly declared, "To hell with it." Then her hands were in my hair, tugging my head to her. She kissed me; hard. Our mouths mashed against each other until we fell into a rhythm that had me exceptionally grateful that she wasn't still in her Little Mermaid nightdress.

Finally, she pulled away, breathless, her cheeks flushed. I felt the same. "You're incredible," I told her.

"Yeah, I am," she agreed. "Don't do what you did again, King," she warned me. "If you've got something going on, you tell me, because whatever it is, we can work it out. Together."

"Together," I agreed. I sank back against the wall, pulling her with me as I refused to let go. "This is the best Christmas ever." Not only had I gotten my second chance with Atlantis, I'd gotten it with Luna too.

The End

The story of Bright Boys will continue in June with 'The Dancer Who Saved Her Soul.' Sign up to Ji Soo's newsletter to keep up to date with all of the gossip from Atlantis Entertainment.

www.JiSooLeeAuthor.com/newsletter

In the meantime, if you enjoyed this story, please consider leaving a review. Those few minutes will really help an author out!

SONGS MENTIONED

1) 4-Minute – Crazy
2) Pentagon – Runaway
3) EXO – Ko Ko Bop
4) EXID – DDD
5) BTS – Fake Love

CHARACTER BIOGRAPHIES

Name: Bright Boys (브라이트 보이스)
Fandom: Dazzle
Colors: Lemon Yellow
Debut: November 20th, 2017

Bright Boys consists of 7 members: Hyunseo, Yongsik, Ryan, Apollo, Dongyeol, Jaehoon, and Seungjin.
The group debuted on November 20th, 2017.
They were disbanded on November 3rd, 2018

Stage Name: Hyunseo (현서)

Birth Name: Sang Hyun-Seo (상현서)
Position: Leader, Vocalist
Birthday: November 20th
Age: 23
Zodiac sign: Scorpio
Height: 180 cm
Weight: 57 kg
Blood Type: A

Hyunseo facts:
He was born in: Seoul, South Korea
Family: Father, Mother, younger sister

Stage Name: Yongsik (용식)

Birth Name: Ren Yong-Sik (런용식)
Position: Vocals, Dancer
Birthday: April 1st
Age: 22
Zodiac sign: Aries
Height: 178 cm
Weight: 65 kg
Blood Type: B

Yongsik facts:
He was born in: Ilsan, South Korea
Family: father, mother

Stage Name: Ryan (라이언)
Birth Name: Tsang Ryan (曾培炎 / 창 라이언)
Position: Rapper
Birthday: January 28th
Age: 19
Zodiac sign: Aquarius
Height: 179 cm
Weight: 60 kg
Blood Type: AB

Ryan facts:
He was born in: Hangzhou, China.
Moved to Busan, South Korea at age 6
Family: Mother

Stage Name: Apollo (네이트)

Birth Name: Yang Joo-Chan (양주찬)
Position: Rapper
Birthday: August 9th

Age: 19
Zodiac sign: Leo
Height: 179 cm
Weight: 56 kg
Blood Type: A

Apollo facts:
He was born in: Jangsu, South Korea
Family: father, mother

Stage Name: Dongyeol (동열)
Birth Name: Jung Dong-Yeol (정동열)
Position: Vocals
Birthday: November 25th
Age: 19
Zodiac sign: Sagittarius
Height: 175 cm
Weight: 55 kg
Blood Type: O

Dongyeol facts:
He was born in: Samcheok, South Korea
Family: Father, mother, older and younger brothers

Stage Name: Jaehoon (재훈)
Birth Name: Kim Jae-Hoon (김재훈)
Position: Rapper
Birthday: April 6th
Age: 18
Zodiac sign: Aries
Height: 179 cm
Weight: 65 kg
Blood Type: A

Jaehoon facts:
He was born in Seoul, South Korea
Family: father, mother
Nickname: Aslan

Stage Name: Seungjin (승진)
Birth Name: Lee Seung-Jin (이승진)
Position: Dancer, maknae
Birthday: April 20th
Age: 18
Zodiac sign: Aries
Height: 180 cm

Weight: 69 kg
Blood Type: B

Seungjin facts:
He was born in Seoul, South Korea
Family: father (Chairman of Atlantis), mother, older
brother (Vice Chairman of Atlantis), older sister (Vice
Chairwoman of Atlantis)

Name: TBC (확정되다)
Fandom: TBC
Colors: TBC
Debut: 2019?

**A new group is coming from Atlantis
Entertainment …**

Stage Name: King (킹)
Birth Name: Lee Min-Hyuk (이민혁)
Position: Vocalist

Birthday: May 15th
Age: 18
Zodiac sign: Taurus
Height: 177 cm
Weight: 60 kg
Blood Type: AB

King facts:
He was born in Seoul, South Korea
Family: father, mother
Former solo artist

ACKNOWLEDGEMENTS

The Zodiac series is designed to be 14 stand-alone novels focusing on 13 different couples, following the members of Bright Boys (and King) as they debut, disband, re-debut, have a comeback single—and everything in between—while focusing on the individual members and their relationships. Needless to say, a lot of planning and plotting has gone into this. Which is why my first words of eternal gratitude belong to Cheryl and Sarah. Between the three of us, using FaceTime / Facebook and a wall of flashcards, the Zodiac series was plotted out. And that took about a week—just for the first six books. It didn't help that after writing "The Girl Who Gave Him The Moon", I realized the characters didn't fit, and therefore the story didn't work. Fun fact: in the original version, Luna was dead, her sister Scarlett had gone to SLA in her place to find her sister's pen pal, and in the process, fell in love with Sungil. The story by itself worked, but it didn't for the series. It was a painful moment when I scrapped that. However, I think this story does work so much better, so it was worth it.

One of the fun parts of the process is getting the book covers. I have an amazing cover artist—Natasha of Natasha Snow Designs. I don't need to tell you that though. You can see it by looking at the cover! What you probably can't tell from looking at it how irritating I'm sure I was with it. As good as I am at words, I can't translate what I see in my head onto paper for a designer to create. Thank God! If my suggestions ever made it to the final cover, it would be a mess. Thankfully, Natasha is exceptionally talented and can create beautiful covers! Thank you, Natasha!

My beta team are FANTASTIC! Adena, Melinda, and

Heather have an amazing set of eyes and pull out an embarrassing number of typos (I'm still hanging my head in shame) but you have also found the inconsistencies before this book became an embarrassing mess. Thank you, beautiful ladies! 사랑해!

I must also add a thank you to Byungchan from Victon. Even though he's never going to see this, his visuals inspired King, and Victon's music helped inspire the story.

ATLANTIS ENTERTAINMENT NEWSLETTER

Would you like to be kept up to date on the antics of the idols and artists at Atlantis Entertainment? Sign up to the Atlantis Entertainment Newsletter, managed by the silent Chairwoman of Atlantis Entertainment, Ji Soo.

Ji Soo will keep you updated on the Atlantis Roster, as well as providing you with a healthy dose of K-pop, some Korean culture, and if she can persuade her 할머니 (that's Korean for 'grandmother', pronounced halmeoni) to part with some cherished recipes, some of those, along with some reading recommendations. There may even be a few insights into her crazy life. But probably not, because her life is very boring …

Find out more at:

www.JiSooLeeAuthor.com/newsletter

ABOUT THE AUTHOR

International Bestselling author Ji Soo Lee spends most of her days lost in a K-Pop haze, which inspired her to start writing stories about her idols at Atlantis Entertainment.

Under the name Ji Soo Lee, you will find YA contemporary romances, with romance levels like a K-Drama.

Under J. S. Lee, Ji Soo writes steamier stories, mainly of Reverse Harems.

WAYS TO CONNECT

Facebook
Author Page:
https://www.facebook.com/OfficialJiSooLee
Atlantis Fan Group:
https://www.facebook.com/groups/AtlantisEnts/

Bookbub:
https://www.bookbub.com/authors/j-s-lee

Amazon:
https://www.amazon.com/J.-S.-Lee/e/B07H353S3L

Instagram:
https://www.instagram.com/ji_soo_lee_author/

Website:
www.jisooleeauthor.com